The Crumbs
Of
His Heart

Sylvia Mosime

Copyright © 2008 **Sylvia Mosime**

All rights reserved by the author. No part of this publication may be reproduced, stored in a retrieval system or transmitted in any form or by any means electronic, mechanical, photocopying, recording or otherwise, without the prior written permission of the author.

All characters in this publication are fictitious and any resemblance to real persons, living or dead, is purely coincidental.

ISBN 9780 9561 5390 6

For Mmamasego Mosime

CHAPTER ONE

"He doesn't love you, hon. It's your pay that's keeping him around."

She tightly closed her eyes because it was suddenly too much. In all her life, she had never experienced the intense pain that ripped through her heart; even that fateful day when her uncle tragically informed her that her mum has passed on. Yes, distraught and aggrieved she was, but this – a whimpering sound rose from her dry throat.

An alarmed Susan asked, "Are you all right?"

Staggering outside she gulped in fresh, calming air.

How could Sue say such an awful thing?

"Mark does not love you."

The words struck her with numbing shock.

"Mark does not love you."

What kind of nonsense was that?

"Mark has to love me. He just has to," Pulane told herself fiercely.

She blinked rapidly as a scorching thought suddenly surfaced.

But has Mark ever told me he loves me? Well, has he?

The fear that gripped her already bruised heart was even more staggering. Christ, she felt so cold. Icy cold. In the blink of an eye, the warm gentle wind that had been caressing her was no more. The warm reassuring breeze that had gently been blowing, calming her down, was no more.

Get a grip; get a grip, she told herself. Sue was just saying that to stir up trouble…saying that to sabotage this good thing she had with Mark; it was nothing to take to heart, absolutely nothing to take to heart. As she dazedly stood there gulping and gulping in the cool air, the thought returned. *But has he ever said he loves me?*

Yes, it's that bitch Sue. She's contaminated my mind to breed these doubts. Now when she badly needed the refreshing puff of air to appease her rankled soul, it was gone. Just like that – done a disappearing act on her! The damn deathly cold.

"How did it get to be this cold?" she gasped loudly as the cold, dreadful wind from Canada whipped her face. Her teeth started chattering so violently it reminding her of the racket that fucking bitch Sue made stirring her endless cups of tea.

Fuelling up to crap on me, she thought.

Pulane ground her teeth hard to cease the chattering – no such luck. With her heart still aching like there was no tomorrow she clutched at her body.

She started rubbing her trembling hands against her long arms in a desperate attempt to diminish the goose pimples that were mushrooming all over her shaking body. But the goose pimples ballooned even further, and the shivering intensified.

She squeezed her eyes even tighter as she leaned heavily against the wall to steady her shaking limbs. "Just cos he doesn't say it, doesn't mean…" *Jesus! What is Sue on about?*

"One…two…" at a snail's pace Pulane kept on. Locking out what Sue had said, she centralised her mind on the counting.

"Th…three," she clung on, forcing her mind on the numerals. When she eventually reached the tenth number – there was a God after all; the pain that had mercilessly been gnawing her heart slightly diffused.

After several deep breaths she was back in control; the pain was gone. She heaved a grateful sigh of thank you to God. What Sue had said was just a load of bullshit, nothing to take to heart – absolutely nothing to take to heart.

How could Mark possibly not love me?

She looked up, but who was that staring at her like she was some kind of an alien? Sue, the mouthy bitch.

"I have the right to his heart."

"Huh?"

"There is no way he cannot love me," Pulane said, glaring at Sue.

"And stop talking such crap!"

"Hmm, truth is the shittiest of all bitches," muttered Sue, nodding her head.

Pulane arched her eyebrows. *What was with this bitch and her grating mouth? Ah well, an annoying bitch she is, but she has her uses.* "Please, Sue, please lend me fifty bucks."

Suspiciously, Susan asked, "What for?"

"I need to buy…" Pulane's voice faltered. "Ingestion med and… stuff," she said.

"Really!" 'You are lying,' Sue's voice really said.

May as well come clean, Pulane decided. "Well, Mark isn't in such a good mood, but I know that if I get him a pack of smokes, he'll be cool."

"What exactly do you mean when you say he's not in such a good mood?" Sue slowly asked.

"He's sulking and not really talking to me," she blurted, casting her eyes down.

"And Mark can only be nice enough to talk to you when you get him a pack of smokes," Sue said knowingly.

Damn Susan and her distorted mind. She was twisting everything. "It's not like that," Pulane weakly protested.

"Why don't you tell me what it's like then?"

"It's complicated. You wouldn't understand," she sullenly said.

Nodding her head as she opened the door leading to the kitchen. "You're right, Pulane. I won't understand."

Yeah, nothing could be further from the truth. Sue was right, she didn't understand. She never would.

How could she possibly understand? When she was standing on a fucking sidewalk, none of the thorns in this road had ever pierced dear Sue's feet. She didn't know about the staggering pains. How much it hurt. How unbearable it was, especially when Mark paraded around with that awful girl.

With great difficulty, Pulane swallowed.

How could she coherently explain to Sue that when she had no money to give to Mark, he blatantly ignored her and was totally indifferent? He didn't even bother to return her good mornings. And the pain she always felt then – well, it cut so deep. She just couldn't handle it. But when she had something to give him, her mouth started to water in anticipation.

She really had to find cash to buy those smokes. There was simply no other way.

Violently Pulane shuddered as she recalled last week when she was too broke to finance Mark's weekend of clubbing. He dropped her flat and settled cosily with a bitch called Cindy. It was as if a knife had been plunged deep in her heart when she saw that loose girl draped all over him.

Inwardly she cursed.

Cindy was a teacher and could well afford Mark's expensive habits. But what about me? Pulane anxiously licked her lips.

Where am I going to get the money to buy those smokes? She was now very frantic.

Damn fucking shit! Pulane helplessly pulled at her hair in exasperation. A simple maid she was, earning five fucking hundred peanuts a month – Definitely not enough to keep Mark to herself. Especially now that the tables had turned on her and she was in fierce competition with a college girl who earned ten times more than her destitute self.

"College girl! Fuck that shit, she's only a nursemaid bitch who stands in front of six-year-olds reciting vowels."

Sure, Mark was working, but she just couldn't find it in her trusting heart to question him on what he did with his pay.

"Who knows, he might be saving up to pay the bridal price for me."

The thought brought Pulane such immense joy that her haunted face glowed elatedly. She didn't really know why, but she always felt kind of honoured when Mark came to her for money. After all, he was Mark, and he could ask any girl, and they would eagerly oblige, but it was her he came to. That meant something, in fact, a great deal of something she emphatically told herself.

Only her lack of funds drove Mark to hang around that transient Cindy.

"Only my lack of funds," she repeated to herself sternly.

If she could only get some more money. God, how she yearned for that day!

But today, yes today she had to get the smokes.

But who was there to understand her emotional predicament enough to help? Sue wasn't helping today. What was it she said? All she wanted was a personal loan, payable at the end of the month. Why was Sue giving her the third degree over a paltry loan of fifty bucks?

She wondered whether she should ask for a wage advance – yes, she was that desperate. Yeah Mrs Chambers, her boss, had a good heart; she would definitely come through for her. But she wasn't home, and Pulane couldn't afford to keep Mark waiting. Every minute counted, otherwise Cindy would overtake her, and....

Pulane closed her eyes in dread.

Anguished, she shook her head. Damn, she always was flat broke, sometimes even reduced to bathing with a dish detergent. What exactly would have become of her if it weren't for her boss's, Mrs Chambers, charitable heart? All these clothes she had been giving her; it was a good thing Sue had let herself go and none of the clothes fit her.

Pulane tightly folded her arms across her chest. Mark was the one and only thing that mattered to her. He was the last thing on her mind when she drifted off to sleep. The first thing she thought of when she opened her eyes. He mattered a great deal to her. She lived for that guy. She loved him so much, and she would do anything for him – anything. And yes, she would rather shower with a dish detergent than deny Mark money to party the weekend away.

And sure, she was well aware of what people would say. Sue had been feeding her that particular crap ever since the day she got together with Mark.

Sue, with her shocked disgusted looks. Calling me a stupid little bitch.

But she didn't give a rat's ass about that. This was her life, and she would play it exactly as she saw fit because at the end of the ride, it was she who was accountable.

Damn. When things were not right between them – with Mark not being the real Mark to her – it was so hard; it gave her such murder pains. She just couldn't stomach it.

It fucking hurt. Really, really hurt. Like that particular morning.

"All right, Mark?"

"Pulane, I need a pack of smokes."

Despairingly she had said, "But I don't have a cent on me."

"I'll call Cindy then."

She knew him well enough to know he wasn't bluffing. In a small desperate voice she'd heard herself say, "Please don't. I'll find a way."

"You better do it fast cos I need them as in right now!"

Where am I going to get the cash?

There was a lump in her throat – she swallowed hard. If only Sue could understand, then she might lend her even a twenty.

Lurching into the kitchen she found Sue fixing herself a cup of tea.

"If I don't get those smokes, Cindy…" she couldn't say the rest. Her eyes welled up in desperate tears.

"No, Pulane, for your own good, this time I will not lend you a cent. If he dumps you, hey, good riddance!"

"Dump me! What are you talking about, Sue?" she shrieked, staring at Susan in stupefying shock.

"You need to forget him, Pulie," Sue insisted.

Glaring at her she asked, "Why?"

"He is a nasty piece of work. He does not treat you right," Sue flatly replied. Pulane gaped at Sue in stunned amazement.

So what if Mark didn't treat her right? Did Sue really think that was enough reason to leave Mark? Besides, Mark wasn't that bad really. It was only that he had these expensive habits they both couldn't afford. And when his craving for smokes was at its worst, he couldn't think straight and got sick in the head, coercing him to do stupid things – Mark had told her as much. She had asked him a hundred of times to quit the smokes, but he said he couldn't; that he'd tried, but still couldn't. So all in all he wasn't bad really, Pulane frantically told herself. It was these damn enslaving habits. If only… *Damn, why do wishes have to be so damn unattainable!* Pulane thought.

But why should she have too many expectations of Mark? Like everyone else, he had his faults.

'Forget Mark?' Where had Susan lost her fucking marbles?

"You need to leave him now, Pulie. Eventually you'll meet a nice proper guy who will really appreciate you," Susan urgently said.

Eventually? How long exactly was that road? A lifetime? Or maybe Sue the psychic had glimpsed God's programme and had the date handy.

"When is this eventually?"

"Just be patient."

"I don't mind practising my patience on Mark."

Sipping her tea Sue said, "A lost cause."

"Mark has all the reasons to love me," Pulane said pleasantly.

Sue looked at her blankly.

"No one can ever love him the way I do."

"You mean no one except you can tolerate the cheating parasitic rat that he is."

"I wish you'd stop talking like that," Pulane moaned.

"He cheats on you all the time. And he doesn't as much as honour you with a backward glance when you're broke. Now, how telling can that be? Pulane, when are you going to fucking wake up?"

"I'm getting out of here," she said bolting out of the main house.

Pulane shook her head as she walked briskly to their quarters. Sue talked crap. Mark loved her. He really did. Still, it hurt to hear her talk like that Pulane told herself as she opened the door to the spacious room she shared with Sue.

Mark does not love me! What the hell kind of shit is that? she thought scornfully.

Opening the small fridge she filled up a glass with water and washed down Sue's unsubstantiated silly talk. Mark needed the cigarettes. She was broke, but Mark needed the cigarettes. Yanking open the closest she took some clothes off their hangers and carefully looked them over.

"My heart is not giving me a break," she whimpered out loud. It's hurting. Hurting very bad, and I'm scouting for something to sell so I can get my fulfilling dose of medication. Let's see – what can I use to buy time before payday? No this is worn out, she thought as she threw a floral dress on the bed. I really love this guy; he makes me feel so fucking good, but this guy does not do freebies, so a girl has to do what she has to do.

"Aha, good stuff," she said, triumphantly pouncing on a short black dress that had been hanging at the back in the closet. Hurriedly she put back the heap of clothes she'd thrown on the bed.

As she was sneaking out with a backpack, she heard Sue's voice.

"Where are you going?"

What was wrong with Sue? Why couldn't she just let her be?

"Flea market," Pulane replied.

"And?"

She decided it wouldn't do to provoke Sue since her motherly years had landed her a senior role. A role she wickedly used to her advantage, mothering everyone and taking other people's business as her own, distorting facts while she was at it.

Mark doesn't love me! Pulane flinched. Sue really should not have said that.

"Pulane?"

With glum reluctance Pulane told her.

"You are going to sell the dress Mrs Chambers gave you out of the goodness of her heart so you can buy cigarettes for Mark!" exclaimed a shocked Susan.

"He needs the smokes," Pulane cried, running her hand through her hair.

She looked at her hands; they were shaking. She really was desperate. Mark teaming with Cindy was way too frustrating. It really hurt.

Sue's mouth had now dropped open, and she was looking at Pulane strangely. She didn't care less about that. That was Sue; always casting such strange looks, especially when it was about Pulane's unending loyalty to Mark.

"My heart bleeds for you."

Now what is that supposed to mean? Pulane thought.

Pulane impatiently tapped her foot on the paved ground. Time was not on her side, and she was fed up with crap spouting from Sue's mouth. When it came to other people's business, people like Sue were very good giving their bullshit opinions. If Sue was such a know-it-all, then how come there was no steady partner cheering in the background? How come they all made a fast exit after a couple of dates? Strangely, that didn't seem to get Sue down. She would dismiss the parting boyfriend with a careless shrug. "He's a rat; he doesn't appreciate me enough!" she would say.

Pulane sighed. *Sue expects too much, her one major blunder. Me, I don't,* Pulane thought, shaking her head. *I make do with what I have. I will cling to the little that I have, no matter how sick that makes Sue.*

"When you don't give Mark money, he drops you, right?"

"Yeah," she reluctantly admitted.

"Pulane, doesn't that at least tell you something?"

"Only that Mark loves me, but he needs money too."

"He doesn't love you, Pulane!"

"I told you never to say that!" she shouted. "Mark and I are a team. If he needs some cash, it's only proper that he comes to me. Why should he bypass me in his time of need?"

"What about you then? How come when you need him he bypasses you?"

"I told you, it's the smokes. When he doesn't have them, he gets this murder headache that messes his thinking."

"Pulane, when are you going to get it together? Mark cheats…"

Pulane knew Susan. On and on she would go. She knew damn well that talk was cheap. You didn't have to pay a fucking dime to utter a word. Whether you talked shit or not, you didn't have to pay a single penny. That's why some people the likes of Sue just talk and talk.

"Gotta go," Pulane said, racing to the gate.

As she hurriedly walked to the bus stop she agreed wholeheartedly with her heart.

More money was what she really needed. If she had more money, she would be able to hook Mark to her for life. Yeah, what she needed was enough loot to bail her beloved from the slut Cindys of this world.

When will Sue catch up with the rest of the world? she wondered as she slung the backpack high up on her shoulder. *Being loved for just you is an extremely rare treat, as for finding that perfect partner. Perfect partner, ha!* Was there such animal? Such stuff was just a consolation myth old grumps had come up with to shield being ridiculed. Once you realise you will die an old maid, you either hibernate or come up with something to wade off the taunting. "I'm waiting for my perfect partner," they said, knowing full well such animal didn't exist. You should see them walking stiffly with grim-sheeted faces when they crossed the street to buy stuff in a supermarket. Of course, marriage wasn't obligatory; it was only when you deeply yearned for it as much as Pulane yet played cheap pretend games, well that was when something started smelling wrong. How were other strays going to know about you? Walking around with such airs, pretending it was all good while the real truth was that you would jump in elation and marry that champion loser like a shot if only he asked.

Leaning against the bus stop sign, Pulane took a deep refreshing breath. Sue better stop being so picky unless… Anyway the bed that you made for yourself was the one that you must rightly lay on. Only she mustn't grate on us with whiny complaints when her face gets crumpled up with age, and she has nobody to keep her warm.

Pulane prided herself on being a nice girl, and the last thing she wanted was to rail I told you so on Sue. Anyway she had decided to team up with Mark because once you were a beggar you simply couldn't afford to choose. That was what she told herself as she jumped on the bus. *Only a handful of people manage to be loved for who they are. Only a handful,* she firmly repeated to herself as she occupied the back seat by the window. If Mark loved her for the measly pay, which she was always eager to hand him, then okay, no worries. Besides she too loved him for his overwhelming magic, the one that made her want to jump up and down like a little kid, the one that put springs under her feet. So this was two-way traffic after all.

Once you catch up and realise that special love where you are loved for just you is not oranges growing on top of trees, you wise up and make do with what you have because you certainly won't find such love by being Ma'am Sunshine and smiling at everyone. It just falls on your lap, only there is not so many laps it falls on.

That was love with no stipulations, but was it happening with her? No fucking way, with her there were stipulations, money stipulations.

Deep in her thoughts Pulane opened the side pocket of her backpack and took out a pack of gum. Still engrossed in her Mark thoughts, she threw one in her mouth and slowly started chewing.

So what was she to do? If Mark loved her for her wages, which she was always more than happy to hand him, then let it be. No way was she going to keep her life on hold waiting for that too rare I-love-you-for-just you love. Of course, it would be cool to have such a good reassuring thing in her life. But what if she wasn't listed in that too small a list? Well, there was nothing she could do about it. What she most definitely would not do was drop Mark because he was only into her when she has something to give him. She was through listening to Sue, muddying her mind with crap, she told herself as she blew gum like a five-pula whore. Besides, it was she who hurt when Mark was with other women. Sue the mouth didn't know shit about that one. And it was she who felt fulfilled when things were right between them. And sure, she had weighed the hurts against the fulfilments and well, she shrugged, what was a little hurt compared to Mark's breathtaking magic? Besides, there was no man who was altogether faithful; this she got from her own mum.

"They all cheat, hon. Only some are good in hiding their trail of sins."

Her mum was a lot of things, but a liar she was not. At least Mark was a firm condom believer. At least whatever shit was in store for her, it certainly wouldn't compare to certain creatures who indulge in condomless sex with their I-love-you partners only to wind up with the everlasting AIDS. Faithfully swallowing I love yous tumbling from his cheating mouth. She shook her head, at least *that* she didn't have to worry about.

The man sat next to her lit a cigarette. Looking up at him she smiled, "You're smoking the same brand my boyfriend smokes," she pleasantly said.

The man grunted.

Boyfriend – it just didn't carry that much weight. *I must start advocating for that ring*, she suddenly decided.

Hugging her backpack to her chest, she wished the bus would abandon its many stops and fucking increase speed. She was very much aware that it was after lunch, school was out, letting loose that… that home-wrecker Cindy!

Pulane just couldn't understand what the fuss was about. Mark was her ultimate happiness – it felt so real when she was with him. And to her that was all that mattered.

Mark loved her for the pay he could easily get out of her; yes, that much was pretty evident. But if she just folded her hands and said, "Ah well, I'm not giving him my pay. If he doesn't like it, to hell with him," who was going to suffer when off he trotted to Cindy? Where else was she going to get that dose of fulfilling magic only he seemed to deliver in her? She wondered about this as she pressed the stop button.

It suddenly occurred to her that she had been doing quite a lot of protesting – too much on the defensive about her deep feelings for Mark. She frowned. Well what did people expect really? Some stuff was really hard to coherently put into words. When it came to real feelings words were too limited. The trick lay in walking this road first then they would catch on, get the drift, about how she loved Mark so much that sometimes it even frightened her. How she felt it was only she who had the right to his heart. And how she would do anything for him – anything.

It wasn't like she was running around like a headless chicken for nothing, her best possible good feeling was what she would get out of it she told herself as she jumped out of the bus.

She quickened her pace to the second-hand clothes stall. "Hello," she said brightly. Today, she was going to beat the schoolteacher at her own slut game. Today, Mark would be solely hers.

"Stop chewing that gum when you're talking to me," the woman in the stall said sharply.

"Sorry," Pulane said, taking the gum out of her mouth.

"So what did you bring me, today?"

"Designer wear. My boss got this dress from Paris," she said as she hastily opened the backpack, bracing herself to haggle over a worthwhile price. A name dress, which meant enough loot to even get a mini party pack for Mark.

"Aha, let me see," the woman said, grabbing the dress from her.

Yeah, the money she got out of the sale of the dress would do she decided, for now. As she waited while the woman carefully checked the dress for loopholes, she wondered about a long-time solution to her emotional predicament. She really, really needed Mark, but darling Mark didn't believe in freebies.

But how to come up with a plan that would guarantee heaps of money? She wondered – a lucrative plan that would finally get a grip on….

"Ten pulas," the woman's voice cut into her thoughts.

"Are you crazy? Feel the softness of the fabric, it doesn't prick like the trash most people sell."

"We don't care about brand names here."

Snatching the dress Pulane said, "Fine, I'll go somewhere else."

"Fifteen," the woman quickly said.

"Okay, twenty pulas, and that's as far as I can go."

"Deal," the woman said opening up her bag.

CHAPTER TWO

Mark, whose real name was Raditonki, wearily pushed a wheelbarrow full of weeds and dead flowers he had picked from his boss's garden.

He was an all-muscles thirty-year-old, and judging by his biceps, he liked displaying that he was one strong young man. He was very tall and had broad shoulders. His complexion was dark, a shade too dark perhaps – the kind that tend to provide camouflage in the dark.

When he first came to the city it didn't take him long to realise he had been saddled with stagnant name. He had discarded the Raditonki then and called himself Mark. It was more user-friendly, and this is what he repeatedly told those who were fond of dragging out the Raditonki he had long buried under the rural woodwork.

He didn't have any real family; the story he told whoever asked was that both of his parents were dead and the rest, he shrugged, the rest didn't matter.

Mr Chambers, his boss, was married to a smashing wife, Sarah, and was blessed with a couple of cute kids. The Chambers lived in a big house located in the rich suburb of Phakalane.

At the back of the main house were the double servants' quarters. Mark lived in a cosy two-bedroom with a fitted kitchen, closet-sized lounge and a bathroom. He had all this to himself since Morgan the cook and Tom the chauffeur were staying with their families in Broadhurst, a high-density suburb. On the other side was a shared spacious bedroom with a neat fitted kitchen and a small bathroom. This was where the housekeepers slept.

The housekeeper, Susan, was just plain and dumpy with the kind of nothing looks you could find on every street in Gaborone. Mark nodded absently; yep, with lady Sue there was absolutely nothing there that could increase *anyone's* adrenalin level.

However, there was twenty-two-year-old Pulane, he grinned. She was a good height, five feet ten inches, slim but not stick thin – just about the right cuddly size of slim.

Her bust was real, the best, the very best, good stuff. They didn't seem to make those anymore. Silicone tits were nothing but shit – too hard. Not that user-friendly, he laughed quietly. The trouble with the world nowadays was that they were in competition with the man upstairs. They thought they could *match* his hand. Ha! Deep in thought he looked at the well-cut lawn. Sure, that Pulane was hot stuff, but the face was just that, a face, nothing there to grab a man's eyes.

He stopped the wheelbarrow, grabbed a twig broom and started sweeping leaves that were scattered over the lawn.

The only hiccup with dearest Pulie was that Mrs Chambers was slightly heavier, and from her own indifference, Pulane didn't bother altering the hand-me-downs she got from her boss. Nice clothes, yes, but they swamped her figure, and with Pulane it was the figure that was *it*. Her little maid dress was good stuff though, nice fit with no blurring of her candy frame. Yummy cleavage, long shapely legs all on show. It was a pity that was the only time one could feast on sexy Pulie unless you had his kind of arrangement.

As he tossed more leaves in the wheelbarrow, he heaved an immense sigh of contentment because today was a long-awaited Friday.

"A weekend of heavy clubbing," he whistled.

He wondered whether Pulane will come up with his weekend cash, but it didn't bother him that much because he already has his contingency Cindy, a nice girl, who was clued up and never cried that she was broke. And no, hell no, he was not the least embarrassed about living such parasitic life. There was nothing like a free meal in life. If the girls found him so exciting, then they should act on their appreciation by paying him. He was Mark; he made them come, so why the fuck not? He was not feeble minded enough to stick to a girl unwilling to cough up money for his charm. Nothing was free in life, and yes not even *come*.

His friend Duncan, a fellow neighbour gardener, was always on his case about it. "Mark, you have to stop this. It's not nice...."

But stuff like 'nice' he could do without. Was 'nice' going to put food on his table? Were the jeans he was wearing under the overalls bought by 'nice'? Duncan should really lighten up, drop his grandpa attitude and come around. If he was craving for a sermon on this 'nice', he knew where to go, only he had no urge to. And Duncan as his friend should be loyal enough to respect that. Give Mark the break that he deserved.

Squatting by the hippeastrums, Mark carefully inspected them and cut the yellowed dried leaves. Watering them would be a waste, such a pity this was their dead season. He couldn't wait for January when he would start to reawaken them into beautiful flowers.

Ah, damn wheelbarrow is too full, if I put more in, it will just fall out. He gently pushed it to the compost heap. As he was dumping the lot, Duncan made his appearance.

"Mark, my man, what's the deal tonight? Are we going clubbing?"

While using his gloved hands to empty the wheelbarrow, Mark replied, "We sure are."

"And I thought the man was broke!"

"I am broke, mate, but one of these girls will have to come up with a plan," he calmly explained.

"And if they too are broke?"

Mark flippantly shrugged his shoulders. "They'll have to make a visit to the cash loan then."

"Give them a break, Mark. We don't really have to hit the clubs tonight. There are other nights."

"Gee, Duncan, you're so thoughtful, but I need money to go out tonight, and I ain't giving anyone a break about it," he flatly said while Duncan trailed behind as he made his way back to the garden.

"But where are they going to get the cash?"

"That's not my problem, Duncan," Mark pointed out, snapping at his friend. "I've done my job, both girls came when I shagged them, so where is my fucking pay?"

"Mark!"

"Don't fucking make me feel bad! I hit the magic spot, they scream in ecstasy. Now it's time for a little thank you." Turning to face

Duncan he continued, "And all the good stuff I say to make them feel good. You think that's fucking easy?"

"Lying to them?"

"They know that, but they still listen. Are you blaming *me* for that as well?"

"Poor Pulane. I feel bad for that kid," admitted Duncan.

"Why?" Mark asked, frowning.

"Cos you are a bastard, and she really loves you. Be nice to the kid."

Widening his eyes Mark asked, "Aren't I?"

"No, you are not," Duncan said flatly.

"But I'm going with her, aren't I? If I were as horrible as you make me out to be, I would have dropped her long back. Pulane's maid coins don't even cover my expenses. I'm only keeping her out of the goodness of my heart."

"Mark, you are a prostitute!"

"Muddy it any way you want, but if it's not me who loves it, I ain't taking any crap, you *pay*."

"You aren't even going out with her, you're only sleeping with her, and that, we mustn't forget, she pays for."

Laughing humorously Mark asked, "So who do you expect to pay for Pulane's pleasures then? I'm a businessman Dun, I can't afford to give free fucks "

He looked at Duncan curiously. "So how come you're here this early? Knocked off already? Man, you are lucky."

"My mind isn't really into work today. That Maria bitch, can you believe her nerve? The bitch ditched me last night."

"So what? Too many fishes out there," Mark dismissively said as he cut dead leaves from some potted plants.

"Yeah, but this is the one fish I still need to keep," Duncan explained.

"She dumped you – see where your goodness has gotten you, Dun?" Without looking up he asked, "What's the story?"

"She wants the 'Mrs Duncan' title – two years playing girlfriend is too long a trial, so she said."

"Marriage!" Mark exclaimed, straightening up.

"Yeah," Duncan admitted.

"But Maria, she isn't all that."

"My point exactly," said Duncan as he assembled the leaves Mark had been cutting into a heap.

"She wants marriage. Un-fucking-believable! What's she going to give you in return? Why are you taking such shit?"

"I don't know, Mark," he said miserably. "I still want her but not enough to marry her."

"Her expectations are too high. Maria has practically nothing to offer you," said Mark flatly. Nodding his head in understanding, he continued, "So ask her to move in with you. Most girls, especially Maria's kind, get off on that. Stay with her and make sure you fuck all the bullshit out of her. Familiarity breeds contempt. She'll soon get on your nerves, and that's when you can easily kick her out."

"I tried that trick, didn't work. She said her parents would kill her if she moved in."

"You shouldn't let a girl get to you this way, Duncan, it's not wise."

"Can't help the way I feel."

Staring at the potted plants he had just pruned, Mark said, "So play her along. If it's marriage she wants, give her that."

"Mark, you aren't listening. I don't want to marry her!"

"Has she ever met your parents?"

"She isn't even important enough to meet my dogs, Mark. Sex is good, but not that 'wow' to marry for." Duncan shook his head, irritated. "Damn, what is it with girls and this 'marry me, marry me' shit?"

Shrugging indifferently, Mark said, "So get a couple of old people to pose as your parents."

"Huh?"

"Just to buy time since you aren't emotionally equipped to deal with being dumped," Mark said. "So here's what to do, it's simple. Hold court with her parents. Negotiate bride price with Maria's parents, and your 'parents' will plead for some time to come up with the bridal price. In the meantime, you have your way with her; fuck her out of your blood. She's full of shit, who does she think she is blackmailing a brother into marriage?"

"That's horrible! That will mean lying to her parents. I can't do that to old folks," Duncan angrily protested. "It will be jinxing my life!"

"But she's the one forcing you to do that," Mark calmly said.

Shaking his head Duncan replied, "No way, mate, I'll never sink that low."

"Suit yourself. It's not me who's so whipped into her," said Mark as he crossed the lawn and picked up some more fallen leaves. "I wonder which DJs will be spinning discs tonight," he said dreamily.

"So you really are set on clubbing tonight?"

"Sure, you can join me if you want."

"I'm broke."

"So what? Pulane with a combination of Cindy will un-broke us," he laughed.

Thrusting his hands in his pockets, Duncan asked, "What happens if Maria's parents wait and there's still no bridal price?"

"You won't be so hung up on her by then, but if you are, you explain how hard times are. You're just a gardener and eight herds of cows is not a fucking joke. Just say you're still saving the money to buy those cows." Looking at him, Mark continued, "She is only a stupid little bitch, not even worth going to all the trouble!"

"I don't mind lying to her, but to deceive her poor old parents, no!"

"Like I said, it's your funeral. Can't believe you're so hung up on this little whore to take such crap," Mark said irritably. "Why, Duncan, why? Does this girl give you money?"

Appalled, Duncan said, "No! I'm not like you, mate."

"The girl has no sense of appreciation, and you still *want* her!" Looking at his friend, Mark said, "So what is it then?"

"I don't know, Mark, it's not something I can explain."

"Oh, a tight little pussy has you completely whipped." Raising his voice in anger, Mark said, "You are a fucking *moron*, Duncan!"

"I'll have another talk with her, and if she stays adamant…I don't know. I just can't marry her. I know I'm only a gardener, but does that mean I should marry a fucking maid? Duncan shook his head mournfully. "Jeez, women, as soon as they come, they start whining! What's wrong with this girl? Why can't she give me a fucking break?" Duncan moaned.

"How does she even get time to make these exorbitant demands on you, Dun?" Mark chided, frowning at Duncan. "You are supposed to be having sex with her, not a cosy little chat. That's the shit that happens when you let a woman open her mouth on you!"

"So, Mark, I'll see you later."

"Sure. I'll drop by at eight. Don't let her get to you." He quickly tossed the leaves Duncan had assembled in the wheelbarrow.

Mark was almost thirty-one years old and still pushing wheelbarrows! No, what he needed was a lucrative change of scene. About time he moved on. Pulane and Cindy were too small potatoes.

What he needed was a clued-up woman with a load of cash, enough cash to bail him out of this wheelbarrow-pushing shit.

As she buoyantly handed Mark two packets of twenty Marlboro and a bottle of Vodka, Pulane's mind wandered off to what Sue the mouth had said when she got back from the flea market.

"You are a stupid little bitch, Pulane!" she had spat.

If Pulane hadn't been in a hurry to see Mark, she would have sat down and calmly explained the whole deal to Sue. She would have sat there until she got through to her.

She would have explained that if what she was doing made her a 'stupid bitch', then no worries, she could live with that. She couldn't help it really, but hey, being a stupid bitch had its own rewards because when she was playing the stupid bitch, there was absolutely no pain in her heart. Mark was cool, and there was no more Cindy to haunt her. It was complete bliss, she felt good and happy.

Yet when she tried to be strong and deprive Mark of her pay, it was pure unadulterated hell.

Disbelievingly she shook her head.

One time she figured Sue knew what she was on about. She figured that with her being old and stuff, she knew better. So she listened.

When Mark came to ask for more cash, she threw him out – exactly as Sue had advised.

But Sue hadn't mentioned the pain; an excruciating pain right there in her heart. It was so deep that she was totally convinced she was going to die. Too piercing a pain, especially when Mark blatantly paraded around with a variety of girls under her nose. It was actually during that time when that awful Cindy entered the scene – all because she listened to fucking Sue!

She had held on because Sue insisted the pain would eventually go away, but it didn't, instead it plunged deeper. Just when Pulane was about to give in, Sue had started another song and dance about stuff called self-worth and dignity. She emphasised how very important those were to anyone, especially a young girl like Pulane. Again, she listened. It was hard, but she listened, grasping at her newfound knowledge of this dignity and self-respect because she was told they were important, and under no circumstances should she let go of them.

A month went by and the pain got even worse because Mark now seemed to be going steady with the schoolteacher. Going steady with the dreadful schoolteacher! "Are things ever going to get any better?" she had sobbed.

"Yes, and remember you were able to walk out with your pride intact," Sue had said.

"What good is this fucking pride?" she had cried.

"Very, very good," said Sue.

"But I'm hurting so much."

"I'm older. It's me you should listen to."

That much she agreed. Sue had been around far longer than her. Still….

Sue said she should walk with her head held high and with a bright smile plastered on her face. While inside she wanted to scream, "I want you so bad, Mark. I want you so so bad. Come back!"

But Sue said, "No, no, don't scream 'I want you so bad, Mark.'" Sue said she must scream, "I'm glad you are out of my life you fucking bastard!"

Hell, but that wasn't what she wanted to scream.

Sue said, "Listen I know what I'm talking about."

So she screamed, "I'm glad…"

Sue said that when she saw Mark and Cindy together she should just walk past with her head held high.

But that wasn't what she wanted to do either.

What she wanted to do was scream at the schoolteacher bitch to lay off her man.

Sue said, "Listen, I've been around long before you…."

At first, Pulane faithfully listened. But as more days past, she grew discontented because it seemed that this dignity thing wasn't that big a deal. It didn't even abate the pain. It made her feel worse; she wanted to die even more than before.

It was like having a nasty headache – no, that wasn't severe enough – an advanced stomach ulcer and staring at your medication yet not taking it because you figured you knew better. But the question was: Where exactly did you get your medical degree? What makes you think you can do better?

That made her think long and hard. She loved Mark, but Mark did not believe in charity. You needed to cough up cash for him, buy him smokes, party packs for the weekend, and all that buyable jazz. And yes, so far it was Mark who held the secret code to her heart. And Sue was saying she should trade her soul food for this dignity thing.

No! Hell no! – That was what she decided.

She went to Mark, said her sorries and just to show how remorseful she was she had handed him her whole pay. And like a miracle, Mark was back to his nice charming self. He told her she was a good girl, and he even said his sorries for straying. He explained how hard it was, especially when he couldn't think straight while craving for some smokes.

Now Sue was mouthing 'stupid' to her, Pulane sighed.

Well, being a stupid bitch wasn't so bad really she firmly told herself. There was her proof, right there before her eyes. Mark's face was grim no more. Mark was smiling at her. Really smiling at her with his love for her shining in his eyes. Wow, she felt the immense joy erupting from her heart. She felt so fucking good she could fly.

"What are you thinking about?"

"You, of course, here's fifteen pulas." She thrust two notes at him.

"Good girl," he said. Not much, Cindy would have to top this up.

"Are you still going to call Cindy?"

Surprise registered on his face. "Call Cindy, what the hell for?"

He eyed the 750ml bottle of vodka she'd brought. He decided she deserved a little reward, so he turned on the charm.

"Why would I call Cindy when I have you?"

"Really?" she felt she was going to explode with happiness.

He was an expert on such things; he knew what was expected of him. He took her in his arms and worked on her with his skilful hands.

Later.

"I saw Duncan this afternoon. You guys going out tonight?"

"Yeah," he admitted, playing with her hair.

"Can I come with you?" she asked, resting her head on his shoulder.

"Come on, hon, a seedy nightclub for such a special lady? Not for you, my babe, that's too trashy a place to bring you along."

He decided to throw her a juicy bone to keep her in line.

"I'll take you out to a nice Indian restaurant. You're my future wife, and you, my dear, deserve the best."

"When?" she eagerly asked.

"Soon." Like hell he would.

Kissing him. "Okay, see you when you get back."

"Of course, sweetie," he readily agreed.

"Pulane," he heavily exhaled after she was gone. One of the reasons she was still around in his life was because she was easy meat, so easy to chew.

Pulane, on the other hand, was floating on air. *Future wife!* Mark actually did call her his 'future wife'!

CHAPTER THREE

Dean surfaced with his body aching all over, and with a bitter taste in his mouth. When he tried to get up, he felt as if his faithful forty-year-old body had suddenly turned on him. But he knew he was reaping what he'd sown.

Lager had always been his drink, but last night he bumped into an old friend who offered him some foreign blue vodka. He didn't ask how strong the stuff was lest his friend get offended. These days one had to be on his guard; even a mere good morning could trigger a flurry of punches on your face. Besides, when you were broke, you just couldn't afford to ask questions, yours was to nod your head in union to whatever the sponsor said. What if his friend was suddenly to lose his sharing spirit? No, that wouldn't do, especially when he desperately need a drink. So he had drunk and drunk the stuff and hoped the hangover wouldn't beat him too hard. Because when you were at his age, your body didn't tolerate certain surprises, especially foreign alcoholic surprises. So who was he to whine? He knew he had an understanding with his body. A lager understanding, not some foreign blue drink!

Slowly he got out of bed and proceeded to the kitchen, where he drank the only thing in the fridge, water – lots and lots of it. Of course, his body had the right to hurt, but the impact of the pain was way over the top. It was making too much noise over an anthill. He didn't have a single cent to his name; he had to take whatever was offered because…his face brightened as he recalled the B-complex capsules and the aspirin in his medicine cabinet. He glanced at the clock after taking two of each pills, eleven in the morning. Surprised? He was not.

"Hi, Dean," she said.

She was standing by the bedroom door in her battered birthday suit. At a snail's pace, she walked towards him purring, her flabby flesh hanging loosely on her frail frame. When he looked at her freckled face, littered with huge pimples, he was reminded of the pizza he at times bought at the fast-food outlet across the road.

He shook his head in disgust.

What had that damn vodka reduced him to?

When he looked at her again, he was completely baffled because Madam Wasted Pizza wasn't in the least bit embarrassed. Very sure of herself and oozing with confidence she slowly strutted to him. Looking at her clothes scattered all over, the kind of clothes one would expect to find…where? Jesus! Not even in a dustbin. But the self-confidence stumped him.

Surely, she wouldn't be daft enough to think she could seduce him now. Sure, last night was last night, he was muddled by that strong drink, plus it was dark, a recipe for disaster that made this revolting thing bewitch his vodka-induced vision. He couldn't recall her name, but that didn't bother him. What bothered him was the fact that he had spent the night, or what remained of the night after all that drinking, with such sickening tub of shit. Bile rose to his throat as he saw the lumpy sores on her wasted body. But Madam Pizza seemed to be in a serious mission as she strutted along, enveloping her used-up arms around him.

Roughly untangling himself he shouted, "Take your diseased hands off me!" Horrified as he smelt her insecticide-smelling perfume.

"What's wrong?" she whined, taken aback.

He looked at the nightmare facing him, and this time he welcomed the vicious sickness that followed. At lightning speed, he ran to the bathroom, where he violently vomited, clutching at his throat.

"I didn't sleep with her. I didn't sleep with her. I couldn't have!"

He felt dirty, humiliated and shocked for linking up with such horror. And his pride – where the hell had that gone? The very day he got broke, it ran out on him.

AIDS!

He gasped in horror as he recalled the lumpy sores and the skeletal figure with its jelly thighs and floppy tits. Hot scorching tears came out because with Mister AIDS there were simply no mercies, no I'll be careful tomorrows.

"What exactly happened last night?" he pondered. AIDS a shit business, no kidding about that. So devious that it could castrate a man, a man his age.

Am I on a death row? Dean thought.

Because no matter how much they glorified those anti-retroviral drugs, you'd still be on a death row. And even if you managed to scoop a ten-year ARV borrowed life, when they finally got around to burying you, it was AIDS that would be having the last laugh.

Thrush in the mouth, diarrhoea so severe that....

He started sweating in terror.

He sunk to his knees and remembered God, the God he had hardly paid attention to for the past thirty years of his life.

"Not AIDS, God, anything else but that. I won't be able to deal with that. He wailed in terror. " I…I will die. Next time I'll…."

Next, time what? He was at a loss for words. He still remembered when he was small and his mum used to drag him to church, so he knew what God expected of him. For a start, he was not supposed to have slept with Madam Diseased Pizza unless their mutual agreement was tied in a nice marriage knot. Very, very worried he now was.

So next time, what?

A rubber?

Beating his head in frustration, he had always stuck to using a condom. The thought of AIDS was enough to sober anyone. So why didn't he?

Why didn't he, damn it?

The terror gave rise to the soliloquy.

"It was that damn fucking strong drink. Hey, no worries. Strong drink is it then. So strong drink is justifiably the one that will contract monster AIDS."

He carried on trying to convince himself. "Strong drink is the one that will get the unending diarrhoea. The one that will be wrapped in extra-large nappies. Only it doesn't work that way, does it? Life doesn't have an ounce of justification. A shred of fairness."

"So why did you do it?" he asked himself. "It was my drunk

wanting dick!"

Lovely, he thought. All it took was a little nudge from the AIDS best buddy – drink. Five of his pals, what had they said as they were lying there wrapped in extra-large nappies? Didn't they yelp the now familiar words? Words he had stumbled on last night. Words he now knew as 'Drunk wanting dick'.

Well hadn't they?

He squeezed his eyes shut as his feeling of terror deepened.

"God, you have to help me, you really have to help me," he begged, stuttering in shock.

"Heavenly Father, I know you are a good God, a real good God…" After praying, he decided to take a cold shower, hoping the woman would be gone when he came out.

Such a battered diseased wreck of a girl! *What the heck is happening to me?* He asked himself the question he knew the answer to. Flat broke was what was happening to him.

"Dean, can I join you?" she asked from behind the closed door.

He jumped out of the shower in alarm and hastily locked the door.

Trying the door she whined, "Dean."

What have I gotten myself into? he cursed.

"Dean."

He could detect the desperation in her voice. He couldn't blame her for that though. With her kind of looks, she had to be really desperate to go on living.

Vigorously rubbing his body with a sponge, he still couldn't get over what he did last night, and without a condom! Looking at his dick, he recoiled. Oh Lord it looked so red.

Should he pray again? He wondered, his eyes glistening with tears. He grabbed an antibacterial spray and looked at his dick again. Maybe sanitising… *For fuck's sake! Am I losing my mind now?* He threw the spray at the wall violently.

Of course, people say, 'Fuck it, we are all going to die.' But not with AIDS, with AIDS you didn't just die. He sobbed. Living an AIDS-ridden life with your heart in your mouth as if someone was putting a gun to your head. Tiptoeing through life like a scared little mouse not knowing when your ARV overdraft would expire.

Terrified he shook his head over and over again.

AIDS having the best picnic inside your miserable self. Springing any tormenting ailments it felt like on you! And last night he had done it; let an urgent wanting dick screaming for release be the deciding god of his life. And that diarrhoea, the horrible blisters, the hair-splitting cough. *Oh Lord!* he thought.

In an instant, he was back on his knees. And in a quivering voice he tearfully pleaded for a second chance with the one he knew could help.

When he came out of the bathroom, there was no such luck. She lay spread-eagled in bed – could there be a sorrier sight?

"Did we have sex last night?" He could be just paranoid; they might not have done anything. Then why the fuck were they both naked? His head started to spin.

"Let's fuck," she hungrily said, licking her whore lips at him.

Swallowing the knot on his throat, "Did we…did we use protection?" he asked in a strangled voice.

"Sure, what do you take me for, a fool?"

Having worn out the little looks you had with your whoring, could it be possible you still have that small brain? "I don't take you for anything," he flatly said.

In a hard whore voice, a voice that had done it all and said it all, she said, "Hey, what's with twenty questions, are you going to fuck me or not?"

Screaming agitatedly he said, "Where are the fucking condoms then?"

She crawled under the bed and dangled a used condom at him.

"Happy now?" she said, heavy with sarcasm.

Thank you, Jesus. Hallelujah! Thank you so very much. Oh Lord, you really are the best deal one can ever have.

So totally relieved he was that he forgot himself. He jubilantly grabbed her and started waltzing her around the room. She misunderstood and started caressing him with her coarse hands. That brought him around, and he jumped out of her deadly claws.

"I think you should go now."

"Why?"

One blurred night, one single night she spent with him and already she was asking him the whys. *Fucking hell!* "Get the fuck out of my house!" he exploded.

"I didn't come last night," she said accusingly.

"Tough," he said, shrugging.

"I'm not getting out of here till I get my dues, you owe me a come, mister," she shouted, pointing a straight finger at him.

Owe her a come! "What you are you going to do then, rape me?" he taunted.

"I don't have money for a cab," she said, changing lanes.

A fucking whore, that's what she was. "That's good cos you'll have to walk then," he said, nodding his head. "It might help in toning that hanging flesh of yours."

"I live too far."

"Get out!" he thundered.

"Okay, okay."

Clever girl, he thought because even though he wasn't in the mood to be physical, it wouldn't do for her to prise a couple of punches from him. Imagine a fucking whore like that giving him grief, questioning him!

She took her time getting up, hoping that he would change his mind about asking her to leave.

Fat chance of that!

He watched his temper progressing to its peak as she slowly picked up a short black dress from the foot of the bed. This was his house. He grabbed her by the hair, dragging her half-naked body to the door, throwing her out along with her shabby dress and trashy shoes.

She didn't take kindly to such treatment. Pretty soon, he heard her pounding on the door, shouting at him; her words spiced with chilling profanities he chose to ignore. He had his own problems, money problems; his rent was due next week. So why waste time on a trashy little whore?

I guess I should update Jomo on my predicament, he thought. He had every right to be optimistic when it came to his brother Jomo. They were both from the grime of a stagnant town called Francistown. With distaste, he began reminiscing of the 'good old days'. He didn't know if his so-called parents were still alive, and the truth was he simply didn't care. When he turned twenty, Jomo twenty-five, they decided they'd had enough of their mother's loud sarcastic mouth and their old man's bullying fists. They left, and that had been twenty years ago. Their parents hadn't come looking for them. Probably a blessing in disguise for them, two less brats they didn't have to look out for again. Dean idly wondered what had happened to their other two wimpy brothers, not that he really cared. As far as he was concerned, Jomo was the only family he had.

When they arrived in Gaborone, they joined a notorious gang called 'Snoop'. It was their only choice since they had both flunked their GCSEs. Jomo, with guts made of steel, soon acquired a higher place in the gang. Quite unlike Dean, whose only mission in life was blowing the money he earned on beer and women. He had already been given several warnings for his lack of discipline and commitment, but the last straw had been a year ago.

He had been with Steve, the big man's son, and two other guys when they robbed the Standard Bank at the African Mall. The heist went down all okay. He was behind the steering wheel, but tipsy as he was his reflexes were impaired. While making good their escape their car hit the wall. An unruffled Steve didn't hesitate; he shoved Dean away from the driver's seat, took over and drove off at full speed. The car was heavily dented and speeding around with it in broad daylight was tempting fate. Along the way, they 'borrowed' a car, and that didn't take more than five minutes. The big man, Chief, wasn't amused when he was briefed on the operation though.

He screamed at Jomo, "I want that fucking prick brother of yours out!"

A week later Chief had summoned him. Two of Chief's ass-licking thugs had burst into his apartment unannounced and bundled him into a car to one of Chief's many warehouses.

"You are a fuck up. A careless motherfucking piece of shit," the old man had coldly said, stroking one of his many guns. "Every ambitious motherfucking cop and its mother wants to nail me." He had grabbed the gun pointing it at Dean. "I am not going down cos of your fuck ups. Are you *listening* to me you piece of shit?" Chief was not into bluffs, he had pulled the trigger on Dean, and the bullet had missed him by inches, embedding itself in the wall.

Dean had thought, *That's it. I am finished*. He had been certain he was going then, he could almost see the demons dancing. Dropping on his knees with mucus flooding tears he had sobbed, "I'm so sorry, Chief. It won't happen again. Promise!"

"Get the fucker outta my sight!" Chief had screamed at his gorillas, whacking Dean repeatedly on the head with the gun.

But Jomo being Jomo had somehow cooled the old man down, and instead of being thrown out, he had been slammed with a suspension. For two whole years, he was told never to darken Snoop's door. Jomo kept pleading on his behalf, but this time Chief didn't budge. He told Jomo without mincing his words that Dean needed a two-year attitude adjustment.

Two years without a job and pay. He still couldn't believe Chief could be this hard. And all because he had a couple of drinks before going on a job!

Yes, besides Snoop, there were other gangs. But Snoop was the most notorious. It was greatly feared and what it said went. It was quite a blow when he realised Snoop suspending him meant he was blackballed. Not a single gang was willing to risk Chief's wrath by taking him in.

What was he to do? The only profession he was familiar with was on the other side of the law. There was nothing legal for him, not with him having flunked his GCSEs. Sure, they were dumb shit jobs out there with insulting wages, but who needed that crap?

Then Jomo got him an assistant manager's job in a restaurant. His job was to ensure the customers' service was top grade. Somehow, he had managed to blow that one. He couldn't quite recall what made the manager to send him packing, but it had something to do with one of the staff's nicely packaged behind, which Dean had been fond of grabbing.

Two fucking years for such a small transgression – Un-fucking-believable! It wasn't like he was *swimming* in it; just a little tipsy, that was all. He needed something to steel his nerves. Did chief think robbing a bank was child's play? The fucking bastard just sat on his fat ass screaming orders and reaping dividends! He'd blown the whole thing out of proportion.

"Don't bullshit me, you fucking moron! You drove onto that wall because you were fucking drunk, you piece of shit!" he'd said.

Fucking hell! Who'd have thought two years could take this long, he cursed. Only a year had elapsed since the suspension, and he really felt he had now learnt whatever lesson Chief had in mind. But Chief wouldn't be convinced. Two years was two years. He'd even threatened Jomo with an extension if they don't quit bugging him.

At eight that evening Dean was at Granada nightclub.

He sat there nursing a glass of lemonade waiting for his brother. Jomo was cool, one way or another he would come up with something.

No alcohol, it was time – time to sober up and tackle life with a clear head. Hell, I know I'm one of them failures. Why kid myself otherwise. Hiding under alcohol stupor, walking the streets as if I'm the man while – ugh, no need to beat myself up.

It happened.

"Forty years of age and Jomo is still babysitting me. Forty flipping years," he repeated, disgruntled.

Fucking hell, what was that?

Three hundred and sixty-five days – and what? Forty times that. Jesus! He hastily stamped the urge to work out the exact figure because he was already too revolted with himself.

This is it, no more fucking around. I'm changing. To think I'm this fucking old! What happened to all those years I'm supposedly to have had? Drink and women – exploring pussy. Took forty of them years to learn the lesson. That pussy is just pussy, you don't lose your mind over that. Fuck the bitch, yes, wipe yourself off and fucking get on with your life. Drugs? Thank God, Jomo had beaten the drugs demons out of him. He'd tried that route, Jomo got some thugs to beat him up and break his ribs. It took months to heal and Jomo hadn't minced his words.

"It's up to you, bro. Every time you take drugs, I will get you beaten up." Shrugging, he continued, "Might beat you to death next time." In a hard voice, eyes glittering dangerously he shouted, "I would rather have you dead than have a fucking junkie for a brother!"

Forty years old. Sighing, Dean slumped his shoulders. *And a fucking failure.*

One of the many reasons he had never heeded Chief's threats before the suspension was because of his brother Jomo; he was always there to take him under his wing. When Dean was suspended he relaxed and acted as if he was on holiday – blowing Jomo's money on beer and women. And the reason he couldn't pay his rent was because Jomo had been paying his rent with a twelve-month standing order. However, the standing order had now expired, and with Jomo being too busy to renew it, he had just given Dean a five-thousand-pula cheque, inclusive of one thousand for rent. That was two weeks ago, the five thousand was all gone now, and dear brother was going to grill Dean for that.

No, it was time, time to do something about his life.

Forty of them years!

Taking a deep breath he thought, Jomo, my queen mother. One hell of a brother, Jomo; but hey, even mothers throw in the towel eventually. Yeah, for real. A long overdue wakeup call.

Taking a sip of his lemonade, he sighed. If he kept on with this kind of life, next time…he shook his head. Yes, AIDS really scared the living daylights out of him. It was not about him being frightened of dying, it was the way it beat you to a sorry sight before dragging you to your grave! No, he couldn't take that.

And maybe that girl this morning didn't have eternal germs crawling in her. Maybe - Stop it, stop right now, his inner voice admonished him. That girl is sick, hell she looked sick. So what's up, Mister, wanna go for seconds? No! He grimaced.

So stop fucking around. Or maybe you miss your mates so much you want to follow suite, hey, it's a free country.

Before his brother had sat down, Dean started.

"I need a job! I can't live like this any more." He spoke as if it was Jomo's fault.

Jomo just looked at him, shaking his head.

"I can't live my life accepting handouts, Jomo. Last night I accepted one handout that nearly cost me my life," he said, raising his voice emotionally.

"Hey, if you want my help, you are going to have to lower that damn voice of yours!"

After he had ordered his drink, Jomo asked, "You were telling me about something that nearly cost you your life."

"I didn't have cash to buy my drink. Some guy gave me this strong Russian vodka and I blacked out."

"You blew the whole of that five thousand already?"

In a small voice he said, "Jomo, please don't shout at me."

"Dean, when are you going to fucking grow up?"

He answered sullenly, "I'm all grown up now."

Jomo's drink came.

"Bring me more lemonade," Dean ordered the waiter.

"You're drinking lemonade?"

"I'm not an alcoholic, Jomo."

"Surprise, surprise," Jomo said as he raised his glass to his mouth.

"Okay, as I've already told you, I need a job." Grumpily, he continued. "Fucking Steve, I thought he was my mate, I didn't know he would run home to daddy and tell tales."

"Drunk on a job and you have the nerve to blame other people!"

Dean shouted at his brother, "I wasn't fucking drunk! Fucking hell, Jomo, I bloody need a job!"

Jomo looked at him. "Ha! 'I need a job'," he mimicked. "What about the fucking job I got you?"

Frowning, Dean said, "What job? Fucking manager fired me cos he wanted to fuck all those girls in the restaurant. Guy is married. How the fuck was I supposed to know his extracurricular activities extended to the restaurant? The whole fucking restaurant for that matter!"

Putting his glass down, Jomo said, "I agree, the guy is greedy, we should raise his rent and teach him who he's messing with." Pointing a finger at Dean, Jomo berated, "But where do you get off grabbing your waitress's ass? Were you fucking drunk?"

Looking in his drink, he mumbled, "It was a grabbable ass."

"You are a fucking disgrace!" Gathering steam, Jomo shouted, "First I get you an in with the big man, fucking go on my knees begging him to let you lead some of our operations, but what the fuck happens? You fuck up! I ask you to keep an eye on massage parlours; instead of girls servicing customers, they spend all their time on you. Telling some of our girls they are now your exclusive fuck, forbidding them to sleep with customers!"

"That was only with Brenda – she's sixteen for fuck's sake!"

"Oh, but it's okay for you to fuck her!" Glaring at him Jomo said, "Telling girls that if prostitution is such an okay trade, maybe Chief should get his mother and daughters into it. Stuff like that getting to

Chief. No wonder he wanted to blow your fucking brains out!"

"I fucking hate Chief. Fucking pulled a gun on me...."

Slamming his fist on the table, Jomo yelled, "Shut the fuck up, you fucking moron! We put you on a job, you get drunk. We ask you to collect the rents, the money comes up short cos you are a fucking thief who steals from the very people helping you out. And all the time who has to kneel down and placate Chief? Me! Fucking me!" He poked his chest with his finger.

Quietly Dean said, "Okay, I'm a bastard, I know that. Sorry."

In a hard voice, Jomo said, "Listen, this is it, I've had it with you. You fuck up, and I ain't holding your hand no more!"

"I really need a job," Dean said determinedly. "Ivan is the only one who can take me in now."

"Yeah, Ivan is the one guy who doesn't jump for Chief, he might help. And he doesn't take shit either, if you get on his wrong side, he will fucking blow your brains out!"

"I won't fuck up this time."

"And how many times have I heard that?" Jomo said despairingly.

Dean said vehemently, "I mean it this time!"

"Anyway, I hear Ivan is abroad," explained Jomo.

"Abroad?"

"Holiday." Jomo emptied his drink. "He'll be back."

"When?"

"Don't know." He shrugged. "Stop pestering me about Ivan."

"After drinking that strong stuff, I woke up to find a fully blown AIDS girl in my bed – well, she looked like she had the eternal curse," he blurted.

Lurching to his feet in shock Jomo seized his brother by the collar of his denim shirt. "You slept with an AIDS whore?"

"But I used a rubber!" Dean hastily added.

Jomo abruptly released his collar and sat down heavily, shaking his head. "Still, a stunt like that..." he said.

"I need something to keep myself busy," Dean explained.

"Are you sure you used protection?"

"Yep."

"Listen, Dean, condoms are not an absolute deal." Leaning forward, Jomo said seriously, "If it had burst, what would have become of you?"

In a small voice Dean replied, "I really am scared of AIDS."

"AIDS is a bitch of a disease, Dean. A bitch of a disease! And this mindless screwing of yours…."

Nodding his head, Dean agreed. "It ate up all my friends."

"And I can see how desperately you want to be next."

"I had a narrow escape."

Jomo said, "AIDS is as much of a shit disease as cancer. But the thing that infuriates me about AIDS is at least if you take care of yourself, you are safe, while cancer you never have that much of a chance, but we still have people like you, blindly getting drunk and indulging in deadly stunts."

"Hey, hey, Pastor, cool it! I know the deal; to stand on my own two feet, get a job. I've done enough sampling of the honeys. Time I settled down."

"You settling down! With who?"

"Go on, laugh. But I'm all ready now, though I haven't met her yet. Come on, bro, help me find a job!"

"I'll see what I can do."

"Anything you can get, I'm your boy," Dean said.

"Good, cos I ain't taking any more of your crap!"

"It's this sitting around doing nothing that's doing my head in," he said, shaking his head. "Hey, I was at your house on Friday," he stated.

"I was out of town," Jomo said as the waiter brought more drinks.

"And why is the garden so messed up, Jomo?" He added, "The lawn is fucked up, and the flowers I planted are all dead. I told you to feed them with an organic fertiliser. I fucking told you that!"

"Organic fertiliser?"

"Yes, Jomo, I left it at your house, remember? Where did you take it?"

Jomo carelessly shrugged. "Cleaning lady probably threw it in the garbage bin."

"What?"

"Give me a break, Dean. I don't give a fuck about that gardening shit."

"Well I care," Dean said emotionally.

Leaning forward, his brother suggested, "Speaking of gardening, here is the deal, why not work as a gardener? You're keen on gardening stuff,".

Dean was too stunned to say a word. Did he really hear his brother right?

"It's the only thing you enjoy doing," insisted Jomo, taking mouthfuls of his drink.

"But…."

Jomo cut him short, pointing a straight finger at him. "But nothing, Dean. This is no time for some stupid pride. And this time I'm not bluffing; either you snap out of your childishness, or you are on your own," he said with an edge in his voice.

"I can't live on such peanut wages."

"What peanut wage?"

"Whatever gardeners are paid."

"I can always help with a bit of cash."

Dean looked at his brother coldly. "I'm not taking any more money from you! It's all your fault I turned out this way."

"Hey, I was only trying to help."

"Giving me money is not helping, Jomo," he said.

"How about I open a small business and I hire you?"

"And I become what, a manager? Not my scene. Can't handle money," he said, shaking his head.

"I've run out of ideas," said Jomo sitting back.

"I can't work for you cos I won't be able to take the job seriously."

"I see your point," agreed Jomo. Looking at his untouched drink, he asked, "Are you going to drink the stuff?"

Dean shook his head. "So?" he anxiously inquired.

"How about a gardening job, and I negotiate to something like nine hundred monthly? Accommodation and meals free. Besides, it's only for this year, next year you will be back with us."

"Why are you insisting on me working in a garden?" Dean huffed.

"What else is there? A waiter? You're too temperamental for that. A labourer? A lazy asshole like you? But gardening is something that you've always enjoyed doing. So it won't be such a big deal."

"A garden boy?" he said, shaking his head.

"That's it! Take care of yourself then," said Jomo, slamming his drink down and angrily getting to his feet.

Dean pleaded his brother. "Please, bro, I need your help here!"

"I told you, try gardening. Remember how I always had to drag you out of my garden cos once you are there you can't stop working. Even in school, you spent more time in the fucking school garden than in classes. You said it relaxes you, you said it!"

"I guess you're right, then," Dean agreed in a resigned voice.

"Good, I'll talk to this guy, Shane Chambers. I was with him yesterday when he mentioned something about looking for another gardener."

"So what are you now? A recruiter for donkey jobs?"

"Don't be silly, he only mentioned that cos he stumbled on me while I was calling the florist."

"Wow, and what did you order," Dean eagerly asked.

"Flowers, of course!"

"What flowers?"

"Roses."

"You are too fucking conventional!"

"I like roses – buy woman roses, she'll spread her legs so wide you'll think she's been sexually deprived."

Shaking his head Dean said, "And I'm the one being told off for screwing around."

"Let's go," Jomo said, getting to his feet.

"To where?"

"My house."

"I didn't manage to pay the rent," Dean confessed.

In a sarcastic voice, Jomo said, "And why am I not surprised?"

After they were in Jomo's car, Dean warily asked, "So what's this Chambers guy like?"

Engaging gears, Jomo said while driving, "Very much okay. Owns Charsecurity Systems."

"I've heard of him."

"And it won't be too much work on account of this Mark guy who is already working there. All you have to do is hold on till the suspension is over."

"I'll try," he said.

"So are you sleeping over?" Jomo asked.

"Yeah," Dean agreed.

As Jomo drove through the gate, Dean said darkly, "It really burns me up the way you neglect your garden."

CHAPTER FOUR

Monday morning at seven o'clock, Jomo was driving a sceptical Dean to the Phakalane suburbs.

"Come on cheer up, it's just a temp thing, you'll soon be back with us."

"Fucking hell, I've never worked as a gardener. If this guy isn't happy with me…" Dean shook his head.

"Yet you're the one who keeps saying gardening is the one thing you love doing."

"Yeah, with nobody breathing crap on my neck."

"Shane knows me as a reputable businessman. We play golf together." In a firm voice, Jomo told him, "Not a word about Snoop, okay?"

"Oh, and what business are you supposedly in?" He glared at his brother. "Drugs and making prostitutes out of little girls?"

"Don't talk shit, sixteen is not so little," Jomo said. "Do you see us forcing them, huh? These girls are nothing but fucking whores. No fucking self-respect, selling pussy like they're selling sweets!" He snorted in disgust. "Why not try cleaning jobs? Or better, get a cooler box camp outside the school gate and sell ice pops. Honestly! I can never understand a girl who resorts to selling her body."

Stretching his legs, Dean remarked, "That's funny talk from a fucking pimp."

As he drove on, Jomo remarked, "Pimp? Me? Don't fucking insult me, bro. We fucking protect those girls, give them good working environment and only get a cut. It's business, pure and simple! And by the way, no screwing kitchen girls!" In a warning voice Jomo continued, "Shane knows you are my bro. Any shit you pull will reflect on me." Looking at Dean sternly, he added, "You better stop with the crap and pull up your socks!"

"I used to like sex, really like it, but this bitch of a disease lullabies my dick to sleep – I don't know, maybe I'm too paranoid about AIDS, but believe me, it scares the shit out of me."

"No one has enough balls to tackle AIDS head on, but you don't have to be scared, careful is the right tactic – know who to fuck." Looking at his brother Jomo said, "And like I said, you'll be working with someone – guy called Mark. Be nice, do what this guy tells you. I don't want to get funny phone calls from Shane about you," he said as he drove through the motorised gate on a paved driveway.

The beautifully manicured lawn mesmerised Dean, flourishing with variety of plants including lilies and huge dazzling roses.

"Wow," he said in admiration, staring at the lawn that was smooth and green with blazing flowerbeds and a series of winding walks.

He jumped out of the car with Jomo trailing behind.

"It's a beautiful garden," murmured Jomo.

"This is it, Jomo, so enthralling. Look at how this Mark experimented with colour and texture by using container gardening," he said pointing at the beautiful potted plants.

"And he has a good head for this. Take a look at this; here he used discarded ice buckets for potting which gives it a rustic appeal."

Jomo snorted, "Discarded ice buckets, why couldn't he just buy a proper vase?"

"A vase is not so cool. Like its colour, you can get tired of looking at it."

Dragging Jomo on, Dean continued, "Now there is a beauty. The aloe; as you can see, it makes orange red flowers that brighten up this place. Even when not in flower the leaves do a good job of adding texture, making a cool plant. There is the pyracantha; it's great for attracting birds in the garden. Most people call it an orange charmer, see that – that is the lavender, and you can see how its lovely flowers boost up this garden," he explained.

"But what did he put in this pot, it can't be water?" asked Jomo, frowning at the tall colourless pot that was filled with orange liquid.

"It's water, he put in a food colour to match the...."

"Sorry, may I help?" inquired a short, fat woman, in a maid uniform.

"Morning. I am Jomo, and this here is my brother. We came to see Mr Chambers."

"Can you come this way, please?"

They were ushered to a huge immaculate study room. "Mr Chambers will be with you in a minute. Coffee, tea?" asked the housekeeper.

"Coffee, black no sugar please," said Jomo. "Dean?" But his brother was marvelling at a framed painting on the wall.

"Oh, I think I can tolerate one more cup of coffee. Black, no sugar," he told the woman, who hastily went to see to their coffee.

"He better not give me grief, Jomo. I won't work for a bitch boss who screams at me."

"Shh."

While they were having their coffee, the man of the house made his appearance, smiling and shaking both their hands.

Dean looked at him critical because he needed to know exactly what he was getting himself into here. There was nothing worse than working for an ungrateful bitch boss who screamed at you and made you feel stupid and useless. And shit like that Dean was not going to take, he firmly told himself. That was the shit that broke a man, and he started taking it out on his loved ones.

The man was in his mid-fifties, of medium height, pot-bellied with big broad shoulders and a receding hairline. Dean kept looking at him because the man being white meant he had to look even *harder*, especially at the eyes because some of the 'misters' were still running their slave network behind the closed doors of their homes. People knew that very well but didn't say it because they would be called whiners. Dean kept looking, searching for that racial gleam because these ones were cleverer than their grandfathers, no slave boats, no whips now – oh no, just like fashion, that nasty trend was no more.

Belittling looks sliding up and down were now doing the whippings. Whipping the insides, penal beating us into a dim world. Fucking hell, was it any wonder some of us had stopped trying? *Stopped trying - another icing on the cake for them,* Dean reflected. *Only we learn that too late. First, it is the anger. Too much of it, meanwhile years are going and the next thing you are pushing forty years. And you find yourself standing in front of one of them begging for a job to push their wheelbarrows and you feel drained, defeated. And you want to weep because you have played right into their fucking hands,* he thought.

He continued to humour the man with a smile, but he kept looking at him.

"Sorry to keep you waiting. So, this is your brother," the man said with a big welcoming smile after shaking both their hands. The eyes were kind, reassuring. Good. Very good.

"He sure is. His name is Dean."

"Nice to meet you, Dean, glad you'll be helping us in our garden. I'm in a hurry for work, but as you know from Jomo, you have the job. Hey, you can even start today."

"Thank you."

"You're welcome."

A few minutes later Dean met the man's wife; a tall blue-eyed blonde with a slim, alluring body. "Honey, this is Jomo's brother."

Dean braced himself, waiting for something to jump in honey's eyes while he shook her hand. Was he being paranoid? He took a belly deep breath – he was black. And yes, he knew the score. And no, he did not want to talk about it. A lot of brothers and sisters had done the talking. A lot of talking. A lot of songs. And where did it get them except being laughed at and called whiners?

"Pleased to meet you, Dean. So when do you think you'll be starting?" she asked, all smiles.

These two really seemed okay; still, you can't judge a picture by its cover like his nan used to say, "I can start today, ma'am."

"You can call me Sarah," she said. "We'd love a much bigger garden."

"No problem, Sarah."

"Mark, that's the guy you'd be working with, stays in a two-bedroom house at the back. You'll stay in another room. You work weekdays only, from eight to five," Mr Chambers explained. "That's the official time, but Mark is usually in the garden as early as six because in the afternoon it's too hot. And of course, he finishes any time he feels like. We don't really mind, as long as the garden looks good. You'll be earning nine hundred a month."

"Thank you, sir."

"Are you okay with everything? Anything to ask?"

Dean shook his head. "I'm fine with everything. No questions."

"Good, but if you encounter any problems while here, please feel free to come to us. We have a good team here: two ladies who see to the house, and Morgan who is our cook. Then there is Mark, the man you will be working with – he is an all right guy. We don't usually tell him what to do, that's how good he is at his job," said Mrs Chambers.

Laughing the husband piped in, "He is the one who tells us what changes he wants to make, and my wife will be like, 'No, Mark not that one, don't take that one out,' and he will say, 'I know what I'm doing, trust me'."

"And he will replace it with a more beautiful plant, making the garden even more hypnotic, and I see myself going back, 'Yes, Mark, you were right. You really know your stuff,'" said the wife, laughing along.

"Dean *loves* gardening," said Jomo.

"And so does Mark," the wife said. "I'm quite sure you two will get along."

He was later led out of a double door leading to the garden area, where he met a tall, very dark guy in overalls.

"Name's Mark," the man said, shaking Dean's hand.

"I am Dean. I love your garden," he admitted in admiration. He still couldn't get over such a beautiful sight – beautiful birds by the pyracantha, and the striking Ilex acquiflium with its glossy foliage. It was truly marvellous.

"Thanks," Mark proudly answered.

"They told me they want to extend the garden."

"Yeah."

"So where should I start digging," Dean asked all eager, picking up a spade that was lying on the ground.

"First you need to change into your working clothes."

"Working clothes?"

Winking, Mark replied, "Health and safety. Come on, they are in your room."

"Oh," he said, following Mark to the servants' quarters. Opening the door Mark led him into a small lounge furnished with four beanbags, a small telly and a portable radio.

"Beautiful," Dean said appreciatively.

Showing him to a small kitchen with a two-plate stove and a small sink, Mark said, "There isn't really that much reason to cook because all our meals are made in the main house. And this is your room."

"It's lovely," Dean said, admiring the fully furnished bedroom.

Mark pointed to the wardrobe. "I put your working clothes there: safety boots, gloves the lot. Our laundry is done by the girls, just put your clothes in the laundry bag, and they will sort it out. I'll be in my room, call me when you're done." Looking around, he asked, "Where is your gear?"

"My brother will be bringing it later."

"Okay," said Mark as he walked out of the room. The room was small but comfortably equipped, and there was clean linen folded on the bed. The bed was fine, a double with a wooden headboard. He sat on it to try the mattress – perfect. Everything neat and cool. Of course, the place wasn't as expensively furnished as his former place, but it wasn't bad. Besides, the only thing that counted was his privacy, a room to do his own stuff.

He quickly changed into blue overalls and boots, and stuffed the gloves in his back pocket. He called Mark and they hurried back to the garden.

"This is a nice place," Dean remarked.

"Yeah, the Chambers family are pretty cool."

Mark showed Dean where to start digging and he got to work. It was true – he really did love gardening. That was where he was at his best; it made him feel so at peace. He knew preparing a garden needed a lot of work because more effort at this stage would sure as hell pay later on. Plants would then have the nourishment they needed to thrive. With renewed vigour, he purposely cleared the bare strip of ground. With Mark busy with the trimming, he cleared the ground, working very hard to prove his capabilities.

At ten, a young woman came over.

"I've left your breakfast on the patio," she announced brightly to

Mark.

She was in a maid's uniform that ended just above her knees. Shit, never had he seen such dynamite legs! He dragged his eyes off the legs to check out the rest of the package. When his eyes rested on the bust, his mouth went completely dry. The face wasn't hot though, just – he fumbled for what word should he use – yeah, passable. Such a body though, a body that made the lukewarm impact of her face not matter at all. His heart started jumping as his eyes were drawn back to the eye-catching cleavage. *Shit! If only I can get those in my mouth.*

"Pulane, this is Dean. We'll be working together." His eyes were still focussed on the magnetic boobs. "Hi, nice to meet you," he said, offering his hand to clinch the greeting.

Ignoring his hand she flippantly said, "Oh nice to meet you too." Her eyes were only on Mark. Smiling at him, she quickly kissed him. "Have to go," she said, totally ignoring Dean.

Oh, so that was it. The girl was evidently Mark's. *How does it feel having those chewable tits squeezed between your…?*

Cutting into Dean's thoughts, Mark explained, "She is another housekeeper."

I can see that. What about the good stuff? About how it feels to have those big mamas in your hands, rubbing them with your dick, coming on those juicy tits.

Before he could stop himself, "Are they real?" he asked, fanning his face with his hand.

Laughing at him, Mark replied, "Of course, she's a maid. Where would she get money to *buy* such a yummy set?"

"What's she doing serving tea with such ravishing tits?"

"That's Pulane for you. No fucking ambition!" muttered Mark.

Sex bomb. Built for sex. Everything about that girl screamed sex. Long, slim, flexible legs promising exploratory indoor games. And Mark said that pair was real. Dean licked his dry lips. Still, she was Mark's and the last thing he needed was some conflicting drama with his teammate. And besides, there was that monster AIDS lurking around the corner, waiting to grab him by the balls. *Oh well*, he shrugged.

Angrily Pulane stomped back into the house.

Who was that pathetic joke? Tongue hanging out staring at her breasts! Bastard, she spat. You'd think he would have a shred of decency, pretending to be a nice guy, playing it cool. This was his first time around here for crying out loud!

Imagine him eating her up like that! She was so put off by his cannibalising show that she only came off with a peck from Mark, a fucking inadequate brushing of her lips on his mouth. She didn't even get to taste his mouth! Bastard didn't even pull her towards him, holding her as he usually did. Parting her lips to a soul-nourishing kiss. All he seemed interested in was her meeting that Dean. Like she gave a fuck about him. Like this Dean would quench the flame igniting inside her. Sometimes Mark could be so…aggravating! Why did he think she went to such lengths, preparing his breakfast bringing it all the way to the patio? Never mind Morgan the cook, when it came to breakfast, he was only interested in the Chambers. Sue didn't bother herself that much: burnt toast, overdone scrambled eggs with tea that looked more like dirty water. She dumped it all on the kitchen table and screamed at them to come get their breakfast. Pulane shook her head moodily.

All the trouble she had to go through with those heart-shaped crispy bread using the cookie cutter, the tricky omelettes. Did Mark think she was doing all this hard work just so she could be introduced to some cannibal jerk? She heaved a sigh. That bossy Susan had ordered her to do the laundry. Argg. Still, no worries, there was a nice efficient washing machine waiting to do all the hard work. She bent down to sort the clothes from the laundry basket.

She had only managed a deficient peck from her one and only.

With hands on her hips, she grumpily looked at the clothes on the floor, which lay in two separate heaps – whites and dark colours. She frowned – it seemed to be quite a lot. And on top of that, there would be ironing!

But that new gardener wasn't bad to look at – very handsome in fact. Not that she was taken in by his good looks. One time she was like that, totally bowled over by such looks, but she had come around – wise up. While the rest were busy bowing down to pretty faces, she had wisely retreated. Pretty faces were nothing really. Nada, zero, nothing.

She sat on a stool thoughts crowding on the new recruit. His face was a picture when she refused to shake his pretty hand. His on-the-prowl antics were instantly wiped off, taken over by major bewilderment – all surprised. As if he sweated to get to look the way he did. What was it he expected from her anyway? A pretty face buttering her up and for what, a birdbrain hulk of flesh that only had genetic luck to thank for it? She had missed out on a soulful hug and a nice, very good kiss – Mark slowly suckling on her tongue with heat running through her. Not those limp kisses she had been forced to put with up until she met up with Mark. She had missed out big time, and this time it wasn't Cindy's doing. It was odd that this was the first time it hadn't been her slut doing. This time it was some pretty boy with hanging tongue and surreptitious eyes full of complimentary expectations. What a jerk!

And now she was feeling so emotionally voracious – so empty. Fuck it, who gives a fuck about laundry? She was horny and she wanted Mark!

She abruptly got to her feet. The laundry would just have to be done later when she was more up to it, she decided. A cup of coffee would help set her mind right. This was bullshit, she whined; they couldn't even steal an hour off work now that Mark was working with someone who might rat on them. She petulantly bent down and quickly bundled up the laundry in the basket. Tramping to the kitchen, she switched the kettle on. Once Sue found out she hadn't started on the laundry, they would be a shouting drama.

Who gives a fuck? she offhandedly shrugged, taking a ceramic mug from the rack and fixing a strong cup of coffee. She could handle Sue by claiming a tummy ache or something. Which Sue would probably not buy right away unless…what?

Aha, she would start with a litany of complaints about Mark. That would be a first; never had she really complained about Mark to Sue, rather it was Sue who didn't seem to tire moaning about Mark.

Yeah, complaining about Mark would catch Sue off guard, and then she would say, "Sue, I don't feel so good." Wow, Sue would probably send her off to bed. Death was the one thing she couldn't get out of, the rest was easy. Pulane smiled to herself. So long as you were tuned in, making use of the brains God had so faithfully handed you. Like her lack of finances – it was a restraint, but not for long, she vowed.

Stepping into the living room, she sat herself down and sipped her coffee. A fond smile, she could hear Mark's voice. All of a sudden, she felt so fulfilled. Mark's voice, her favourite music, soothed her soul. It was beautiful. Of course, Sue did not agree with her, but then Sue had this crooked picture of Mark.

She smiled once more.

Mark was the king of her soul. He made her feel happy, like she was walking on air. The guy gave her one hell of a good feeling – so fucking good, so soul-nourishing, so out of this world. Mark really was the magic to her heart. Even the days when they were having their high and lows thanks to that nursemaid bitch Cindy. Well, in those tough periods, she would station herself by the window. Her rampant heart on the loose, refusing to give her a break. In those Mark-less days she would stand by the window and watch him before she resumed work. She would stand there and stare at him – and salivate.

She would faithfully stand there until she felt better.

Looking at him, just that was enough to tone her mood. She would stare at him and marvel at how manly he looked, marvel at the way his touch had brought the magic in the garden – just as it had brought the magic in her. And if it happened that just looking at him was not enough to appease her, she would…Mark!

She shook her head as she felt her heart jumping about. Yeah, sometimes just looking at him wasn't enough. Especially when he had been with another girl the night before. She would stand there by the window, looking at him, but the girl's face would keep clouding her mind, keep interfering with her medicinal vision. Desperate to feel better and get on with work before Sue started screaming, Pulane would turn back the clock to the sizzling yesterdays. With a touch of imagination, of course, rewinding and rewinding to the passionate yesterdays, to the more than quality time she had with him. And the more she polished her yesterdays with her skilful imagination, she had felt what? Well, good really, and more anticipative as payday crept closer.

One morning she had rushed to the window for her looking-at-him medicinal session. She had felt torn inside when she found Mark missing. Sue had found her huddled in the corner crying her heart out.

"Just to look at him, Sue. I'm not saying he should talk to me or something. All I want is for him to report to work faithfully so…so I'll be able to see him. Is that too much to ask, Sue? Is it?"

She took another sip of her coffee. Her friends were saying all kinds of stuff. Questioning her state of mind. "Are you okay in the head?" Some had even gone as far as calling it the 'works of witchcraft'. Fuck that shit. Because when you had lived your whole life bleakly, you learned not to expect much. If you had enough brains you knew the difference between a little bit of something and a complete nothing. Once you realised your bleak situation, you got to your feet and grabbed whatever crumbs fate threw your way. And yes, Mark was full of shit. But, she took a deep breath, at least she did have the crumbs, which, when you came right down to it, were better than nothing. Besides, there were sadder things than this. Crumbs, no matter how full of shit they were, were not simply a write off. Once you wise up, gobbled up that constricting pride you would see what she was on about.

And it wasn't like Mark beat her up and stuff; she was no battered wreck. It was only that sometimes he needed the smokes got all sick and bothered.

"Pulane!"

She jumped to her feet. Luckily she was finished with her coffee drinking.

"Are you done with the laundry?"

"But, Sue, I'm having premenstrual cramps," she whimpered.

"And do you know why, Pulane? That wad of toilet paper you've been using just so you could spare cash for Mark to get beer…."

"Sue, please don't start on me, not now," she cried as she sat down.

"How many times have I talked to you about this, Pulane?" scolded Sue.

"What?" she asked, expertly twisting her face in pain.

"The wad of toilet paper you stupidly use for sanitary pads."

"I'm sorry, Sue. Mark is a lost cause anyway. I'm thinking of dropping him,"

A job well done; Sue gaped at her. "Huh?"

"He's a nasty piece of work, Sue. You were right all along."

"Oh poor babe. You go rest." Sue kindly patted her on the shoulder. "I'll bring you aspirin."

"Thanks," she said, painfully getting to her feet.

Sue said as she climbed the stairs, "I'll do the laundry. Just rest."

Pulane allowed herself a conspiring smile. She had pulled it off; she congratulated herself as she dropped the mug in the sink.

As soon as Pulane got to their quarters, she whipped off the dreary apron, sprawled in bed and lazily stared at the ceiling. She had forgotten to collect the breakfast tray on the patio. She would tell Sue to it and make use of today. It wasn't every day she was this obliging.

After a short while Sue came in, gave her two pills, which Pulane hid under her tongue, and a glass of orange juice to wash the pills down. Then she left for the main house after promising to bring Pulane lunch.

As soon as Sue was gone, Pulane stripped off her sick cover and sat up in bed. She took out the pills from her mouth and threw them in the glass of juice.

She took a nail file and clippers from the table and started clipping her toenails.

Mrs Chambers told her she went to the beauty salon just for this.

"I'm off for a manicure," she had announced.

She had looked at her boss blankly – it wasn't her fault she had been a fresh country recruit then.

"My nails," Mrs Chambers had patiently explained.

"Oh, I can do that for you," Pulane had eagerly offered, figuring a quick way to make some easy cash. Not for Mark then, they hadn't yet linked up. Mark had been busy playing indifference at that time. He hadn't realised what he was missing out on. He hadn't yet noticed the good thing that she was.

"Don't worry Pulie, the salon will do it for me "

'Pulie', that was what the Chambers call her – a modernised version of Pulane. She was a good boss, helping Pulane out by toning down the rough edges of the rural name she acquired while holed up in that stagnant village. 'Pulie', if only other people had enough sense to call her that. She had gone to the government office, requesting to change the 'Pulane' on her ID card. She had neglected to ask her mum while still alive what 'Pulane' meant exactly. No, not neglected, dreaded was more like it. She had always had this deep-seated suspicion that dearest mummy blamed her for her dad's disappearance.

"Your dad left me while I was still expecting you."

There was nothing new there. A lot of rats had hightailed it into thin air after shooting off their daddy seeds, leaving the trusting mums in a daze, not knowing what could have gone wrong after all the pillow talk promises. Well, things were a bit different now. AIDS was doing a pretty good job of clearing the world of unscrupulous swarms of daddy rats, pity about the victims though. The be-faithful crash course AIDS had so wisely made mandatory – where you fuck at your own eternal risk. There was no such thing as a rewrite in AIDS house.

Still, her mum would give Pulane a funny look and speak in a hard voice when something went wrong. Pulane could be called paranoid, but she knew what she was talking about. She had been there and heard Mummy dear's voice turning shrill and accusatory. She shook her head, she never really had she a chance with her mum. Every bad thing that used to happen back home had been totally her doing. Even when she hadn't been around, her mum would wait till she got back, the same way she waited while she Pulane still in the womb.

"What happened to Uncle Theo?"

"Left. It's hard to find a partner when you have such a big daughter. Men are wary of daughters, especially ones that aren't even theirs."

"Are you saying it's my fault?"

And Mum would give her that look – the one that roughly assented her suspicions.

So her embedded suspicions were not baseless after all. What exactly did this 'Pulane' name mean, she suspected it meant something dodgy like her dad. She could ask the other Pulanes, but she only knew a handful, two in fact.

There at the government office they asked her all sorts of questions, the way they probed you would think it was a federal offence to change one's name. Finally, she got weary of the whys on the paperwork they ordered her to fill in. Yes, she was embarrassed with herself when she hit the city with her lagging-behind way of life, deteriorating in a stone age era while city people were... she fidgeted, she really had been embarrassed by her rural ways. Still, it wasn't her doing – if only God had made things easier for all of us, made us choose our own folks. Church people said it was made that way for our own good. Well, forget the church people. They have such big mouths; a lot of talking was the only thing they were good at. They would tell you a lot of weird stuff and talk till they were blue in the face with their holier-than-thou litany of 'don't dos'. However, behind your back it was a whole different ball game, they would feast on the same stuff they had fiercely told you not to play with, laughing at you, taking you for a stupid fool. You would think that would be enough, but no, they would continue to rail on you, tell you that you were next in line after the crispy frying of Hitler. Why am I even thinking about this? she abruptly wondered.

Clip, clip. She smiled when she remembered how insulted she'd felt when Mrs Chamber's turned down her offer to cut her nails. Whites, who the fuck did they think they were anyway? She had automatically blamed Mrs Chambers' refusal to do her nails on her black colour. Why not? It was the easy way out – like others she too had been caught up in the scapegoat trick. Why battle over differential calculus when you can just whine your way out? Especially about poor Grandma, who spent her life on her knees slaving, scrubbing their fucking floors.

Lost in thought massaging her toes, Pulane nodded her head agreeably. *Flunked out? Don't despair, that's the height of their expectations of you.*

Ah, damn fucking shit, who was she trying to fool here? She lurched to her feet with sudden rage. Exactly where had covering up her idleness by ranting about ancient history gotten her except crippling down all her ambitions?

Dearest Mummy was set on Pulane getting her education, selling tomatoes in the street for her school fees. She told Pulane many times not to wind up like her, but what did she do? She swallowed hard. While the rest of the world was relying on sitcoms for that belly laughter she heard was medicinal, there she was Pulane the asshole maid entertaining them with her free comedy shows! Damn, she moaned. Jeez, to think mum was on the right plot all along! I'd better watch it, better get it together.

Once she was done with her side-of-the-track pedicure, she lay on her back luxuriously.

A nice vacation today, but was only one thing missing – Mark, of course.

Mark, real, a true and loyal African. Pulane had heard of sisters bleaching their skins! Well coconuts were not only found in supermarkets, she had noticed.

And thank you God for those small favours. Mark was not into traitor creams; he was content with his skin colour. He moisturised his cute face only with vitamin E enriched lotion. She smiled dreamily; he really was good fun. Physique – Oh my God! Such maleness. He dressed cool too, not like the pathetic guys she had seen around town in their sagging jeans Saying things like, "What's up, dogg?"

When she was fresh rural material, she had been completely stumped. How could people go around calling each other dogs? Since she hadn't wanted to be stamped 'Betty comes to town', she had tried hard to keep an open mind. She had cautiously told herself that maybe there was a hidden dignifying thrill to this 'dogg' thing, because it wasn't just the doggy hello, she had heard. 'You are my dogg' was what they said when it was time to hand out the compliments. Convinced she was missing out on something enlightening, she had started to look hard at the Doberman, the Pekinese, German shepherds...was it the fur or the hair, the extraordinary sense of smell? Well, what was it really. But just when she had felt she was on the verge of a breakthrough, the dog had turned on her and barked ferociously. Quite disgusted she had been then – simple looks setting them off like that. That had struck her as unreliable; was the vicious barking their way of hiding something, something questionable?

Still, her Mark was neither of those things. He was his own man, and he did his own unconventional stuff – an original in his own way. That was another of the reasons why she had taken him for a better deal. Here in the city the pathetic guys with their cheap tired lines were not getting them a break. "Hi, babe, are you tired cos you've been running around in my dreams." *Jesus Christ!*

At least Mark was straight enough to put his cards on the table. "Pulane, I'm calling Cindy cos you ain't buying me the smokes." No cheap lines there, and it showed he had balls. And in the long run if Mark scattered her heart in pieces, this is what she would say, "At least he is real."

And no, she was not saying Mark was a nice agreeable guy. Mark was full of shit. He really was. And yes, sometimes he hurt her pretty bad; so bad that she would be convinced she would never recover.

Her eyes clouded.

Still it wasn't like that *all* the time. Sure Mark did crap on her, and crap on her a lot, but come bedroom time, he delivered real good. Hey, this guy knew his stuff, fulfilling her in every possible way. With Mark they was no fumbling blunders, no one-minute wonders, and no pretend orgasms.

She jumped out of bed, clapping her hands, full of energy.

It was time. Time to hatch on a big plan that would bring a bucketful of that lovely money. It would get Mark to settle down instead of running around wasting his talented moves on some transient bimbos.

It was not long before Dean clicked with Mark. And the way he played girls – Dean tried to caution him about that, but Mark was Mark. He only laughed at him and told him, "Hey, lighten up, mate!"

"Dean, you live such a placid life. You need to loosen up, mate," Mark facetiously said as he filled a terracotta pot with soil mixed with stockosorb and bone meal.

"I'm merely being cautious, with AIDS waiting to devour us, you don't have a choice."

"But there is always a rubber."

"Not completely safe, mate."

"Nothing in life is completely safe, Dean."

"I agree. Still, with AIDS you have to cover the entire base," he said as he watered the ground he had just finished clearing. "I've decided to drag any girl I intend to sleep with for testing."

"Girls don't have time for such shit."

"No problem, I'll say my goodbyes then."

"Goodbye! Before you fuck her, are you for real?"

"Yes, goodbye." He turned and looked at Mark. "Ever met an AIDS beaten down victim, Mark?"

Mark nodded sadly.

"Think any girl is worth going through that?"

Mark said, "If you use a condom, you won't."

"And if it bursts, what's going to be your backup, Mark?"

"It doesn't always burst," Mark protested.

"AIDS is the bitchiest disease that can ever happen to anyone, Mark," he said viciously. "I refuse to unconsciously crown AIDS the deciding God of my life!"

As Mark planted some flowers in the pot, he said, "Well, there always are those drugs, ARVs."

"But they aren't a cure," Dean violently protested.

"I didn't say there are." Looking up, Mark said, "At least when the shit hits the ceiling, they are dependable."

"You'll still be on death row, Mark," he quietly said. "The deadly monster will bide its time. Planning its attack. While you are busy celebrating cos your CD count is up, AIDS will be there listening, planning. Once it brings out its full reinforcement, you may as well start digging."

"Aw, come on, stop talking like that. You talk as if there is no hope. Listen, we have ARVs, the state is giving them for free…."

"The government, Mark! The government is all talk to swindle more votes. You never know the real story with those guys. ARVs are free so they say. But what happens when you go to the hospital? They start telling you stories. 'Your CD count is okay. You don't need the drugs now.' They give you paracetamol, tell you to go home and eat boiled fish and spinach." Nodding his head emphatically, he continued, "Now that a lot of people are testing positive, they are holding onto the ARVs cos the stuff is expensive. They now only give them when you are far-gone."

"No, that's not true."

"Not true? What about these big companies that provide ARV drugs to their employees? How come their percentage of AIDS-related deaths is much lower than those relying on the government for ARVs? Why? Because, dear Mark, those companies know with HIV one has to act fast. They know they can't afford to hire and train people every fucking day."

Mark didn't say a word.

"Don't sell yourself short by trading your life to those drugs, Mark. They don't even cure AIDS, just wet-nurse it to prolong the cobra in it."

"Still ARVs are the best shot we have so far."

"No, Mark, that's where you are wrong." Dean shook his head at Mark. "Protection against this monster is the best we can ever do."

"But if protection fails, we have ARVs to fall back on," insisted Mark.

"I'll tell you something, Mark. When you've tested negative, never ever think of ARVs. Live your life as if there is no such thing."

"You're losing me now, mate."

"Listen, when you are fully heated up for sex, the mood is urgent, the mood is now. You simply cannot think rationally cos even your brain is screaming 'sex now'. And if they are no condoms, and the tightening in your pants is intense with her pussy all heated up, you'll start thinking, 'Ah well there are people who still live a fine life with ARVs.' But you are not those people, Mark! You are you. Your body can turn on you and build up some kind of resistance against those drugs. You could be one of them unlucky ones."

Mark adamantly said, "But they do help - really truly."

"I'm just saying only when you've tested positive, that's when you should think anti-retroviral, but while you are negative, live your life as if there aren't such drugs." Dean looked up and saw Pulane, "Pulane! Please turn the tap off, for me. Nice girl she is, what's the deal between you two?"

Mark casually shrugged his shoulders. "Not much. I make her come, and she compensates me in return for such good and satisfying service."

"Fucking hell, mate. This girl loves you!"

Carelessly Mark said, "Well, who told her to love-love me? Not my fault, mate."

"Some people can't help the way they feel."

"All the time I've been shagging this girl, I never once said 'I love you.' She is fucking mental." Raising his shoulders Mark continued, "I don't know where she gets such ideas from!"

"Bet it was when you shagged her and she came. Girls take an orgasm very seriously."

"Everyone is on my fucking case cos of this Pulane! 'She loves you, Mark, be good to her'. She better give me a fucking break of those mushy I love yous! I will fucking dump her," shouted an enraged Mark. "Dumb fucking bitch making me feel bad!"

"So you don't really love Pulane?" Dean asked.

"Pulane is too fucking penniless for my liking, mate," Mark recklessly told him.

CHAPTER FIVE

Two months elapsed with Dean still a committed employee of the Chambers. Whatever Mark told him to do, he fervently did. He was keen and he learnt quite a lot.

"Instead of using a basket, a trendy alternative is to fix a trellis to a wall and tie pots to it. But the plants that you choose should flower at different times."

Nodding his head Dean replied, "Yeah, to make it interesting."

"That's the idea, and the pots should have good drainage holes. Then put a layer of drainage chips in the base. Afterwards you fill them with good potting soil." Dean listened alertly. He even learnt about balancing and every day he put fresh colours in a vase, which matched the colour scheme of the interior decorations.

Mark taught him everything.

He could even make vases more stylish now by wrapping a headscarf around them. Place the vase in the middle, pull the fabric around it and tie it with a ribbon. Other times he used a crepe paper, even a gift wrapper. He didn't even know about using lukewarm water because according to Mark it contained less oxygen and thus prevented air bubbles in the stem of the flower that could block water uptake.

"Except for tulips, they prefer cold water," said Mark.

"Where did you learn all this?"

"Five years experience and the occasional courses the Chambers take me to," said Mark as he picked a bunch of orange and Barberton daisies, expertly putting them in a tall vase.

"Maybe Tracey will help," Pulane reassured herself as she tiredly reached the main gate.

"Hi, Madam Mark." Duncan, who was busy in the garden, smirked at her.

What a rat. "Is Tracey in?" she asked.

"Sure. And why aren't you at work? Oops, I forgot, you need a small loan to buy my mate's dick. But not his heart, Pulane. Even you wouldn't be stupid enough to think that." He dropped the spade he had been digging with and looked at her contemptuously. "Hey, you better top up that small money you are always giving him. Things have gone up, girl. Otherwise my mate will drop you for a more agreeable babe."

"Duncan, you are such a bastard."

"Bloody hell, Pulane, girls like you disgust me. Where is your pride, girl? I'm only crapping on you to shock you out of your stupidity. Lose Mark; he is not for nice girls like you. What's going to happen when your friends stop lending you money to pleasure him? Are you going to end up stealing just so you can keep him?"

Taking a deep breath, she asked, "So who is this girl?"

Waving her off he replied, "Ah, Pulane, don't even ask."

She shook her head and proceeded to the kitchen, where she found her friend.

"Tracey, I need money to get out of town."

"Why?" asked an alarmed Tracey.

"Just for the weekend."

"Has something happened back home?" asked her mate.

Tracey was cool. Pulane couldn't lie to her. Miserably she said, "It's Mark."

Tracey's face darkened. "Of course it's Mark. It always has to be him. What has he done this time?"

"Some girl by the name of…" she hiccupped, "is coming over for the weekend. He doesn't need any drama from me, he said…"

"What?"

"I wouldn't be able to control myself, Trace. That's why I have to get away," she snivelled.

"He really is a shit bastard!"

"I know," she sadly admitted.

"So why don't you cut him loose?"

"I don't know," she moaned.

"What do you mean you don't know?" Tracey shouted.

"My head isn't feeling right, Tracey. Do you have a headache pill or something?"

"I asked you a question, Pulane!"

"But you know I can't," she wailed.

In an icy tone Tracey retorted, "No, Pulane, what I know is you won't."

Resting her head on the wall Pulane swallowed the knot in her throat. Christ what was with Tracey today? She knew damn well she couldn't. Her desperate attempts in getting Mark out of her life had always been futile.

The first time she was all set, she thought she could do it. She had found Mark in bed pumping up some bitch. And Mark just smiled at her and said he had always wanted to try out a threesome.

She had run all the way to Tracey's, who told her Mark was a mean rotten bastard and she should rid herself of him. It had made perfect sense then. That was before she caught up with Mark the next morning.

"Mark, me and you should talk," she had said as she found him bent over his precious flowers.

"Oh, sure," he said, straightening up and focusing on her with his almond-shaped piercing brown eyes.

She really had been all set. She had even rehearsed her dumping line. 'Mark, listen it's been great but it's over.' Just that, no wasting of words, Short and clear-cut. But before chanting her dumping lines, she had looked at his face. She still wasn't sure how it happened, but the alluring come-to-bed eyes had grabbed her. Diverted her to a honey-lovey world, and allowed her to totally forget her dumping line.

"Pulane," Mark had impatiently said.

"I love you," she said.

"That's what you wanted to talk about." Mark had looked at her strangely.

She had just nodded.

"Fine, now can I please get back to work?"

"Sure. I just wanted you to know that."

"Thanks," Mark had said dryly.

It was only when she got to her room, where she found Tracey waiting, that she remembered her dumping plan.

"Did you do it?" Tracey had demanded.

She had licked her dry lips. "His eyes…I never quite realised how arresting they are."

"Dammit, Pulane!"

"I couldn't do it, Tracey, not with those eyes focused on me. The words…they refused to come out. Only 'I love you' came out."

"You told him you love him?"

"Well…it's true."

Tracey had made her write a Dear John letter. "They call it a wimpy way out, but better this than having a devious rat like him in your life."

Tracey had personally sealed the envelope. "Drop it in his room while he's still in the garden."

But Mark's door had been ajar, and there was Mark with his shirt off displaying his mouth-watering six-pack.

"Hi again," she had stammered.

"My babe." He honoured her with his bewitching kisses. As hard as she tried, she couldn't repel his flaming touch. The kisses had rapidly progressed to bedroom gymnastics.

Later he'd asked, "What's in the envelope?"

"Oh nothing, it's Tracey's," she had quickly said.

Tracey had refused to sympathise with her. Refused to understand.

"I can't," she said once again. "Tracey, you really have to come through for me with bus fare. Mark said if I ever embarrassed him in front of this girl with my jealous antics, he'd never talk to me."

Suddenly Tracey's face brightened, "Well, that's good, then let him not speak to you."

"Tracey, please."

"I don't have a cent on me, Pulane."

"Damn," she said. "God, Tracey, I really do love him."

Tracey looked at her, concerned. "Is he still using condoms on you?"

Pulane nodded.

"What happens when he ditches the condoms? What will you do then?"

"What? I'll refuse," she said in shock.

"What if this love daft you into condom-less sex? What then. It's already suckered you to accept his serial cheating. What are you going to do when Mark teams up with those guys who don't like condoms?"

"Female condom," she said promptly.

"What if he says he doesn't like it too? What will you do then?"

Pulane lurched to her feet. "I got to go."

"What?"

"Bye, see you later." She reeled out of the back door.

Tracey talks crap. She grimaced wryly. There was a whole lot of stuff one can impulsively get stupid about. A hell of a lot, but AIDS, Jesus Christ! She shook her head. Ah, why was she even hurrying back to that stupid work anyway she suddenly wondered, slowing down her pace. Damn this scrubbing of floors shit, it just wasn't her scene. *I should have tried harder back in school.* Lately she had been through a lot, and she decided she deserved a break. She sat on the bench of a small shelter that advertised a mobile network.

Condom-less sex with Mark. It just showed Tracey didn't know shit; all mouth but she knew nothing. Footsteps cut into her thoughts. She looked up.

Cindy!

Damn fucking shit! "Where are you off to?" Pulane jumped up in sudden rage.

"To see Mark."

"See Mark? What for?" she demanded in blazing rage.

"For some love," Cindy said, amused.

"Love! You really think Mark could love a tub of shit like you?"

"And what are you, a nothing maid who Mark fucked out of teamwork and you are now what…acting like you have some kind of claim on him?"

"Fuck you! You nursemaid bitch!"

"Beats scrubbing floors in some honky's crib," Cindy snapped. "Get out of my way. I've stuff to do."

Blocking her way Pulane said, "You think your paltry pay blinds him from seeing the tub of shit you really are. Drowning my boyfriend in your folds of flesh. Who the fuck do you think you are?"

"Well, Mark is already fucking me. Fucking me a lot, so yes, I think my pay does come handy to lover boy." Cindy jovially smiled at her. "Now, maid girl, out of my way!" She roughly elbowed Pulane aside.

Jumping back and blocking her path she said, "Oh no, you've had your picnic for far too long. Mark is mine, and you are to stop coming between us."

Cindy looked at her peculiarly. "You are Pulane, aren't you?"

"Of course I'm Pulane!"

"See, you really are losing it. Mark only slept with you because he felt so sorry for you."

"You are making me very angry, Cindy," Pulane said quietly.

"Like I give a fuck what I make you. Listen, Mark only told me about a girl called Jen. He never mentioned any Pulanes to me. Wait a sec; he did mention one stifling maid he slept with. He said I mustn't take this maid's hysterical shows for anything else except for a horny little bitch who can't accept 'over' as truly 'over'. I take it that horny little bitch is you?"

Pulling Cindy by the hair she smacked her face. "You are lying!"

Freeing her hair Cindy said, "I have far too much respect for myself than to fight on the street over a man. No wonder he hasn't time for you, not even a complimentary fuck once in a while!" Nastily shaking her head, Cindy added, "You really are a hysterical little bitch!"

"I am warning you, Cindy." She pointed a threatening finger at her.

"You are just a horny disgruntled bitch cos Mark refuses to give you an occasional fuck." Cindy looked at her strangely. "I'm actually surprised cos the Mark I know is very accommodating." She shrugged. "Must be your clingy, embarrassing antics. Grabbing Mark's visitors by the hair, claiming him all to yourself," Cindy spat.

"Cindy," Pulane warned.

"What's the problem? Your maid pay has run out and Mark's delicious dick is out of bounds? Hey, I don't need this bullshit! Go ask him for a fucking credit and stop giving me grief!"

Bursting into tears she said, "I fucking hate you, Cindy! Why can't you just leave us alone?"

"Listen, let's go ask Mark. I swear he only told me about this other girl."

Wiping off the tears with back of her hand Pulane agreed. "Aha, let's go."

"Fine," Cindy said impatiently. They burst into Mark's room.

"Ladies, what's up?" he said lazily.

"I was on my way here when this little tramp pulled me by my hair and told me to stop coming between you and her."

Sitting up in alarm he said, "What?"

"Give it to her straight, Mark. I'm your future wife and you only put up with her lumpy company cos she boosts you with cash," Pulane charged.

"Mark, I thought you said there was only a Jen."

"Of course, babes. Cindy I really am sorry about this." In a hard voice he turned to Pulane. "You are going to have to apologise to Cindy."

Pulane's stomach tightened, "What?"

"Yes, Pulane, I fucked you. But you don't fucking own me!" said Mark, looking at her straight in the eye.

"Mark, you shouldn't sleep with such obsessive trash, next thing she will be nagging you to marry her. She even smacked me, stupid little bitch!"

"She smacked you?"

"You said you liked me. You called me your soon-to-be wife," Pulane said in a daze.

Laughing, Mark replied, "Me, marrying you? Man, what a joke." He raised his voice in anger. "Why would I fucking *marry* you, Pulane?"

"Shh, lower your voice," hissed Cindy. "I don't want to be caught in your lovers' squabble."

"She talks fucking crap! Me marrying her? Jesus!"

"I didn't come here to watch you fighting with your maid girlfriend, Mark! I came here for sex. The sex I fucking pay for."

Frowning at her, Mark said, "Don't be a bitch, Cindy."

Ignoring Mark, Cindy turned to Pulane. "Listen, honey, Mark is not into free fucks." Waving her off she added, "Run along and get some of your maid pennies."

"But…" Pulane spluttered.

Throwing herself into bed, Cindy said dismissively, "Mark, get this girl out of here. She doesn't understand your language. Probably thinks her cow boobs will bewitch you into a free fuck."

Flinching Pulane desperately said, "Mark, I love you."

Laughing, Cindy exclaimed, "Love? Not with this bloke, dear. Hard, cold cash is more like it."

"Get out, Pulane," Mark coldly said. "Me and Cindy have some private game to get into." Sitting on the edge of bed he took Cindy in his arms. "Just looking at you flames my body. Now why is that? How about a cooling down game?" Totally ignoring Pulane he proceeded to unbutton Cindy's top.

Pulane quickly lowered her head to keep from fainting, gripping the headboard to steady her jelly legs.

"Mark, what's this girl hanging around here for? Didn't you tell her to go?"

Mark jumped up and threw Pulane out of the room, hastily locking the door behind her.

She staggered out with Cindy's laughter ringing in her ears.

CHAPTER SIX

"I'm cutting Pulane loose," announced Mark one afternoon as they were busy in the garden.

"Why, she being difficult?" Dean asked.

"Sort of," Mark ambiguously replied.

"Poor Pulane. This is going to kill her," sympathised Dean.

"The problem with Pulane is…she is too into me," Mark dryly admitted as he added a handful of super phosphate to a potted green plant.

"And you don't like that?"

"She is nice but…" Mark shrugged his shoulders.

"Oh."

"How about I shift her to you?" blurted Mark.

"What?"

"She is a nice kid," he insisted.

"Really, then why is this nice kid being dumped?"

"Greener pastures," he explained.

"But you've never been faithful to her. She must have gotten used to that by now. So why dump her?"

"I am dumping her," he said flatly.

"Why?"

"She is too suffocating," he said shaking his head. "I tried forcing her hand to do the dumping, but I guess she is one of them who doesn't have any pride."

"Yeah, there is nothing as tasteless as a woman with no pride. Tell me about this greener pastures that you've found," Dean said as he was tying a ribbon just below the heads of some long-stemmed narcissuses in a tall pot.

"Jen, cashier at Nando's, the one in Game City," Mark said dreamily.

Dean was not impressed. "What's so special about her, aside from her earning more than Pulane?"

"The fact that she earns more makes her special enough," answered Mark, who was now sprinkling the organic fertilizer on the green lawn.

"You like money too much."

"What else is there to like?"

"I still think you are making a mistake letting Pulane go," Dean said as he tied another ribbon below the heads of the narcissuses.

"Good work," complimented Mark.

"Thanks," Dean replied, beaming.

"Anyway, Pulane is not indispensable to me."

"Check out this Nando's girl, at least for a couple of months before any letting away of Pulane is done. We call it insurance," Dean suggested.

"Fuck insurance. Damn! She changed. Cindy told me Pulane beat her up," Mark told him as he wiped his hands on his overalls.

"Beat her up?"

"Yeah, told Cindy I said I was going to marry her. Imagine her blurting that bullshit to my cash cow!" said Mark recklessly.

"Is Cindy getting dumped too to give way to this Nando's girl?" Dean inquired.

"Nope. Cindy is cool, knows the score better than that penniless volatile bitch. But Pulane, she has to go. Shit, she used to be such a nice understanding kid. But these days…" he shook his head regrettably.

"So your mind is really set on letting her go."

Mark nodded.

"I like Pulane, she's a nice girl and I still think you are a fool to let her go."

"So grab her," said Mark, unconcerned.

"No fucking way, it's unsettling the way she's so much into you."

Almost shouting Mark said, "Well I don't want her no more."

Mark dumped her. Dropped her flat.

Just looking at her could break a person's heart. She was a whimpering wreck. All of a sudden she was seriously ill, and she couldn't even walk properly. She didn't eat any food, and she said there was a big knot sitting in her throat, making even swallowing saliva a trial. Mrs Chambers was so alarmed that she told Pulane to rest for a full week.

Dean really felt for the poor girl. He tried talking to Mark, but the selfish bastard flatly told him over was over, and it was not negotiable.

Poor, Pulane. She made one huge mistake, and she fell for the wrong guy.

Dean sighed.

All in all no strings sex was best because when it was over, it was over. They were no reviews that would keep popping into your mind, no wrestling with your emotions.

He shook his head. Mark was an emotionally devious player. The same way he himself had been. So how come Pulane wasn't off celebrating? Couldn't she see that being dumped by Mark was the best deal she could ever have?

After a week of emotional recuperation, there she was, back at work. Dean decided to cheer her up. He found her stacking plates into the dishwasher.

"Hi, Pulie. How's it going?"

"Not so bad," but her voice said something else.

Christ, such a nice kid. She deserved better than wasting her grief on the no good Mark. Of course, Mark was a mate of his, but any girl setting her mind on him was asking for serious drama.

"Pulane, Mark is no good, and you are better off without him."

"Oh."

"He doesn't care about you, Pulane, and you ought to forget him," he advised. Okay, that was a bit harsh, but hell, he had to get through to her.

She leaned against the sink because she was suddenly dizzy with sickness.

Doesn't care?

What was Dean crapping about? He may drink and hang out with Mark, but did that make him knowledgeable on Mark's feelings? She looked at him coldly. Liking him even less.

Mark doesn't care!

What kind of bullshitting was he on about? If this rat bastard wanted her body, why couldn't he just come out and say it? What was with the bullshitting? But then being the rat that he was... *Fuck it!* She was Pulane, and she was too old and wise for mind games.

"Dean, can you please go. I'm kind of busy here," she said darkly.

He breathed heavily. He had been around for far too long, and what was she, twenty? He could read her like an open book. Damn, what was with girls? They had such a penchant for lies. And since he prided himself on being the perfect gentleman, he decided to play along and spoon-feed her the lies she craved.

"Mark really loves you, Pulane. It's only that he is...um... confused."

In an instant Pulane's face was glowing. "I know," she said radiantly.

"Sorry about what I said. It's just that he made me angry by letting this girl get to him."

"That's okay."

Hey, he really was a nice guy. Look at the good job he had just done. The girl was actually smiling – a beautiful smile. *Good job,* he complimented himself.

"So how about we go out tonight? Cheer you up." Then he saw her face, "Just friends," he hastily added. He had now switched back to the truth. The last thing he needed was a rebounding Pulane to mess with his heart. *If it was my former self before AIDS crushed my balls, making me into such a paranoid puppy, I could check you out for a one off.*

"But what will Mark think?" she exclaimed.

"I'll level with him, will that be okay?" *Actually Mark would be very happy.*

Gratefully she nodded.

"Don't you want to make him jealous?" Dean teased.

"Too risky. He might be disgusted and take me for a cheap slut, no," she emphatically said, shaking her head.

"Okay, so I'll pick you at eight." He gave her a hug. The girl was stiff, so she thought he had a hidden agenda. That slightly irritated him. What hidden agenda could he possibly have, especially on Mark's leftovers?

So he wasn't the bastard of a rat she took him for. How very refreshing.

She still hurt terribly.

She looked up. The sky was very black, blanketed with clouds. So black you wouldn't suspect they were stars behind the clouds. But she knew they were there. She was no doubting Thomas. She didn't have to see them to admit they were right there, hidden by the clouds.

She took a deep breath.

Just like God. He was there all right, very much the same good God, no matter how hard her bleak circumstances tried to convince her otherwise she warmly told herself.

Somehow the thought of God calmed her down. She heaved a deep grateful sigh and sat there with her arms folded. *God is fair and just. He will come through for me*, she keenly assured herself.

Closing her eyes she prayed. She glorified God for being the God that He was. Then she asked God to bring Mark back into her life because she loved him so very much.

Remaining seated, enjoying the cool refreshing breeze that was gently blowing, she fiercely told herself, "Mark has to come back to me – he just has to."

This was no condolence dream. God was out there, and as long as He was there, there was hope because God could definitely bring Mark back.

Okay, God could do it, part of her acknowledged, but the question was would He do it?

What if He started saying he was her father, and he knew what was best for her and this hurricane relationship she had with Mark was just not it?

What then?

Was she going to argue with the father of wisdom? With He who knew better? Was she?

Her Christmas thoughts evaporated as her breath came in laboured gasps. She was suddenly frightened; frightened of the fact that He may not do it. Tightly she shut her eyes and nursed the choking pain in her chest.

He may not do it, she wailed. Yet it wouldn't be such a big deal to Him. It wasn't like it would be a tiresome task, just a snap of His two mighty fingers, but still He may not do it.

She swallowed hard.

"It would only take a millisecond of His time, but He may not be bothered to do it," she said out loud.

A sob broke from her.

Only a snap of His finger and Mark would miraculously be back. But still, a chance existed of Him not doing it.

But why?

She hiccuped, life with no Mark – could that be possible? Nah, not possible, she just wouldn't be able to go on.

"I mustn't think that," she desperately told herself with her arms tightly folded across her chest.

No, she shook her head vehemently. She was just being silly. The God that she knew would never spring that on her. He was a good God, a real good God, and as long as He was there, hope was also there.

"Pulane what are doing by yourself in the dark?" Sue suddenly interrupted her thoughts.

"Nothing," she mumbled.

"I've been meaning to talk to you, Pulane. Ever since that piece of shit left you, you've been miserable, why? Don't you see how much of a blessing this is, Pulane? Look at the bright side. Life is going to be more fun now. Your pay will be solely yours. You'll be able to afford toiletries, no more bathing with dish detergents. I really can't understand what the long miserable face is for. You should be jumping up and down, thanking your lucky stars the parasitic rat is out of your life!"

"Mark isn't that bad," she said pensively.

"I'm going to pretend I didn't hear that."

"I love him so much," she said, bursting violently into tears.

"Pulane, when are you going to get this into your head? He is a complete bastard and you need to let go."

"Why?" she asked between tears.

"I just told you, cos he is a parasitic, womanising bastard!"

Angrily she turned on Sue, "You mustn't talk like that. You're so insulting! Mark isn't any of those things!"

"Really!" Sue said in complete disbelief. "I can't believe you are defending him. What is this, selective amnesia?"

Arguing with Susan wasn't on her agenda.

"I have to go, Dean is taking me out."

"Now, that is what I call a good step," said Susan, fondly patting Pulane's shoulder.

"Well it doesn't mean anything except to cheer me up."

"He's a nice guy, unlike that Mark rat."

"I have to go and dress up. He'll be here any minute now," Pulane said as she stood up.

Dean dragged her to a club by the name of Vision. When they were seated, she sipping a cider with Dean drinking lager, a guy came over to their table and talked to Dean. She took another sip, ignoring Dean, who couldn't possibly calm her pain.

She was bored and cursed herself for agreeing to this fucking nonsense because no matter how extra nice Dean could be, he was no Mark – end of negotiation.

She sighed deeply.

It had been one hell of a week. Mark's sudden departure out of her life had nearly killed her. She had tried to lure him back with all her pay.

"No thanks. I have someone else taking care of my financial needs," were his cold words.

"The Nando's girl?" she had spat.

"Yes, Pulane," he replied, as cool as a cucumber.

She had burst into tears, hoping this would emotionally blackmail him enough to reconsider. It didn't work; he was a tough bastard.

"I warned you, Pulane. Told you to take it cool, but no, you went right ahead and beat up my woman."

"Your woman!"

"Yes, Pulane, my woman."

"Mark please…I'll be…cool."

"No, Pulane, I don't feel you anymore."

"Mark how could you do this to me?" she said between sobs.

"Hey, Pulane, it's no big deal."

"No big deal?" she had gasped.

"What we had was just a sexual arrangement. An arrangement that I just terminated." He paused, fixing his bed-hijacking eyes on her. "And it's about time it was terminated," he added.

If she hadn't quickly sat down, she would have collapsed on the floor in shock.

The impact of being ditched by Mark hit her so hard. All of a sudden she was sick, every muscle in her body ached. Even Mrs Chambers was alarmed and asked what was up with her. Pulane had to lie and claim tummy ache. Mrs Chambers urged her to go and see a doctor. Hell, she even drove her to the doctor herself. Then she sternly told her to rest for a whole week.

She pressed her hand to her chest as she recalled how Mark never came to see her all the while she was confined to her room. And Cindy? How come she wasn't dumped like her? What was her crime? Her maid job, was that it? She forced back the tears.

During her one week of rest, she wrestled so hard with her emotions; she tried really hard to hate Mark.

It didn't work.

It had bothered her then that she still dreamt sweet dreams of Mark. It bothered her a great deal because she so desperately wanted to hate him.

Then for some inexplicable reason the intense anger had somehow disappeared on her. She didn't know how that came about, but it happened. She just woke up one day to find the anger gone. That was when she started to look forward to the sweet honey dreams. They were good, darling dreams because in her world of dreams they was no 'it's over Pulane', no slut third parties. By the time she got back to work she had realised one thing – she was in love with a bastard and there was absolutely nothing she could do about it.

She tapped her foot as the sounds of Usher filled the club. With a sudden jolt of anger her thoughts dwell on Sue. Today Sue was having one of her motor-mouthing days, she said Pulane was in denial.

"Mark doesn't love you, he never will. And he will never come back to you." Sue said as she was dressing up for her date.

So now Sue had acquired psychic powers. How cute.

She took a sip of the non-consoling cider.

Mark getting back with her was probably not on the cards, just as the prophet Sue said. She wouldn't be surprised, not even a tiny bit. Pulane had long ceased relying on fate. It was too biased, and its favouritism sickened her. All this time she had been battling her ass off to get Mark to the altar. But what did the treacherous fate do? Produce a girl with the most haunting face she had ever seen and a figure bewitching enough to…damn!

So what was expected of her? Sit and cry. Crying and agonizing over fate that didn't seem to have an ounce of kindness, especially when it came to Pulane.

No, this time it was going to be a whole lot different. She fully intended to stand firmly on her own two feet and create her own luck. She was through with crying and feeling sorry for herself.

She was jolted from her thoughts by what Dean's friend said.

"Snoop suspending you was a shit shock. Where was your big brother?"

Pulane blinked rapidly, and for the first time she saw Dean in a different light.

Dean shrugged his shoulders. "He tried talking to Chief."

"But what's this shit about you working as a gardener? Come on, man. How can you really work as a gardener?" exclaimed the stranger.

"I love gardening."

"But that doesn't mean you should work in a garden. No, Dean, that shit is not for you. Why didn't you come to me? You know I ain't one of these guys who have to kiss Chief's ass."

"We did think of you, but you were on holiday."

"Yeah, I haven't been around, but I'm back now. So call me," and with that he stalked off.

In a casual voice Pulane asked, "So what was all that about?"

"Oh that, he's drunk. Never mind him."

Drunk, do I really look that stupid to him? All of a sudden she was energetic.

She excused herself and headed to the ladies' room.

Snoop!

Her face brightened as she saw a small light in her tunnelled life.

Snoop!

The most feared and powerful gang in the country, and Dean was one of them, well, suspended now.

God was nobody's crutch; He only helped those who helped themselves.

What a break! What a beautiful break!

Who could have figured the quiet Dean was a Snoop? As she happily splashed cold water on her face, she dismissed the surprise; it was plain stupid to judge a picture by its cover. She grabbed a face tissue and hurriedly wiped her face.

She plunged her hand in her handbag and rummaged inside.

She took a face powder and a lipstick from her Prada handbag, another product of madam's golden heart.

Mark and his love of money. If she ever laid her hands on real money, she would be able to…she broke into a bright smile.

And there was unsuspecting Dean, whose Snoop skills could be quite handy.

A very nice guy this Dean, she nodded her head as she stared at her face in the mirror. She knew his kind. When they fell in love, they fell real hard. You instantly became their god.

She smoothed her hair down and broke into another smile.

What a perfect pawn Dean will make.

What was it he said? *"Just friends."*

Once again, she smiled.

No, platonic wouldn't do as of now – too damn restrictive. It wasn't possible to graduate a pawn out of a platonic deal.

With an exhilarated air she powdered her face.

She needed to get him into bed to bias his rationality and catalyse his pawning career.

Lure him into the sucker trap.

She looked up as Tracey came through the door.

"Why are you so stuck on losers, Pulane?" said Tracey crossly.

"Dean just took me out, there aren't any strings attached."

"At least he's no Mark."

Pulane shrugged offhandedly.

"Maybe you should attach some strings on him, practice yourself on him until you're in the best form," Tracey said.

She nodded. "Yeah, Dean will make a good nursemaid for my

broken heart."

"I still don't understand how a pathetic shit like Mark could break your heart. But maybe you should hook up with this Dean. Make him your recuperating tool. He looks good, good enough for your self-esteem," Tracey said on her way out.

Now back to Dean.

How should she play it?

A couple of bed sessions should be enough to seal the sucker deal. She knew without doubt the transformation would be awesome. He was a nice guy, definitely not the kind to bed a girl and make a fast exit. He simply didn't possess such ratty balls.

Afterwards he would be overwhelmed with guilt because she was such a nice young girl who had just had an emotional hurricane.

The guilt would turn him into an eager-to-please somebody. And wow, into the palm of her hand he would jump, and remain super-glued there.

She heaved an immense sigh of contentment.

She hurriedly applied her lipstick and off she breezed to her future pawn.

"You look cheerful for a change," Dean observed.

"That's cos I've finally realised the truth."

"What truth?" he softly inquired.

She borrowed Susan's words. "I've been in denial. Mark doesn't love me, he never will. I've been having a little chat with Tracey, who made me see some sense."

"Oh," he said cautiously.

"I think it was just a case of battered ego cos it was him who did the dumping."

He looked at her. "So you didn't love him?"

She lowered her eyes. "I used to, but he killed it long back with his habitual womanising."

"I see," he said, nodding his head in understanding. With a radiant smile, she opened herself up for hopeful predators. "And now I feel so free," she brightly announced.

"That's nice," he said, smiling back.

"So enough about me," she said, staring straight at him. "Tell me about you." She was never interested in his life before, but now…well things had changed.

"What do you want to know?" he asked.

Damn this guy and his lukewarm stance. The smile was a nothing smile, no spark of attraction. The fool was still under the impression they were on platonic ground. She cursed silently.

"I've never seen a lady friend visiting you. Where is she by the way? Stay too far away to visit?" she asked, hoping he wouldn't think she was too forward. It wouldn't do to scare him off.

"I don't have a girlfriend."

"No girlfriend?" she exclaimed.

"Nope," he answered, nodding his head.

She smiled inwardly. Someone had just been handed to her on a silver platter.

"I'm still looking for the 'One'."

"Don't lose patience, Dean, she'll come along." *In the form of me*, she silently added.

"I intend to wait till she comes along. Especially now that there is AIDS."

"Yeah AIDS is a scary shit," she admitted.

"I can't afford to take it casually. The stakes are just too deadly high," he bitterly told her.

She said, "AIDS is the worst thing that can ever happen to anyone."

"I get tested every three months, that's how scared I am," he admitted, gulping his lager.

"And when's the next test due?"

"Monday," he said.

She reached out for his hand and covered it with hers. "I've never had unprotected sex. I may be young, but I'm not that stupid. Still one can never be too sure. I want to get tested too. Please, Dean, may I come with you on Monday?"

With a worried frown he asked, "Are you sure?"

"Completely," she answered in a firm voice.

She now knew which cards to play. His fear of AIDS would be her weapon.

So at the testing centre she would insist in him being present during her test. That would definitely break the ice between them. And when he saw the negative line…another smile. The steel door guarding his cautious heart would miraculously swing open. People were too scared of AIDS, and once they knew you were negative, well, they considered you a real find. And Mr Paranoid here was no different.

"Okay I'll go with you," he said.

things had changed.

"What do you want to know?" he asked.

Damn this guy and his lukewarm stance. The smile was a nothing smile, no spark of attraction. The fool was still under the impression they were on platonic ground. She cursed silently.

"I've never seen a lady friend visiting you. Where is she by the way? Stay too far away to visit?" she asked, hoping he wouldn't think she was too forward. It wouldn't do to scare him off.

"I don't have a girlfriend."

"No girlfriend?" she exclaimed.

"Nope," he answered, nodding his head.

She smiled inwardly. Someone had just been handed to her on a silver platter.

"I'm still looking for the 'One'."

"Don't lose patience, Dean, she'll come along." *In the form of me*, she silently added.

"I intend to wait till she comes along. Especially now that there is AIDS."

"Yeah AIDS is a scary shit," she admitted.

"I can't afford to take it casually. The stakes are just too deadly high," he bitterly told her.

She said, "AIDS is the worst thing that can ever happen to anyone."

"I get tested every three months, that's how scared I am," he admitted, gulping his lager.

"And when's the next test due?"

"Monday," he said.

She reached out for his hand and covered it with hers. "I've never had unprotected sex. I may be young, but I'm not that stupid. Still one can never be too sure. I want to get tested too. Please, Dean, may I come with you on Monday?"

With a worried frown he asked, "Are you sure?"

"Completely," she answered in a firm voice.

She now knew which cards to play. His fear of AIDS would be her weapon.

So at the testing centre she would insist in him being present during her test. That would definitely break the ice between them. And when he saw the negative line…another smile. The steel door guarding his cautious heart would miraculously swing open. People were too scared of AIDS, and once they knew you were negative, well, they considered you a real find. And Mr Paranoid here was no different.

"Okay I'll go with you," he said.

CHAPTER SEVEN

Sure enough, their HIV tests turned out negative, and just as Pulane had predicted, the test opened the cemented door to his heart.

Dean was so scared of AIDS – not that she could blame him, AIDS was serious shit, and he was so relieved to find she too was HIV free. To the trusting Dean, that sealed the deal, she was a good clean girl. So finally, he loosened up.

Only last week when they were coming from seeing a late-night movie, instead of the usual peck, he had surprised her by gently prying her mouth open for a long tongue kiss. Hmm...she went along with him, she wasn't stupid enough to protest about a mere kiss. A kiss was just a kiss. What was there to lose?

Still, she was counting on mind games in her recruiting crusade. The game hidden up her sleeve was not to easily give in to his sexual demands. Yeah, that was where her game playing was reserved because that was where she had plenty to lose. And no way was she going to stoop to the level of a cheap slut for nothing; she was way too smart to spread her legs for zilch. No, what Dean had to do was prove his capabilities first. Besides, the test had already done such a good competent job, and this was why she sat down and reassessed her strategy.

Snoop was one notorious gang; even the cops were terrified of it. To be a member meant your nerves were of cast iron, she acknowledged. But just because Dean was a Snoop, no way was she going to jump to any conclusions. Supposing he was just a tea boy there? She wouldn't be surprised if there was some truth in judging a book by its cover. That was another reason why she wouldn't go further than a kiss with him, what could a tea boy possibly do for her? Serve her tea – Puleese. Besides, caffeine was no good to her – it gave her palpitations.

She frowned. But that guy mentioned something about a suspension. So maybe Dean was a real Snoop after all. But she refused to raise her hopes to even the next notch. Desperate she most definitely was, but there was no deficiency in her brain cells. He could still be a tea boy, probably spilled tea on their fiery-tempered gang leader, who pulled the suspension on him. Besides, it wasn't possible – okay at least feasible considering the brutality of fate, for one to fall from a gang such as Snoop to a mere garden boy. Nevertheless, she had decided to play him along, get to know him. Test the waters. Find out what exactly he could be worth. He couldn't be worth nada; he had to be worth something, she firmly told herself. That was why she still wouldn't drop him, even if he happened to have cotton wool balls. A girl had to keep her options open for insurance. Hey, he could still run a couple of errands for her, and most importantly he could introduce her to more hopeful candidates in Snoop.

Still, Dean was so quiet – it was hard to believe he could be a Snoop. On the other hand, why not? Still waters ran so deep.

And she wasn't fooled by the likes of Dean, oh no, she wasn't the least fooled, especially by this dramatic transformation with him beaming at her. "I'm glad you're negative too." And all of a sudden the hugs were abrupt no more, his eyes all the time focused on her cleavage and his tongue jumping around, but she wasn't the least bit fooled. If she had tested positive, he would have dropped her like a hot potato and called her a bitch diseased slut.

She inwardly shuddered, she really did sympathise with the victims of this monstrous disease.

She shook her head; the stigma associated with AIDS was even more horrifying than the AIDS itself – more *deadly* than the AIDS itself.

"Oops," she exclaimed as she saw how dirty the water she had been scrubbing the floors with was. If Sue found her using such dirty water, she would start with the shouting.

She stood up and hurriedly changed the water. Then she put in a handful of powdered soap and shook her hand inside to produce the

foam. She sourly knelt down and continued scrubbing, wondering why Sue was adamant in her refusal for her to use the mop. Rigid old-fashioned Susan claimed the mop wasn't that effective. Bullshit, her knees were getting marked by all this kneeling.

"Aha!" she said triumphantly. There was a mat in their room, next time she would rest her knees on it. Better not mark her knees, the only part of her body she could now count on were her legs. She used to think her bust was good, but Cindy's nasty remark about her boobs still rankled. 'Cow boobs,' that stung.

She kept on scrubbing, knowing full well inspector Sue would order her to do the floors again if her microscopic eyes were not satisfied.

"Pulane, what's that faraway look on you? How can you make a good job of cleaning the floors if your mind isn't on it?" Her sharp eyes fell on the floor and pointed accusingly. "What's this black spot?"

"It won't come out," Pulane said wearily.

"No, Pulane, it will come out. Come back and redo this part. And finish up quick. I want you to clean the windows too."

A month later she decided Dean was ripe enough to put her plan into action.

She started with phase one – sobbing violently.

Troubled he asked, "What's wrong?"

"I'm scared," she said, still crying.

Enveloping her in his arms, he gently wiped off the tears. "Don't cry, babes. It pains me to see you like this."

"I do love you, Dean, but I'm scared you'll leave me."

"I won't," he fiercely promised.

"Just like Mark."

"Well, I'm not Mark."

"Birds of a feather flock together," she hiccupped.

"Pulane, please."

"I need some kind of assurance. Marriage assurance," she blurted.

No answer came from Dean.

"So you don't want to commit," she cried even harder.

"Pulane, you could be on the rebound. Can we at least wait a while?" he gently said.

She gaped at him, completely taken aback.

"Rebound from whom?"

"Mark."

"It was nothing that deep with Mark. He was just a mistake I've now wisely put behind me."

"Are you sure he is completely out of your heart?"

Irritably she said, "Come on, Dean, he never was in my heart!"

"Ah, so you slept with him all this while, and he was nowhere near your heart." He looked at her suspiciously. "What does that make you, Pulane?"

Oops. "What I'm saying is that Mark is not and was not the love of my life."

"Dun was telling me that you are too into Mark and never will you get him out of your system."

"That's Duncan, full of shit," she spat.

"He has known you far longer than I," Dean said quietly. "I…"

She cut him off. "Don't listen to Duncan. He is just sour cos his girlfriend of two years has kicked him out."

"Maria, you mean?"

"Yeah, and now that he has no girlfriend, he's sabotaging other people's relationship. What a rat!"

Trusting Dean visibly relaxed. Their relationship had progressed to cuddles and kisses, but that was about all. As far as she was aware, he hadn't yet done anything to earn himself further than that. Of course, he tried to go further, but she was way ahead of him, fed him the 'too soon for that' line. After a couple of weeks the line didn't seem to work that much. He would storm out in the middle of the night and spend the next day sulking.

"Dean, please don't get mad at me," she would plead.

"You say you love me, but the lack of action in the bedroom makes me wonder…."

"Dean, please don't talk like that, I love you." Since she didn't want him to slip through her fingers before he served his purpose, she had quickly polished up her line.

"Just give me a little time, sweetie. I didn't want to tell you this, but I have this fear of you bolting out after the big moment. I know you love me, and you'll never pull such a stunt on me, but, Dean, I can't help myself. I will sleep with you. All I need is a little time. Please, let's not rush into this. We love each other, Dean. The first time has to be special, memorable...."

That clinched it – for now.

"Where would I get money for the bridal price?"

She started whining. "If you love me, you'll do it."

"I do, but my pay isn't enough to tie the knot on," he explained.

"Can't you go back to Snoop?" she wailed.

He sat up in shock.

"Snoop! Where did you get that from?"

"I got ears," she retorted.

"Whatever it is you heard, it's all lies," he said flatly.

"The first time you took me out."

"Oh that guy at the club. Come on, Pulie, he didn't know what he was saying. He was drunk," he said awkwardly.

So he thinks I'm stupid. Big surprise coming his way.

"You disappoint me, Dean. I'm not stupid, and I never knew you could so blatantly lie to me."

The supposedly pawn just kept his eyes fixed at the ceiling, remained tight-lipped.

"I love you, Dean. This is supposed to be a relationship, a two-way street. But if you don't trust me enough to tell me the truth, then we may as well call it quits."

"So you want to dump me," he said in a strangled voice.

Supposing he heartedly agreed to the dumping, shook her hand and wished her the best in future endeavours?

What, then?

Damn, she had as sure as hell overplayed her hand this time. She started hitting the bed with clenched fists in frustration, bawling her head off.

"Pulie, calm down," he said, enveloping her in his wimpy arms.

She decided to lay the guilt trip on him. "You are just like Mark," she sobbed.

"Okay, I was once a Snoop, but I'm suspended now," he reluctantly admitted.

She wiped the tears with the back of her hand. "I want you to know that you being an ex-Snoop will not make me think less of you."

"Thanks," he said.

The bastard was so relieved thinking this was the end of it.

"So let's start saving. This month end I'll give you four hundreds. That way we'll get married soon," she tactfully said, luring him into the sucker trap she had cunningly set up for him.

"But you'll be left with only a hundred!"

"Enough for toiletries," she said.

"No, I can't allow that," he said sternly.

"Oh, I can see you don't really want to marry me."

"I do," he said.

"If I put four hundred, and you put six for ten to twelve months…" She jumped out of bed and shrieked. "A year! I'm not willing to wait that long."

"I could go back to Snoop when my suspension is up," he said slowly.

"How long before you finish serving your suspension?"

"Six months."

"But, Dean, even after the suspension is over, they'll be watching you like a hawk. How did you get this suspension anyway?"

"Drinking on a job."

"How do they operate there?"

"Not your business, Pulane!"

"I don't want inside info, Dean. What I want to know is what cut they give you after a job."

"Oh, it depends on what they assign you to do. You either lead the job or gang up with the rest of the guys to carry it out. When you lead to ensure everything is smoothly carried out on that job, you get ten percent of the gross. While the other guys are given a negotiable cut."

"Did you ever lead a job?"

"That's why I got suspended."

"I see. What kind of jobs do you do at Snoop?"

"You're asking a lot of questions," he said, scowling at her.

"Sorry."

"Snoop is into big stuff, no grabbing of handbags from helpless women or pick-pocketing. Those are too petty for us."

She was thoughtful for some time. "So after this suspension, it'll take you a while to get back to where you were."

"Yeah, I'll just be one of the boys."

"For how long?"

He shrugged. "Don't know."

"In the meantime, you'll just be getting a small cut for even more dangerous jobs."

"That's why my brother assigned me to lead. It's less dangerous, you do the planning and the boys do whatever you tell them."

"Jomo is a Snoop too?"

"Not so loud, Pulane," he said angrily.

She made her mind up. "Okay, Snoop is out. Too dangerous, let's try another angle. What's the name of that guy at the club?"

"Ivan."

"You do business with him only once, something not too risky but enough to finance our life. I don't want our kids to end up like us. I want private schools and good neighbours for our babies, Dean."

He kept quiet.

"Has this Ivan ever been caught?"

He shook his head.

"Good. We risk his association, but only once. Something worth the risk, but not too dangerous. I don't want to be a widow before I have the chance to wear a bridal dress. It has to be a one-off, Dean, not an everyday deal. I'm not going to risk the life of the only person I've ever loved."

"But," he hesitated.

She saw the hesitation. Almost home, she plunged ahead.

"Dean, please, you are the best deal that ever happened to me, and I desperately need a Mrs Dean title. So check out this Ivan, see what he has to say. If it's too risky, we drop the whole thing."

Like hell we would.

She started kissing him to fully convince him; it didn't take that long.

"Okay," he said after a while.

"It's for a good cause," she said elatedly.

"So my relationship with Pulane doesn't bother you?" he asked Mark.

"Bother me? Why would it bother me?" he answered, completely baffled.

"Well you used to love her," Dean said stubbornly.

"Don't be silly, Dean. I only slept with her," he said indifferently.

"You make her sound like a cheap slut," he shouted.

"Why do you keep on and on about this girl, Dean?" Mark exclaimed in alarm.

"Well I love her." His voice rose emotionally.

"You what?" Mark stared at him like he had lost his marbles.

"I'm serious about her," Dean said, his eyes welling up with tears.

"But what is there to be serious about in Pulane?" asked a puzzled Mark.

"Everything," he said in a firm voice.

"Like what?"

"I can't explain it in words," Dean glumly admitted.

"That's cos there is nothing to explain," remarked Mark triumphantly.

Dean stalked off without saying another word.

Mark caught up with him.

"Why not hook up with another girl? That way your concentrated feelings for Pulane will get diluted. Then you wouldn't be so hung up on her," Mark advised.

"Are you saying I should cheat on Pulane?" Dean screamed in shock.

"Well, it's the only way to bring you together," said Mark.

"I don't want to talk about this anymore," he said, throwing Mark a scathing look.

"I was only trying to help, mate," Mark said defensively.

"And I appreciate your 'help'."

"How come you are so touchy these days? Another shit influence from your maid girlfriend," spat Mark.

"If you were really my mate, you'd respect the fact that I love her."

"Well, I'm your mate and I'm concerned about what's happening to you."

"What exactly is happening to me?" he asked icily.

"You've changed ever since you teamed up with her."

"Well I'm sorry then," Dean said.

Mark shook his head and went to his room.

She idly flipped through a magazine. 'How to sexually win him,' one page blared at her. *Nonsense*, she thought, turning to another page. *What about men, how come nothing ever falls on their shoulders, why does it have to be a woman who has to win him all the time?*

She then admired skinny turn-up jeans on a celebrity style page. *Great stuff, better pull up my socks, put more work on Dean, then wow! I'll be able to flaunt around in one of these,* she nodded. *With a body-hugging top plus strappy sandals like this, no way will Mark brush me off.* Dean was such a good teammate, so agreeable, eager to help her out with her tough love life, she laughed, leafing through the magazine.

"ONLY LIKE-YOU." Her eyes caught the heading, curiously she settled down to read.

"The gentle kisses,
Your touch so - absolutely right
Stroking my thighs
Exploring
Flesh flaming against flesh
Tongue entwined against tongue
Hearts dancing together
We enfolded . . .

In each other's arms we lay,
I love you, I said
I like you, you whispered
While you slept, I lay beside you burning
I feel fulfilled no more
I feel right no more
The celebratory beat my heart had been dancing is no more
My flesh is cold in dread
Only like me, you said
I feel that's too invalid a word
I feel that's too lacking a word

Only like-me

A too deficient a word
A nothing mocking word
A non-quenching word–"

"Pulane!"

She jumped up in alarm. "Sue, I didn't hear you come in."

"I knew I'd find you here, lazing around!" she shouted, snatching the magazine from her. "Didn't I tell you the Chambers are hosting a dinner party tonight?"

"But, Sue, I was only taking a five-minute break," she whined.

Firmly holding her hand Sue frogmarched her to the dining room. "Break is up, now let's get back to work, young lady."

"What now?" Pulane wearily asked.

"The bar, get a notepad and make an order of drinks."

"Yes, ma'am," she said, her voice laced with sarcasm. Looking up she asked, "Which drinks must I order?"

"Where is your common sense, Pulane? Dinner is for eight people so order enough drinks, the same drinks we usually order, but get a few lagers in case they ask for it, get more Heineken. We wouldn't want to run short."

As she listed the drinks on a notepad her mind drifted off to what she had been reading.

"She is too hard to please," she said loudly.

"I'm not hard to please, Pulane, I simply want everything ready while there is still time to rectify stuff we overlooked."

"Not you, 'Only like-me'."

"Huh?"

"Mark didn't even say he likes me when I told him I loved him."

"At least he's no liar."

Biting her pen thoughtfully, Pulane said, "I wouldn't have minded an 'I like you' from him."

"Pulane, listen, you've had a narrow escape with that bastard. Start thinking smart, get him out of your head."

"It's not so automatic, Sue," she cried.

"You have Dean, what can you possibly lack for in a guy like that?" Sue said irritably.

"In that magazine you're holding, this writer is complaining that when she says 'I love you' to her partner he only whispers 'I like yous'," she said conversationally.

Curiously opening the magazine Sue read, "'No single 'I love you from him'."

"Nope, only the lacking 'I only like yous'." She looked up at Sue. "It's titled 'I only like you' in bold, you won't miss it."

"Aha, I found it."

While Sue was engrossed in the magazine she muttered, "Her mind is rabidly suspicious."

"Why is his tongue too tangled up to say 'I love you'? Why does he have to use tasteless mini words over a serious thing like 'I love you'?" Sue said, pausing in her reading.

"She should be grateful, 'I like you' is better than nothing."

"That's selling yourself short, Pulane!"

"Well…if the competition is too stiff, you need to lower your expectations, otherwise nobody will buy you."

"There is nothing worse than settling for a loveless relationship, Pulane," Finishing up she said, "Anyway, if you had carefully read this through, you will know the writer is not actually complaining over the exact 'I like you' words. Her problem is the love she had over some rat guy who was clowning over it. Why, I say she is right to get worried." Putting the magazine on the table, she said, "Poor girl, so in love, but the guy only fancies putting his dick in her, but take her home to mommy, hell no!"

"I bet if she was here, you'd say leave him."

"Exactly," she said, missing the sarcasm in Pulane's voice. "It's up to a woman to wise up, Pulane, because a man will never cut down on his options for having free sex by dumping you. Never," Sue said flatly.

"Mark dumped me," Pulane said bitterly.

"Because you were a loose cannon beating up his women."

"I did try to cool it as he said but…"

Sue pulled up a chair and in a serious voice said, "Pulane, listen to me. I was once in a rubbish relationship. People told me to cut him loose, but I refused to listen. I told them if he didn't love me, he would leave me. But he never did leave. Slept and slept with me. Ten years, Pulane, can you believe such shit? In the end it was me who had to limp out. I learnt the hard way, dear child. A man will never dump you no matter what unless you do something drastic like halving down their sex rations by harassing his other women. Forget the fact that he doesn't love you – most of the time he's groaning and grunting on top of you, love is the furthest thing from his mind. He'll sleep with you, yes, sleep with you again and again till you are completely ruined merchandise. But to leave you, nope. You will of course hear he has married a fresh college girl, but he still won't lose you. Sure, stuff will tumble out of his mouth to shut you up and keep you opening those legs; 'I was forced into it. Her parents are friends with my folks. But you, only you I love. Look at how far we've come. Years honey, don't let your anger blind you in throwing away the many years we had together. I love you'."

Glumly shaking her head Sue went on, "You'll go to the mirror, stare at yourself. Stare at your faded looks. Count your grandmother age. Count the many years you spent with him, waiting to exhale. His words will come back to you, 'Only you I love'. Your heart will greedily gobble that up. Suddenly his words will taste so unbelievably yummy. Your face will be like that of the little rural people who have just tasted Kentucky Fried Chicken for the very first time. You will wolf down every speck and lick your fingers one by one, wanting more – marvelling at such deliciousness. And if your friends try to caution you, that's who you will hate. You'll call them all the derogatory names in the world. 'Jealous bitches', you will say, while the real truth is there is no single person in the world that can ever get jealous over the 'other woman'. No one, Pulane."

Slamming her fist down to emphasize her point Pulane said, "No, Sue, jealousy is everywhere. People are always jealous of one another."

Stubbornly shaking her head, Sue said, "Not in this one, Pulane. People will either laugh or pity you. But jealous – never."

"Sue!"

"Unless you censor out the real story by feeding them buttered-up stuff. Leaving out the serial cheating he flaunts at you, the insults and icy attitude when you don't have money to buy his charm. But once they get access to inside info, no way."

"But, Sue," she protested.

"After digesting his yummy words, you'll continue to sleep with him. Embracing his cheating life. And if you needle him to leave his wife, he will sulk on you. Start some shouting drama on you. Complain you don't understand. Soon you will be too scared to ask him when he is leaving his wife. And yes, Pulane, you will die exactly like that, still waiting, waiting to exhale life. But the truth is you will never exhale, Pulane, unless you take that courageous step and walk away. Men are selfish bastards, Pulane, no kidding about that, they will never free you no matter what. It's up to you to make that survival decision and rescue yourself. That's why the pain of leaving him is always ten times better than the pain of staying."

"Mark was adamant in dumping me."

"That's one hell of a piece of luck, not all women are that lucky to be dumped by a shit bastard. They either have to do the dumping or they are stuck for life."

"Mark…" she painfully shook her head. "I still don't get it, why do I love him this much?"

"Pulane, if you are not careful, you will fall into the same sucker pot Dean pulled you from." Standing up, she continued, "Be careful of your heart, Pulane, it's the most traitorous part of your body."

Irritably kicking the leg of the dining room table, Sue continued, "I once dumped this man cos he cheated on me. A week later my reserves crumbled, and I went up to him and begged him to take me back. I still remember the amusement in his eyes when he said 'no problem'. It still burns me up that I sunk that low."

"What happened?" Pulane asked curiously.

"He became even worse."

"And?"

"I eventually came around and dumped him for good."

"You probably left him when he was on the verge of changing."

Shaking her head Sue said, "Sleeping with Mark has really damaged you, Pulane. When you're done with the list, go tell Mark to bring up some fresh flowers to spice up this place." Suspiciously, she looked at Pulane. "Nah, on second thoughts don't, I'll tell him myself."

Squatting in the garden, Dean examined the yellowed leaves of a green plant.

"Magnesium deficiency, I'll apply Epsom salts on the whole garden tomorrow," he decided.

Aimlessly, he looked around, what to do next?

Forty. He sighed; he'd never fallen this hard. It was unnerving because he was used to calling all the shots with women. None of them had managed to nail him till… Still, Pulane was a safe bet, not some of these bitches who would pull a fast one on you if you weren't careful.

Women! He shook his head as he drew a long drag from the cigarette he'd just lit. A lot of them were more trouble than they were worth, especially the ugly ones. The insecurity there was shocking; it could break any man's balls. An ugly broad would never accept your female friends, you say 'hi' to a girl in the street, and you are in a shit load of trouble. Shaking his head he thought, Christ, you'd think less looks would be less trouble, but hell no! Girl wants to swallow you, listen into your phone calls, choose your friends, and if you ain't with her on a weekend night, then you are sure screwing around on her!

An ugly broad, he drew a disgusted breath, get one of those in your life and the shit that would crowd your ass would make you start thinking God had in it for you. And why was Pulane whimpering that it was too soon? Well fuck her! How come it was never too soon to take her out to Chinese restaurants and stuff? Did Pulane expect him to stick around and put up with such shit? He spat. A piece of her was stinging him, then she turned around and told him she loved him! What the hell kind of shit was that?

AIDS or no AIDS, he had no intention of putting up with her nunnery games for long. Definitely not. Especially not with a killer bust like that. He couldn't even think straight; he was all hungry and impatient for a full course of indoor games. His hands were shaking, yearning to grab those tits and chew them till…shit!

Why do this to me? he thought.

Kiss, kiss and when he was hot and ready, she shut him out and chanted that it was too soon. Too soon! She better come around and start opening those legs.

As if that wasn't enough, his heart refused to take it slow, plunging right ahead, and now he was completely hooked. He felt chained, cornered. Confiding in that pompous brother of his would spark some fireworks. And Mark – well Mark was in a Nando's chicken world, and when he did talk to him, he didn't seem to understand.

His heart was so stubborn, ruling his life like he had no say in it. He didn't have a choice; his heart forced him into it. He started thinking long term. Hell, he needed assurance as in yesterday, not with these almost daily nightmares that were plaguing him of Pulane bailing on him.

And marriage would be such a perfect refreshing solution. And… that brought him to Ivan.

No need to postpone this further, it was about time he saw Ivan, he decided, and find out what he had in mind.

"I've decided to marry her," he told Mark late that afternoon.

"Who?" asked Mark blankly.

"Pulie of course."

"What?" exclaimed Mark in horror. He was drinking water from a glass. It slipped through his hand and shattered on the ground.

"Mark!" Dean bent down and picked the pieces.

"Dun and them are going to kill me for this," wailed Mark.

"Why?" Dean asked, all surprised.

"They blame me for you linking up with her."

"Why is that?"

"She has got you whipped, Dean, and we are all not amused."

After throwing the pieces of glass in the garbage bin, Dean came back to Mark, who still stood there with his mouth hanging open.

"Close your mouth, Mark, flies will get in."

Mark looked at him. "Dean, why are you doing this?"

"Cos I love her."

"It's unnerving the way you are into this girl," remarked Mark.

"What do you want me to do, Mark? Fuck her and walk, the same way you did?"

"At least I could handle her, but you can't. You aren't emotionally equipped to link with this girl, Dean."

"Oh!"

"You haven't even slept with her, Dean, and you are already talking marriage."

"I don't have to sleep with her to know she's the one."

"What the hell has this girl done to you, Dean?"

"I love her," he calmly explained.

"Okay, I'll talk to Jen. She must have a couple of single friends."

"I'm not interested," he said flatly.

"Dean."

"There is this guy I need to see. Later, buddy, as usual it was such an inspiration talking to you," he said.

This pretend game was sure as hell getting to her.

It wasn't as easy as she had naively assumed, Pulane grumpily thought as she made the bed in the master bedroom. She abruptly dropped the satin sheet she was about to spread on the king-sized bed and went and stood before a full mirror, scrutinising herself. "Dramatic weight loss," she grimly muttered to herself. Bags under her eyes, the little good complexion she had was all gone. Dean was too demanding, too clingy. Something she had not contemplated, and it was a major snag. Expecting her to come to his room every night for a cuddle, which wasn't much really considering the big job he would be doing for her. Still, she thought, screwing up her face, a daily snog in a house he shared with Mark.

It was hard.

And the worst thing was that when she went to his room she had to pass through the lounge. She swallowed the tightness in her throat. Sometimes Mark would be there working on his girl. The girl would be tangled up on his lap on a beanbag. Always engrossed in one another, they never seemed to hear when she mumbled a bitter 'hello'. They were oblivious to her, hands entwined, tongues working on each other, dancing to their lusty beat. What was her probably diseased tongue doing in her man's mouth? Contaminating her man. Well, it ripped her heart to stumble on such lusty exhibitions.

By the time she reached her destination she would be pretty shaky. And Dean, a shit bargain in his sucker voice inquiring what was up with her, would just about set her off. The smell of money to bail her out of her emotional predicament would quickly simmer down the rage building up in her, though. "Mustn't lose it, mustn't lose it."

And thank God for those small favours his big brother, Jomo, had bought him. A Philips brand mini hi-fi, and if you played it loud enough it helped, helped quite tremendously, drowning the sounds of.... But it was never that easy really because Mark's room was right next door to his, and sometimes Dean would complain and tell her to lower the volume. That was when she would hear the lusty moans, the sounds of ecstasy – damn those thin walls. And to top it all, Dean would start touching her. That was when, *'Zoom'*, her acting talent ran out on her. How could she really go along with Dean's fumbling moves when she could hear that girl moaning a sure sign that she was...? She forced back the tears, if only she wasn't sharing her room with Sue, then she would ask Dean to do the visiting.

But you could say she was coming to terms slightly with her peculiar situation because the first weeks were really hard, harder than hard. A mere hand holding from Dean would set her off, and she lashed out, "I need time, dammit!"

Time for what? Just for your boyfriend to hold your hand! That was how bad it was. And Dean would gape at her, more puzzled than angry. "I don't understand you." Call that more of an understatement she too didn't understand herself these days. She had been pretty certain everything would be plain sailing.

Those first weeks! She shook her head; she had nearly blown her cover. Those were the days she flatly refused to lower the volume of the hi-fi. Too vulnerable she had been then; she was right on edge. Too scared to risk it and find out what those sounds would do to her. But there were those seconds when the song being played would end and another track would start. That was when she would hear those heart-tearing sounds. The first time she completely lost it and jumped out of bed blazing, "Why is she moaning like that? What are they doing?" Her hands had clenched into fists. "What are they doing?" she said, violently bursting into wrenching tears that tore her heart apart, hysterically beating the bed.

Dean had grabbed both her hands. "Pulane."

She had looked up through her tearful eyes; his face had instantly brought her around.

"Get out of my room," he had said darkly.

"Huh?" She responded.

"My name is Dean, not anything near Mark to make me his

substitute."

"Oh, so that's what you think."

"Get out, Pulane, my patience is wearing thin."

"Dean, you have it all wrong. Do you really think I could still be pining for Mark after what he did to me?"

"Really, so what was the hysteric show all about?"

"Because it's hard. We are trying to do the right thing by not rushing into that. But they are not making it easy for us, these porno sounds emerging from his room. You'll feel left out and I'm…scared I could…lose you. Oh, Dean, if only you knew how much you mean to me." She solidified it with more tear shedding. He had wrapped his not so soothing arms around her and sobbed out his sorries, hell, he even got her some fancy apology card the next day.

"Oh, Dean, you really shouldn't have gone to all this trouble."

"I'll go to all the trouble when it comes to you."

Nice words. She had smiled inside. Good, slowly he was progressing to the agreeable stage she had so tirelessly been recruiting him for.

"Thanks, Dean," she said, hugging him.

She had watched him go from the kitchen window, his walk more like a bouncing tennis ball. So full of life, smiling at the butterflies attracted by the garden. She had watched, her arms folded, she sighed and finally understood her part. The trick was simple really, to play her part convincingly. That was all there was to it. Firmly she had put on her mask. The same mask men had no trouble wearing once they figured you would only do nicely for sex. Oh yes, inside there was a raging battle, her heart was screaming for Mark, wanting Mark. But no worries, her heart would catch up on the game that soon Mark would be theirs for keeps if they bided their time and played their cards right.

Still it wasn't as hard as before, she consoled herself.

CHAPTER EIGHT

As soon as she breathlessly stepped into the room she said, "Honey, what did Ivan say?"

"I can't tell you," Dean said without meeting her eyes.

"What?" Was she hearing right.

"I do not want you involved." This time he spoke in a serious and firm voice.

"I see." She shrugged her shoulders and let it go.

He visibly relaxed. He was lying in bed on his back. She sat next to him and ruffled his hair. Soon her magnetism charged him up.

"Lie next to me," he said.

She shook her head. "No."

He sat up, startled. "No?" he repeated, apparently he didn't expect that from her.

This was good because she too didn't expect an 'I can't tell you' clause in their nice loving relationship. What was this, shutting her out on her major plan? A plan he would never have the balls to come up with if she hadn't lured him to it. The guy was supposed to be eager to tell all, singing the sucker song that was going to bail Mark out of the claws of that slut Jen. Damn, why was Dean not sitting in the palm of her hand, an underestimation on her part? She blinked, a bit sceptical. A glass of water was on the coffee table; to buy time she grabbed it and slowly drank from it.

"What's with you?" he irritably asked.

She took her time drinking the water. Okay, she admitted, she had used all the verbal tricks she could ever think of. It was time to be more practical. She had to work on him real good to totally wipe off this smart attitude he seemed to have developed. 'I can't tell you,' what the hell kind of talk was that from a pawn?

"You don't trust me enough to confide in me, so why should I trust you enough to lie next to you?" she said.

"Scared, I'll get you to sleep with me?" he asked recklessly.

"You need to get your mind out of the gutter, Dean."

She stood up.

"Hey, where are you off to?"

"My room."

He jumped out of bed and grabbed her. She sighed deeply. Never had she met anyone as predictable as this guy.

"I hate people who play games with me," he said as he kissed her fiercely. She let him, and even kissed him back.

"I'm so hot for you."

She cringed; that was a weird choice of words. Anyway, the spark seemed to be on him because she sure as hell couldn't feel any heat.

"Pulie I love you so…" he moaned.

She was not naive, and she knew her part well. "And I love you too," she moaned, even louder than him.

He undressed her, she didn't protest. Her plan was for him to first see what was on the menu, dangle the carrot so to speak.

"Very beautiful," he groaned as he kissed her breasts.

Breathing heavily, he lifted her. As she lay there in the middle of bed, his hands and tongue all over her, she wondered what he was like before he had adopted this placid behaviour. He had mentioned something about his former wild days to her. What was he like back then? Ah well, whatever he was it wouldn't have done her any good; he would have long ago caught her at her deceitful game. He was actually cool, as he was very trusting and serious. And he probably wasn't as drab as she made him out to be, she admitted. That was just a biased summation because she was in love with some bastard who had decided a cashier at Chicken Land was a better deal than her.

"Dean," she said, already bored.

"Shh don't talk." His clumsy hands were all over her. The excitement in his voice was rightly at its peak. Good, he had seen what he was missing, and would continue to miss unless he delivered something worthwhile. Abruptly she pulled away.

"We shouldn't be doing this," she said as she grabbed her clothes and quickly dressed. Why should she sleep with him when he hadn't earned that stage? She needed more before succumbing to him, especially since she felt he wasn't much in bed.

"What do you mean?" he shouted. He sounded as if he was about to lose it.

"We are not ready," she calmly explained.

"You mean, you are not ready," he exploded.

"Oh no, it's you who is not."

Now he really was surprised. "What?"

"There is no trust between us."

"There is," he said flatly.

"Ivan," she said.

He stared at the ceiling.

"Let's build the trust first," she quietly suggested.

"I trust you."

"Prove it," she said in a no-nonsense voice.

No single word came from Dean.

"I don't blame you for not trusting me though. One has to be cautious on such things," she admitted.

"I just don't want you involved," he said wearily.

"We are a team, Dean. The fact that you are involved has automatically involved me."

"He's after the money Charsecurity guys collect from shops and hotels to take to the bank the next day," he whispered.

"But you don't work at the security building," she said, frowning.

"Exactly, they will never suspect me."

"How much money are we talking of here?"

"Could be millions if we target the day after public holidays when they take all collections for bulk deposits to the bank."

"Are you able to help him then?" she asked. Finally, her adrenaline was pumping in excitement.

"Haven't made up my mind yet, but Ivan…he will make a good partner…knows his stuff."

"And he has never been caught?"

Dean shook his head. "He is too good. The cops don't even suspect he's into shady deals."

"How does he explain his money, a cover job?"

"A rich family," he answered.

"It's a good plan," she said eagerly.

He looked at her. "Pulane, sometimes you surprise me."

"Dean, this is about us. Marriage." She took a meaningful pause, "Marriage means kids and a house, and for that we need money. We need stable surroundings to have kids. What kind of an example will you be setting for your kids if you are still a thug with Snoop?"

Resting on one elbow he said, "Mark does not want me to marry you," he said.

"How come?"

"He doesn't think you're worth that much."

"Who cares what he thinks?" she said, appearing not in the least bothered. Another piece of good news – how could Mark possibly agree to him marrying her?

"You used to be so much in love with him."

"Used to, Dean. That is the key word. I was too stupid to know better. Anyway, let's talk about Ivan."

"I'll be the first suspect," he explained.

"Why? Do you have a record?"

"No, but if they find out I'm a suspended Snoop, they'll be on my case."

She thoughtfully tapped her foot on the floor.

How should she play it now? What he said was highly plausible; the cops would not give him a break once they knew he was a Snoop. And she being his supposedly girlfriend they would be linked - they could both end up being chief suspects.

She buried her face in her hands, suddenly discontent.

God, but she had been so close. So close to reaching her one and only dream, the dream that all along had seemed so unattainable. All of a sudden she felt like weeping.

She watched in dismay as the only chance of getting Mark back flew out of the window. Life without Mark. She tried, really tried to look further than that, but what she saw was frighteningly bleak. The tears were finally released, burning and spilling out of her eyes. She buried her face and wept.

"Pulane, are you okay?" Dean put his arm around her shoulder.

As tears poured into her mouth, she wondered what his useless arm was doing clasped around her shoulder. They had now come to the end of the act. It was now real; she had just quit her act, an act she'd had to adopt in order to recruit him. An act she had been forced into because if she put her cards on the table, said it like it really was....

'Look here, Dean, I don't really think much of you. Mark is the one I'm interested in. So how about being a pal and helping me out? Use your Snoop's skill to steal money for me to boost my relationship with Mark.' No way would he have played along. Yet they say truth can set us free, free from what she wondered, and who came up with that saying? Turn to the truth, and you'll be crippled in your ambitious parade.

Truth was a bitch – it hurt. Right now the joy in Dean's face was... what, a lie? Dean really believed they were altar bound. *Yuck,* she recoiled. But the thought somehow made Dean happy, so who was she to deny him that? If she started on a truth crusade, she would remain a tramp maid till the day she dropped – a fucking stagnant life to a shit nowhere. Nobody would ever say at least she was no prostitute or thief, commending her for earning her pennies. Nope. What they would do was laugh at her, 'So you are still a maid, hah, hah.' But if she bent the truth, acquired money in the process, no matter how shadily she got that money, she would be everybody's sweetheart, win a popularity trophy. This was why she had to pathologically lie. Pruning his rationality till he was exactly where she wanted him.

Only now there was a major snag, his murky past had seen to that, once the cops found out he was a Snoop, all hell would break loose. And a ball-less rat like him wouldn't stand the heat. Once they started on him with the rubber hose, he'd be singing soprano so loud he'd be heard all the way to China. Secrets would be flying off everywhere, and come a day or two, she too would be charged. And once you were there, it was all doom, no such thing as a picnic once your ass landed in jail – you would be marked for life. Even after serving time it would still hang onto her. Her so-called friends would develop amnesia over her real name. Ex-con they would spit till the day she dropped dead. When it came to such stuff, their brains wouldn't mind doing overtime, extending the memories for as long as forever. Another shit drama she didn't need hanging on her head, her problems were endless as it is – so why was his arm pinning her to him like this, as if they had a certain understanding? Whatever understanding they had expired a little while ago, so what was the catch? Exactly where was her compensation for being pinned like this to the point of suffocation.

What was in it for her? What was her reason for tolerating such nuisance crap?

Fucking hell! She roughly shook his arm off.

"You really do want to marry me," he said, sounding surprised. As usual he had gotten it all wrong. He rose from the bed and planted himself next to her. Then he gently covered her hands with his.

Her body shook uncontrollably as she cried heartily. All of a sudden she couldn't stand him, and she cringed when he covered her hands with his. Ah, she nearly forgot, there was absolutely no reason to tolerate that now – roughly she disentangled herself.

"I didn't know you wanted to marry me this bad."

What was the bastard on about now? She dazedly wondered. She was just about to end his Christmas by dumping him right there when she felt the intense ache in her heart. Ah, that would have to wait until the pain...she screwed her eyes shut.

Dammit Mark, why can't I just have you?

"Okay even if they suspect me, it's no biggie. I don't even work in Charsecurity. They can't arrest me based on suspicion only. It has to be something solid enough before they can even think of pulling that." His voice faintly reached her.

"What do you mean?" she managed to find her voice.

"And my brother, he has this lawyer, if they make any silly mistake, he'll make clowns out of them in court."

"What are you saying, Dean?"

"I'll do it," he said, wiping her tears with his fingertips.

That was all it took to mysteriously end the sharp pain.

"No, it's too risky. I love you too much to let you do it."

"And I love you too much to deprive you of the life you deserve," he said.

So well had she rehearsed her part, she stood up and started pacing around.

"I'm scared," she said in a small voice.

"Don't be. I'll be fine," he said, taking her in his arms.

"How much will be our take if you manage to pull it off."

"Depends how much we get, forty percent after we pay overheads, two or three million. Ivan is collecting sixty percent net cos he's providing the manpower."

"Overheads?"

"People who will help make it happen."

Her mind started to race. Mi-ll-ion! Not one, but two or three, shit this was better than she ever imagined.

"But these people, Dean, can they be trusted?"

"Ivan has used them before, so yes, they can be trusted."

That night she let him go all the way. She was finally convinced he had earned that intimate stage. So there she was, she had started the long drag of servicing his raging hormones. She cemented that by doing his laundry and scrubbing the floors of his room. It didn't stop there, she started calling him 'husband', and it worked like charm.

The sucker gobbled it all up.

Every single day, they went over their plan, searching for the loopholes, which they expertly smoothed out till they were confident enough to dream.

Except for the torture she had to endure at night, Pulane was totally at peace. She could even afford to smile at the chicken girl when she came over for her sex dose. Why not? Whatever she had with Mark was about to expire. Soon it would be her turn, her eternal turn.

Dean contentedly folded his arms across his chest, wondering whom he should choose as his best man. His peers were all gone thanks to that bastard of a disease. Jomo was too much of a snob, he definitely wouldn't approve of Pulane. And that left who…yeah Mark, he was the closest thing to him, next to his brother, of course. He shrugged his shoulders as he thought of that snobbish brother of his. He would have to come around and embrace Pulane as his sister in marriage because he really did love her, and he needed her too badly. Last time he mentioned Pulane to his brother, Jomo had blustered something about Pulane being a tramp bitch. Jomo better ditch with the insults because Pulane would soon be the missus of the family, which he probably won't tell Jomo till the deed was done. Who knew what Snoop strings he might pull to stop the wedding; he had better tread cautiously.

"The boxes they collect the money in are simple boxes with padlocks, no ink bombs installed inside. Bullet-proof vans of course," Dean said, making notes on a notepad.

Jubilantly Pulane kissed him. "And no one will suspect us, we don't even work there, we are just the little people who scrub floors and tend the garden."

Abruptly getting to his feet, Dean said, "We've decided to grab the money on April sixteenth."

"But that's two months away?"

Raising his hand to silence her protests, he said smiling, "That's the earliest date after public holidays. Four whole days collecting money from shops and hotels till the bank opens. The sixteenth is a winner day. That's when they take all those collections to the bank for bulk deposits."

"We need an inside guy," she said.

Frowning, he asked, "What for? He might lead them to us."

"One of the guys who goes with the van to the bank needs to be in our pocket, Dean. Even if we get someone to drug them, we need our guy inside that van when it leaves for the bank."

"But not just anyone is allowed to go with the van, Pulane."

"Yeah, but what if they feel drowsy from the drugged coffee and radio in for help before passing out? We need an inside guy," she insisted.

Dean shook his head dismissively. "No, an inside job will definitely lead the cops to us. Let me think…Ivan already got some girl who they hired as a cleaner today. On that day she will put something in their coffee. Not anything to make them pass out, something that will blur their concentration. Anyway we've already laid out the plan," he said tearing up the paper he had been scribbling on.

"There is a bush between Lejara Road and Fifth Avenue at block five, we will be staging the robbery there," he continued, looking at her pointedly. "One person is going to have to lie in the middle of the road covered with what looks like blood, not a man, that will look suspicious, a woman, you, Pulane."

"But you said they are under strict instructions not to stop anywhere else except the bank."

"With you, they will stop, a woman covered in blood. They will both jump out of the van to try and help. The drugged coffee will scramble their sixth sense."

"And?"

Speaking in a low and urgent voice, he said, "They will stop, thinking you are a victim of hit and run, and that's when we will strike. When the security guys arrive at the bank, they have to radio in, reporting their arrival. That's why timing is critical. We have to act fast, Pulane, and that means you are not late in lying on that road. Police will be alerted if the office don't get their routine report."

"Can't you radio in, pretending you're one of them to buy us time?"

He shook his head. "They use a complicated code which they change every day."

"This sound so ominous, Dean. What if another car comes before their van while I'm lying there?"

He smiled reassuringly. "Won't happen, two boards barring motorist from using that road cos of danger ahead will be erected on both sides of the road five minutes before the van comes. And just for good measure, we will have a man wearing police uniform standing by each sign directing motorists to use the other road. We take the sign out seconds before the van comes, and put it back till the job is done."

Clapping her hands cheerfully she said, "Wow!"

"Perfect timing is what bothers me, this has to be timed accurately, and we mustn't be even a second behind. Ivan will be timing their routine every day from now on; we can then properly draw up our own timetable. What about the money? Where are we going to hide it while the heat is still on?"

"How about the bush?" she asked.

"Bush! This is Africa with them traditional doctors. Suppose one herbalist is out in the bush scouting for a traditional herb and the source of this herb happens to be a small tree which has grown on top of our treasure?"

She shuddered. "Yeah, that is highly possible," she said. She fidgeted uneasily. "We can't put it in our room."

"Of course," said Dean sarcastically.

"Damn!" she said in exasperation.

"I could ask Jomo to keep it for us," he said thoughtfully.

"What? Dean, this is between the two of us."

"Jomo can be trusted," he soothed.

"No!" she said, almost screaming.

"He is my brother, Pulane. What the hell do you think he'll do, run away with the loot?" he shouted.

She was wise enough to recognise dangerous territory when she encountered it. She had to be careful; blood was far thicker than sex. Quickly she changed lanes.

"Don't get mad. But you told me how Jomo had always been overprotective to you. So if you tell him about our plan before we execute it, he'll probably force you to give it up, saying it is too risky," she softly said.

"Yeah, Jomo will never let me do it, especially since he seemed so friendly with the Chambers," he admitted. "So I'll play it like this and give him the money to hold for us after the robbery."

"After the robbery! You mean you'll be running around looking for Jomo with sacks of money? What if he isn't home at that particular time? Where would you put the money?" Shit, this was important; the last thing she needed was an interfering brother, especially a gangster one.

"I'll make an appointment with him to ensure he's home the time I bring the money."

His stubbornness irritated her.

"But he'll be alarmed if you all of a sudden ask to see him, he'll probe until you level with him."

She went on, this time in a silky voice.

"Dean, you need to show your brother you're now your own person. Prove to him you can manage your life well enough without him. Imagine how nice it will be when you wait until everything cools off and you visit Jomo with thousands of Pulas to show him the man you've grown to be. Your brother would be like wow, he'll be so proud of you cos you pulled something like that alone without his help," she said, touching his face with her fingertips.

She took a very deep breath.

Talking had never had much of a favourable effect on him. She resignedly put her arms around his neck and resumed the kissing – she didn't forget to groan and moan.

Later her head was buried in his neck.

"Okay, no need to involve Jomo, but where can we hide the money?" Dean said.

"I'll think of a better place," she promised.

"What about a graveyard?" he suddenly asked.

"Graveyard?" She was puzzled.

"Sure, what's the nearest rural area from here?"

"Gabane," she answered, frowning at him.

"We dig a hole, enough to mistake it for a grave, and bury our treasure," he said triumphantly.

"But there are also cemeteries in town," she protested as she rolled over.

"This is a city, honey. People are always moving about. Day and night, same shit. We don't want to risk anyone seeing us as we bury our treasure." He got out of bed and started pacing around.

"It is a small village, no electricity. People who reside in a rural area are poor. Staying awake in the middle of the night for no good reason is out. Kerosene for their lamps means digging into their practically empty pockets."

She jumped out of bed and hugged him.

"Good idea," she said, smiling at him.

"Cemeteries in town are guarded by the city council, but in a rural area it's just a plot, sometimes not even fenced. People are dying like flies ever since AIDS took over. So nobody will question about the freshly dug grave. The grave doesn't even need to be marked. We bury the sacks and pile stones on top. All we need to do is take measurements so we know its exact location."

"But, Dean, surely you've heard about crooks who steal coffins from cemeteries and resell them." She started shaking in dread.

"These guys don't just dig any grave, especially not the one that looks like it belongs to a destitute person. And usually these thieves are the same people who would have sold the casket in the first place."

"But where do we keep our share while we are waiting for the dark? Ah well, we'll see," he said as his hands started on her, kneading and charging her up for one more session.

It still wasn't easy.

Her mind drifted off to the potholes she had once more encountered in her plan as she vacuum the TV room.

She never thought it would be this tough.

Her pawn-recruiting crusade counted heavily in her pretend capability, she admitted. But Dean! He was too insatiable to keep up with.

The servicing of his rampage hormones had created another major snag, and put doubts in her pretend capability. She had thought closing her eyes would help, but she had found herself on numerous episodes berating him while he grunted on top of her.

"When are you going to come?"

Was it something in her voice that instantly deflated his manhood? Probably. Dean would get off her, sulking miserably.

"What's wrong with you?"

A good question. What exactly was the matter with her?

Sex was supposed to be the main attraction in her strategy. So what was going on here?

The time to sexually give in was now, she had shouted at her inflexible body.

Then she had a brainstorm.

How about recharging her non-cooperating body with glasses of wine before she retired for the night to boost her waning pretend ability?

It worked. Especially when she erotically used her imagination and told her mind it was Mark. It was a good thing she never got the stupid habit of yelling Mark's name in bed. 'Keep on tiger' was what, among other stuff, it always had been. And none the wiser, Dean would groan and grunt on top of her to the end without her losing her cool.

She wearily switched off the vacuum cleaner, took a feather duster and started dusting around.

Still, Dean and his non-differing moves in bed were helping, catalysed by the wine of course. A big plus was that Dean was a rigid old-fashioned lover; somehow it had worked to her advantage. When it came to pretend, it was thumbs up for the missionary position. Any woman getting busted in that frigid position after a wine catalyst would be a hopeless case. She may as well leave the pretend field and try her luck in the kitchen. Gramma did say the best way to hook a man was by filling up his stomach. But Dean was a tough one, too horny, so unquenchable; he wasn't that into food of the mouth. Gramma was probably talking about the gone ancient times. In the now era it was sex that called all the shots. Only some people were not too eager to play bed with inept candidates they didn't feel too deeply for.

Circumstances, yes, that. Damn circumstances blackmailed her into this sordid mess. They forced her to join the whore brigade, she silently cursed.

Shaking her head, she mulled over her nightly routine of lying on her long-suffering back, plus the wine opening up her vocal cords, like her fellow whores she followed on cue, making loud moaning noises and faking multiple orgasms. And the non-suspecting Dean basking in paradise. "I feel you so deep," he would say afterwards. Then he would honour her with one of his nothing kisses.

"Was it good, babe?" he always asked.

Well *Cosmopolitan* magazine had already alerted her to that one. They all revel in good reviews Cosmo had stressed. Since her reviews were nothing to rave about, she had wisely assumed that what Cosmo meant was that if for some weird reason you still needed the loser around, make up good reviews. She would of course singsong him that he was the best lover she had ever had. The joy lighting up his moronic face would reassure her that things were firmly under her control.

But Dean was an insatiable dog. Meaning she needed glasses and glasses of wine to get her through the night.

It was a problem – a big mother of a problem. It was the Chambers wine she was boosting her pretend talent with. Pretty soon they would wonder about the disappearing bottles. She had tried switching to Mr Chambers' brandy. A dangerous move, and she had blacked out. Not good, she had an awful lot of secrets to watch out for. Secrets she couldn't afford to blurt out in an alcoholic stupor. Especially when the next day Dean had coldly told her she had such a loud grating mouth when drunk.

Loud grating mouth?

That must have been very insulting to Dean.

But what happened when her loose mouth ran out of insults? What then?

It could unearth her well-guarded secrets. She was not willing to take the chance.

She had gone back to the expensive white wine. Of course, if she could afford the wine, she would gladly get her own, but she was just a maid, and she couldn't possibly afford such luxury. The cheap ones she could afford tasted awful with a horrible smell. It was only Mrs Chambers' wine that helped, lifting her mood without loosening her tongue too much.

Still, the wine consumption bothered her. What if Mrs Chambers complained to Sue? No way would Sue be nice and angelic like the time she transformed the dish detergent into bath foam.

What was she to do? When she didn't take the wine she got more irritable with Dean. It seemed his sexual demands brought out the worst in her.

Then she had accidentally stumbled on her cousin.

Cousey all dressed up in those fancy clothes.

"I'm doing very well ever since I wise up," Cousey had announced.

"Ah so you did rewrite your GCSE," Pulane had mildly inquired.

"Nah," was Cousey's flippant answer. It turned out little Cousey was playing house for an ancient married man who showered her with all kinds of expensive gifts.

"You are in love with a married man!" Pulane gasped.

Cousey had burst out laughing. "Me I ain't in love with no ancient bones. All I did, Pulie, was caught on to the trick."

Still it didn't sink in. Cousey had taken her to Spurs, where they feasted on mega ribs. Afterwards Cousey had confidentially let Pulane in on the trick. She called it the survival trick. It was a trick little Cousey was adamant men were more of experts in.

"The trick is in knowing there is and always will be a sky-high wall between love and sex."

"What?" Pulane had said, goggle-eyed.

"Put the two in separate packets. Know who to love and know who to just sleep with," Cousey had whispered.

"I don't understand," she had whispered back.

"It's called the survival trick, and I was lucky to bust it at such an early age. Great and plentiful sex is not always the deciding factor for him to slip that band on your finger. No man will ever cheat on his wife with a girl who doesn't know her way around the sheets because he certainly is not lying to wifey for your good communication skills. You should see my old man; before he rings the doorbell, he is already loosening his tie. By the time I open the door, he's unbuttoning his shirt. Mumble a quick hello heading straight to the bedroom. Sometimes he completely forgets to ask about my well being, but he never, ever forgets about the sex," Cousey had whispered to Pulane.

"What a dirty old man," she had said disgusted.

"Unlike others I know, I will never get him to leave his wife. I know sex no matter how good is transient thrill, a too cheap thrill, a too casual thrill. Because come five minutes after that earth-shattering climax, he is thinking *wifey*. Thinking how many dozens of roses he should order for honey wife. While you read Cosmo till your eyes burn looking for tips to please him in bed, it's wifey that gets the credit. While you spend your time on your knees servicing him with that mind blowing oral sex – never mind that wifey is a dismal failure in that very department, it's her who gets the flowers."

"What a rat, you should leave him."

"Leave him? I'm actually capitalising on his love for dear wifey. Every cheating episode, he gets so generous. I get loads and loads of guilt money."

"I thought you said wifey gets all the credit."

"I'm saying no matter how wide I spread my legs for him, it's wifey he will always love. Sex and love are oceans apart."

She had listened attentively to little Cousey.

She thought about her reluctant attitude in sexually servicing Dean. Did her problem revolve around packaging sex and love in one bag, disregarding the steel door in between?

"I guess that's the trick prostitutes use," she had said, deep in thought.

"And a trick a lot of men use. And if men can get away with it, so can I," Cousey had fiercely said.

Cousey had gone on to tell her that players of this trick of survival even owed their lives to it. That was why it was called the trick of life. While fools were parading around saying, "My man loves me, never will he cheat on me," and AIDS continued to reign.

Shaking her head vehemently, Cousey said, "Not us, with us it's the condoms we have handed our trust to. It doesn't matter whether we are standing on a love platform or merely the sex one. We use them all the way because we know about that woman Eve. We know for real she bit that apple. If it hadn't been so, there would of course be no survival tricks. But she went right ahead and bit the apple. Chewed and chewed and swallowed it all the way down her throat. We know about how she had everything she could ever wish for with a man who truly, truly loved her, and was one hundred percent faithful but she nonetheless went ahead and bit the apple." Cousey had told her this before saying her goodbyes.

A sky-high wall in between.

She had sat and extensively coached her mind. Wrestled with her inflexible mind till it started thinking productively.

It took days, weeks, but she persistently kept on haggling with her rigid mind.

Love and sex.

She trained her mind about the dividing wall.

And yes, she would admit it; the first brick had been very hard. In fact it had been near impossible, but so determined had she been.

She had then proceeded to lay the second brick, the third...up until she had her survival wall. She had joined the team, and stopped using the wine as her crutch. She expertly put sex and love in their rightly separate packages. Of course soon she would be called a bitch of a slut. But sticks and stones... And it was no fault of hers that Dean didn't know about this trick.

Dean was like most women, living in their own fairy tale world and bundling love and sex in one package. And yes, she refused to take the rap for Dean's daft beliefs. Taking her silky 'I love yous' as the real deal. Her groans with her legs locked around his neck while he lay on top of her sweating and grunting like the pig that he was added up to love. Jeez! Well a fault of hers it was not.

She took a deep breath. Sometimes she felt so sorry for Dean. If it weren't for the fact that she needed his shady skills to catalyse her love life, she would have let him in on the trick. She would have come clean.

Well, now she was a certified team player. They were absolutely no whining remarks of what was the matter with her. Not anymore.

Dean was suckered into an all-trusting and non-doubting lover boy.

Smiling triumphantly. So fully pruned he now was that all she needed to say was, "Jump!"

After dancing their coupling ritual, they went over the plan.

"Both of us can't be in at work that day, but it's a working day. How are we going to get out of this one?"

"Susan will be drugged with a small dose of tamazepam. In twenty minutes she would be asleep, it only works for four hours, enough to get her out of the way, by then you'll be back from our little adventure."

"How is she going to feel when she wake up?"

"She will only have a small headache. Trust me she won't react badly to the drug. Just two months ago she had been prescribed diazepam."

"What's that?"

"A sedative, it's from the same family of tamazepam."

"Sue can be such a bitch sometimes especially when the Chambers are away. Pulane said. "She just sit and bark orders at me!"

"Aha, and it won't seem strange that Sue decided to take a nap in the morning while you slave and do all the work yourself!"

"It's not fair!" She whined.

Smiling at her, Dean said, "On that day, my dear, it would be very fair. Her nap would earn us millions! And the bottom line is Sue won't be alarmed she fell asleep on the sofa."

Snuggling up in his arms, she said, "You are such a good arranger."

"Does Sue get up usual time even with the Chambers away?"

"Yes she does, only 'cos she worries they might phone."

"Perfect. Two weeks before we carry out our plan, I'll show the

Chambers a doctor's appointment card at the general hospital where they deal with lots of patients. A friend will go to the reception at half past eight in the morning with my medical card and register me, there is no photo in medical cards and no photo ID in their computers so why not? I may as well capitalise on that loophole. My good friend will then queue for me till I'm finished. There are so many patients at the general hospital that by the time they call me to see the doctor I'll be back. The money will be counted after I've seen the doctor."

"You're leaving all that money with Ivan without knowing how much is in there?"

"It has to be *me* who sees the doctor, Pulane!"

"I don't want us to get cheated out of our share. Why can't your friend see the doctor for you as well? It's a general hospital, the doctor won't know he is not you."

"That's my fucking alibi, and I'm not taking chances on this one. A stupid receptionist yes, but not a doctor! I'll make an impression on him, cos I need him to remember me. He has to *remember* me, Pulane!"

"Don't make it too obvious an impression. It might dawn on him you want him to remember you!" Shaking her head, she went on, "But leaving all that money…"

"I will know the number of boxes we got. Ivan will not break the locks till I get back."

"Let Susan wake up on that day, you will give her the pill in a cup of tea at eight."

"They won't put two and two together. Susan won't know you have been missing for an hour. When you come back, wake Sue up and ask her if she is okay, make her comfortable on the couch and get on with your chores. *All* your chores, Pulane."

"Morgan, he is in the kitchen all the time," she wondered, worried.

"Don't be silly, the Chambers never spend Easter holidays here, so who will Morgan be cooking for?"

"Wednesday is not a holiday," she retorted.

"But they are coming Sunday, after our big day, Ivan checked that out."

A few days before the robbery, Dean borrowed his brother's car and drove to the village. Pulane insisted on accompanying him.

"I have to keep you company. A graveyard is a scary place in the night with ghost parading around."

Like everything else that came out of her mouth these days he bought that as well.

Tuesday night

"So what are you going to do with all this money, I'm getting you?" he asked.

She knew him well enough to know what he wanted her to say. "Half of it will be spent at our honeymoon." She dangled a juicy steak to his hungry heart.

He rewarded her with a glowing smile and a peck on the cheek.

"I love you," he seriously admitted.

Good that alone would tighten the screws for his full dedicated cooperation. She had to admit the plan was foolproof, but then it took only one silly mistake to ruin everything. Not that she cared if he landed his ass in jail, only one major hitch with that, the millions would accompany him there. She bit her nails, feeling very worried. Did he really have the balls for such big job? What if he messed up? Come on, the guy was a member of the most notorious gang in the country, he had been there for two decades, that should amount to something, right?

A wind of apprehension blew over her. Hell, this was a one-in-a-million chance. Never in a lifetime would she ever meet such an agreeable candidate. Her dream was within reach, and she would be damned if ruthless fate sabotaged it. Dean had to get the lovely money; he just had to.

So what should she say to activate him? She looked up at him with a pained expression. "What? A peck from my near husband?"

"Sorry, darling," he said, thrusting his tongue in her mouth and kissing her.

"Oh, Dean, how I love you," she groaned, clinging to him. "But, Dean, what if something wrong happens to you tomorrow?" she said, bursting into tears and refusing to let go off him.

"Don't worry, nothing will happen to me."

"It's too dangerous, Dean, maybe we should forget the whole thing," she said, sounding concerned and frightened.

Fright she didn't have to feign. She was deadly afraid.

Was Dean really equipped with enough balls to execute this with no hitches?

"I can't back out now. Ivan is counting on me," he explained.

"Are you sure you will manage?" she asked in a shaking voice.

"Hundred percent," he said. He clapped his hands. "Now let's have a look at my tomorrow attire."

She didn't need to be asked twice. She dragged a heavy suitcase from under the bed, rummaged through and put a pile of stuff on the couch. He stood up, completely naked.

"Hand me my belly," he said calmly.

The pillow was made of foam rubber with elastic straps on both sides. He put it on his abdomen and secured the straps on his back. Then he put on polyester track pants. On top of the track pants he wore a black baggy pair of jeans. An extra large blue shirt followed and a grey overcoat. A wig, with streaks of grey and receding hairline was put in the head. The hair in the wig was short and coarse.

She gaped at him in total astonishment.

"You look like a grandpa!"

"I stole this disguise at Snoop, good thing the weather is slightly cold," he said.

"You really do look different," she exclaimed.

"That's the idea; remember, those two guys have to *both* come out of the van before we can strike. We will smear your face with red paint, so they won't get to see your face. Wear baggy clothes, not jeans Pulane, a dress, not a short one and something to make your tits look a little smaller. I'm getting you a nice plaited wig. One of our guys will take you to some place where you can clean yourself up; you can then make it back here before Sue wakes from her little nap."

He opened a drawer and took out a brown paper bag.

"A gun," she gasped.

"We ain't killing anyone," he explained as he put it back and stripped off the disguise. "I will sure look different tomorrow."

"I'm only coming back after I get our share, we'll have to stash it somewhere in this room. I will sneak in through the gate at the back when Mark is still in the garden," Dean said.

"In the room?"

"Who will know it's here? Besides, I'm supposed to be sick, and I'll personally guard it till dark."

"When will you be back tomorrow?"

"By midday I should be here."

"And the graveyard?"

"Graveyard is dark time. Ivan will be lending me his car."

"He knows about the graveyard?" Pulane jumped up in alarm.

"Of course not, all I asked for was the use of his car for a couple of hours."

"I want to come with you to the graveyard."

"No," he said flatly.

"Why not?" she asked, sulking.

"You'll distract me, I need to stay focused," he said, silencing her with a kiss.

Wednesday dawned with, of course, its drama.

"When you are about to go on a job, ditch the fear. Fight it because fear will only make you stumble to carelessness."

A winning piece of advice indeed, Dean nodded as he drove steadily. Still, when he was a Snoop, his lack of fear was more to do with complacency, he admitted to himself. He was very aware of the non-wavering insurance of his brother hovering over him. He knew the jobs he was given were carefully sampled from the dangerous ones.

He knew he had absolutely nothing to get scared of.

Everything had gone as planned, thanks to Ivan, the professional. I have real balls after all. His problem it seemed had all along been Jomo. He was too motherly over Dean, air-bagging his manly balls. He paid his rent, food; hell, he even gave him recreational cash. Jomo babied him all the way to forty years of age, kid-gloved him by sampling easy jobs for him. And when Dean shunned discipline, Jomo continued to do his own thing, disregarding Chief's threats – there was Jomo on the defensive. Even on the day of the hearing, "It's my fault. I made him exile himself from our entire family. He misses the family, that's why he drinks so much…"

Miss the devilish family! Dean had almost laughed out loud.

Pulane had resurrected his balls, and turned him into a real man. Yeah, she really was the best thing that had ever happened to him, and sure, he owed it all to her. The village was only ten miles away – in no time he was there.

Then he took out five heavy sacks.

Five million Pulas, he smiled broadly. They had left the boxes with the heavy coins in the abandoned security van with the two unconscious loyal employees, who they pistol-whipped.

A ticket to a good life with Pulane.

"We really are a team Pulane and I," Dean said to himself.

After he securely tightened the strings round each neck on the sacks, he gently lowered them down into the hole. Then he quickly buried the fortune.

He triumphantly clapped his hands.

A job well done. The graveyard wasn't so big, and it had a wooden fence. And most of the graves were not marked, just like his. Some were identified by a small cardboard box covered with plastic with the name of the deceased scrawled on it. At the centre of the graveyard was a big thorny tree and two meters from it towards the east was his grave.

He looked around before lighting a match on the disguise he had worn.

He never thought it would be this easy, he marvelled as he put sand on the burnt evidence to hide it.

He had pulled it off. He had Really pulled it off. He bounced jubilantly to where the car was parked.

He dropped off Ivan's car and crept back to his room, where he found Pulane still awake.

"How did it go?" she anxiously asked.

"Fine."

"And the five biggies?"

"Safe at the grave we dug out on Friday."

She jumped out of bed and hugged him.

"Oh, Dean. I'm so proud of you," she said.

"You should be."

He quickly showered and climbed into bed. He couldn't sleep, as hard as he tried, he cursed the too much caffeine from those energy drinks him and Ivan had fuelled up with while they were counting the money. But he didn't get out of bed. Pulane didn't seem to have his insomnia; she was already fast asleep.

"Are you sure about this Pulane, Dean, cos I sure don't want some bitch ratting on me to the cops?" Ivan had said.

"I'm marrying her."

Ivan had seemed convinced. "Yeah, that's the only way to keep a woman quiet."

"And the cleaner?"

"She'll have to work there for six more months, don't worry about Dana, I've used her before, she knows the score."

Dean looked at his sleeping queen. He thought she would give him more of her as a congratulating gesture. But no, the pretty baby was asleep. Fondly looking at her, he decided to let her have her sleep; soon they would be in a Mr and a Mrs 'Have all the sex they would ever want.' No more quickies in the morning because they had to rush to work. Now they were set for life. They could stay in bed and indulge till they were full of one another. He nodded in the dark, for once in his life he had stolen for the right reasons.

CHAPTER NINE

"There's been a robbery," Sue announced. "I knew something was up when I woke up this morning, I could feel it in my bones."

"R...Robbery? What are you talking about Sue?"

"It was on the radio, some men hijacked a Charsecurity van full of money on its way to the bank."

Gaping at Susan with an open mouth, Pulane said, "Hijacked! Did they kill people?"

A distressed Susan said, "No, but to actually do that, in broad daylight. What is the world coming to?"

Taking hold of Susan's hand, she led her to a couch. "Sit down, Sue, I'm making you a cup of tea."

"How did it happen, what did they say on radio?" she asked as she handed Sue a cup of tea.

"Not much, just that it happened at ten in the morning yesterday by Lejara Road at block five," she said. "They got away with thirteen million."

"Thirteen million!" Pulane exclaimed in shock.

"How did they know there was so much money in the van that day? I'd say there is a little thief at Charsecurity," Susan said in deep thought.

"But, but..." Pulane said pretty shakily, but because her lips were now shaking vigorously the words came out in gabble.

Deep in her detective thoughts and failing to notice the fear in Pulane's eyes, she went on, "The cops mustn't look further than Charsecurity's office, they must grab every one of them with a rubber hose until they start talking."

"Thirteen, Dean, and we only got five!" she shrieked.

"Hey, hey, who came up with the plan? Ivan. Who scouted people to help us carry it off? Stop acting like a little bitch, Pulane, you are starting to burn me up," he snapped.

"Sue is adamant it's an inside job."

Dismissively he answered, "So? We knew they would all think that."

Agitatedly wringing her hands, Pulane said, "If they question Charsecurity personnel, and they come up with zilch, they might extend their suspicions to all Chambers' workers." She lowered her frightened voice. "And they might come across your Snoop background."

He stepped forward and enveloped her with a comforting hug. "I won't give them reason to snoop on my before-now life. You mustn't lose your nerve, Pulane; cops smell fear a mile off and to them fear means you are guilty. Besides, I don't have a record. Take a deep breath, my baby, tell yourself you refuse to be afraid," he coached. "Let's go to my room, sex is good for stress."

A terrible coldness swept through her. "The cleaner, what if they get to her?"

Losing his temper, he said, "Would you stop stressing! She didn't even make coffee for them that day, all she did was sneak in to put the drug in their coffee and then went back to her cleaning job."

"I'm scared, Dean," she stammered.

Dean was disgusted with her. "Will you hold your nerve?" He grabbed her and pinned her against the wall. "I'm sick of this shit, I didn't even want to do this. But you started putting on a show, crying every flipping day, making me feel bad till I gave in. You better pull yourself together, Pulane!"

Shaking herself free, she said, "It's just that…okay, I will try."

"Don't give me that 'try' bullshit, you do it. If the cops ever come her and ask questions, remember be consistent. Stick to your story, you were in the house cleaning. You don't change your story no matter what! Sue will vouch for that she won't admit to taking a nap cos that will be trouble for her.

"I'm still scared."

"Cops are only trained to catch people at lying. No matter how many times they question you stick to your *story*. You were upstairs cleaning the rooms while Sue was cleaning downstairs."

And from now on, we don't discuss anything about that day, walls can have ears, Pulane!"

She nodded her head. "You're right, Dean. As long as you are with me, I won't lose my nerve. You are my husband, my source of strength." She locked her arms round his neck.

"Good girl," he said, grabbing her ass. "Now let's go and have some sex, show me all about why I must marry you."

"A fucking *maid*! What the fuck is the matter with you?"

"You wouldn't understand," Dean said wearily.

"This is bullshit, Dean. Hey that dumb shit job was to keep you busy till the suspension was up, and now you want to marry this... this thing!" Dean looked at his brother coldly. "Tough, bro, but I love her," he said.

"Sex is just sex, Dean; you don't marry a fucking bitch just cos she can suck your cock to wonderland."

"Love."

"Love, huh?" Jomo spat. "She is a nothing girl, Dean. You should never have slept with her," Jomo viciously said.

"Well it happened, and I'm stuck," he admitted miserably.

"Fucking hell, Dean, why do you want a maid wife for? Think about it, all the time whining to your mates, 'she is not that bad, guys'. Correcting her, wary people are laughing at you. Nursing her insecurity cos she is a tasteless maid tramp who will want you all the time chanting reassurance to her! A fucking ashamed life cos that's what you will be when the novelty of her mind-blowing pussy wears off!"

"Hey, hey, I will never be *ashamed* of Pulane."

"You better fuck her out of your system, Dean!"

"It's not her fault she is a maid," he said defensively.

"I don't want us to talk about that girl anymore."

"Give her a chance," Dean pleaded.

"She is too cheap for my liking, Dean, and I will not allow you to associate with her."

"Jomo!"

"End of discussion," he blazed in rage.

Maybe Jomo thinks he is the mother of the family, about time he found out how wrong he really is, Dean thought.

Marriage, he just couldn't keep away from talking about it. "Mark, marriage is not just a piece of paper, it's a bond blessed by God."

"It sucks, especially if you wind up with rubbish woman."

"When I do the deed, it certainly won't be for the sex. Sex is a cheap thrill, mate, I wouldn't know what to do with her once I come. Love is it."

"And when love fades, what you gonna end up with?"

"The kind that won't fade, Mark. True, true real love." Dean took a deep contented breath. "Like me and Pulane."

Jesus, he felt like singing…and jumping!

This was it. Finally, he knew what the songs were all about.

Mark looked at him peculiarly.

"Dean, why are you so obsessed over this girl?"

"I love her." He closed his eyes, not knowing why everyone seemed not to understand this fact.

"This girl is no good, Dean."

"What do you mean?" he asked in a shaky voice.

"You need to get this girl out of your blood, mate," said Mark quietly.

"What's this shit? Have you teamed up with my brother, too?" he exploded.

"Don't be silly."

"Silly? Then how come all of a sudden you prattling the same crap?"

"We're worried about you. This girl is giving you more trouble than she is worth."

"The course of true love is never smooth."

"Don't get smart with me, Dean," said Mark, frowning.

"But it's true," he insisted.

"Dean, when I handed you this girl, the plan was just to amuse yourself for a short while."

Somehow it didn't sound right for Mark to say he handed Pulane to him.

"Handed? What the fuck are you talking about?"

"Whatever. But the thing is you are fixated to a transient bitch who is going to fuck your brains to the pits." Mark pointed a finger at him. "That doesn't go well with me, Dean. Hey, I'm the culprit who instigated your being with her."

"Well I'm all happy now that I'm with her."

"Dean, get another girl," beseeched Mark.

Turning on Mark he ferociously said, "No fucking way."

"Why not?"

"She is the only girl for me."

"She has gripped your balls up, Dean," he flatly stated.

"Pulane is the best thing that ever happened to me."

"Dean!"

"I love her," he said.

In a flash, Mark was on his feet. "I'm getting out of here," he said with such distaste that he was suddenly embarrassed.

"I love you, Dean," she purred.

I love you.

What could be more appropriate and reassuring than this? Never before had he felt such joy. No girl could ever do it to him the way Pulane did.

This was serious shit, he told himself as he felt the trembling inside him.

"I love you too," he said in a serious and firm voice.

Six months elapsed.

He remained content and blissful. Why not? He had finally met up with the woman of his dreams.

They told him this thing about that special one was nothing but a myth. And to think he nearly bought that! This proves that a man should do his own thing, go with the flow, and stop listening to a bunch of cynics and their pessimistic crap.

For once in his life things were perfectly right.

He has his woman and millions of pulas stashed away.

What more could a man ask for?

After serving his suspension he went back to Snoop. He was a good boy this time and did everything he was ordered. He chilled and waited for the year to pass. They hadn't chosen a country to elope to yet.

The good competent cops never thought of looking in his direction about the robbery before he quit his job to go back to Snoop, there he was right in the Chambers' garden, humming a tune and they never even bothered to ask who he was and what he was so happy about.

Gardener and forty years old, Jeez! Now there was the biggest failure one could ever be, they had recoiled. He had seen the disgust in their eyes when they came in to see Mr Chambers. Passing the little nothing gardener with their air of superiority – masterminds of central investigators. Ha, Ha!

Mark, still his mate, didn't see much of him though. They didn't see eye to eye when it came to Pulane. Mark so gratingly condemnatory, refusing to accept his true love for Pulane. He kept on with the 'she is not good for you' bullshit. *So who does he think Pulane is good for, Jeez! Stuff that comes out of Mark's mouth these days.* He was probably losing his mind or infested with jealousy. The last straw, he mused, the last straw was two weeks back when Mark came over and insistently asked him to kick Pulane out of his life. Dean had shrugged because there was nothing new there. All his friends, even his real brother, seemed to have conspired against his love life. They all wanted her out of his life. Why he asked, but he still hadn't met up with a coherent enough explanation. What ignited the fight was that Mark didn't shut up and let it go. He kept going on and on. Then he had the balls to say Pulane had been all over him, asking for a second chance.

Jesus holy Christ!

A second chance of Mark?

No woman could ever be that stupid.

Mark was his friend, but he didn't appreciate such blatant lies about his fiancée, and that was what he told Mark in cold fury.

It was evident Mark was jealous, very jealous. Well, whose fault was it? He had his chance with Pulane, and like the fool that he was he blew it.

Now why should he bother asking Pulane about this second chance she had supposedly asked for? Why should he when he knew it was all a lie?

Then three days later, Mark was back. Dean was quite glad to see him because he figured he had come to clear the misunderstanding, apologise for those brutal lies, but did he? Nope. He pep-talked his way through as if there was nothing amiss. But Dean refused to play along; he sat there stonily and didn't utter a single word. He waited for the apology to come out, a genuine one, no hasty 'I'm sorry' was going to cut it this time.

Did Mark realise the impact of what his lies could have done if he had bought his fucked-up story? He could have lost Pulie, the one and true thing that had ever happened to him.

No, Mark owed him a big time apology; otherwise it was bye, bye pal. If you had a friend like that, making a sick story like that, Pulane all over him! You sure as hell didn't need enemies.

CHAPTER TEN

Eight months after the robbery

"Honey, I'm going to the village tomorrow to visit on my aunt," Pulane told him one Thursday night.

"Have you told her about me?" Dean asked pleasantly.

"How could I not? I love you, man," she exclaimed.

"And I love you too, so when are you leaving?"

"Tomorrow. I'll be back on Sunday. If it's not too late I'll come over and see you then."

"I'll miss you," he said.

"Not as much as me," she said, kissing him.

She didn't come over on Sunday; he figured she arrived late from seeing her aunt. Tuesday morning he called the Chambers' house.

"She quit her job," was the curt reply from Susan.

"When?"

"Friday."

"Are you sure?" he asked in alarm.

A click, the bitch had hung up.

Bitch cunt, he wouldn't put it past her to lie to him. But still – quit her job, could that be possible? Apprehension blew over him. No, Susan was up to her usual troublemaking. Apparently being a housekeeper and bossing Pulane around wasn't enough. What Susan needed was a pet boyfriend to…Friday, she said.

A very uneasy feeling crept over him and kept eating him up. Finally it got to be too much. He rushed to the Chambers' house and stayed by the gate until he saw Susan.

"She's gone."

"I don't believe you."

She hurriedly opened the gate for him. "Come on in."

They went to the room she shared with Susan. She yanked Pulane's wardrobe open.

It was empty.

Jomo found him on the floor, cradling a half-empty bottle of Johnny Walker whiskey.

"What's with you?"

"She is gone, Jomo. She really is gone."

"What are you on about?" Jomo asked, frowning at his brother.

"Pulane."

Jomo visibly relaxed. "So what? I say good riddance to that rubbish," he said, offhandedly shrugging his shoulders.

"I must have unconsciously done something bad to her. She couldn't just leave me like that," he said, hitting his head with both his fists.

"What are you doing on the floor, Dean?"

"Didn't you hear me? She is gone."

Jomo yanked him to his feet and threw him on the couch. "Why are you so intent on making this girl too big a deal, Dean? Ever since you sank your teeth in her you've refused to let go," berated Jomo.

"That's because I love her," he hiccuped.

"No, Dean, she is too cheap a slut to fall for," Jomo viciously said. Dean took several deep breaths. "Do you think she ran off with some guy?" he fearfully asked.

"Of course, she is a fucking bitch," Jomo said, nodding his head.

Sweat beaded his forehead. "But we had such big plans."

"How about having such big plans with a clean decent girl?" suggested his brother.

Dean vehemently shook his head. "No, that money belongs to Pulane and I."

"What did you just say?" asked Jomo, his eyes widening in alarm.

"Nothing," he quickly said.

"Don't you nothing me, Dean. What money are you talking about?" he screamed with bulging eyes.

"The five million pulas, Jomo," he said, evasively, knowing he should have told his brother long back.

"What the fuck are you talking about?"

"Charsecurity hijack." He paused, letting it sink in. "It was me and Ivan."

Dropping on the couch in shock, Jomo said, "Jesus Holy Christ!"

"I was going to tell you when I delivered you a one-million surprise package."

"Start at the beginning."

He told him, omitting Pulane's part.

"Chambers is my friend, Dean," he shouted.

"But, Jomo, it's no big deal, insurance has paid them off."

Pointing an accusing finger at him, Jomo shouted, "He lost a lot of clients because of that hijack."

"Ah, Jomo, come on, man, cut me some slack," he whined.

Shaking his head, still stunned at his brother's revelations, Jomo said, "I did wonder who did it, but it never occurred to me it could be you."

"Shows how much you don't know me; to you I'm still your brother the wimp," he rudely muttered.

Turning on him Jomo said, "And why didn't my brother the wimp tell me about this?"

Dean's temper was rising. "Aren't I telling you now, Jomo?"

"Don't get smart with me, why am I hearing about this *now*?"

Dean was distracted. "But where could Pulane be?"

"Dean!" his brother warned.

"I told you, I was doing an element of surprise on you." Dean looked at him accusingly. "I was banking on a congratulations from you."

"Fine, congratulations, now let's talk about the maid bitch." Jomo leaned forward. "Why do you feel she too is entitled to the money?"

Suddenly remembering Dean sat up. "Where is Pulane?"

"Never mind her. I need answers here," Jomo admonished.

Looking at his brother darkly he said, "That's easy for you to say, your heart is sitting comfy in your chest, mine isn't here."

"Your fault, you shouldn't have let your heart run loose with a tramp bitch."

Taking a deep breath, Dean said, "It was our plan."

"Was this girl involved all along in the hijack?" Jomo slowly asked.

"Yeah," he wearily admitted.

"Why wasn't I told about this?" Jomo harangued once again.

"You didn't ask," Dean said defensively.

"I want the truth!" he thundered.

Shifting his eyes to the floor, Dean answered, "Well, Pulane asked me not to tell you."

Jomo completely lost it. "And what this bitch says goes, right? What the fuck does this bitch have between her legs, Dean, that she can just make you forget we are family?"

"Okay, I'm sorry."

Blood drained from Jomo's face. "Does she know where the money is?" he quietly asked.

"Yeah, we dug the grave together."

"What grave?"

"The money is in the graveyard," he impatiently explained.

"Shit! Shit!" exclaimed Jomo, springing to his feet and seizing his brother by the collar of his denim shirt. He pinned him against the wall.

"Jomo, I don't need any of your usual bull. Pulane is gone and I need her back," Dean said as he shook himself free.

"She took the money," Jomo flatly told him.

Dean grinned at him. "Nice try, bro," he said, not in the least bothered that there could be an element of truth in what Jomo was saying.

Jomo grabbed him and dragged him to the door.

"We are going to the graveyard," Jomo announced.

Dean went along, directing Jomo all the way to the graveyard. Not because he believed Jomo, no not that. He only did that to show Jomo how wrong he really was about Pulane. She was one hell of a great girl, and shit like that she would never pull.

Finally, they arrived and headed to his millionaire grave with the cynic Jomo trailing behind.

Instead of a safely buried grave, they found a big empty hole.

Dean fainted on the spot.

When he regained consciousness, he was lying in bed with Jomo hovering over him. He just couldn't digest this whole thing.

"Fucking hell! Dean, I'm going to comb the whole world till I find that thieving bitch."

"Would you really do that for me?" Dean asked in a faint voice.

"Five fucking *million*! And she grabs it and runs, just like that. Does she think her maid pussy is worth that *much*?"

Shutting his eyes against the gripping pain in his heart, Dean said, "Check with her aunt at that small village – Gweru."

"I'll ask my boys to start there. I need details here! What's the fucking bitch's family name? I'll need a picture of her too," said Jomo, all business.

Pulane, imagine her pulling such stunt on him.

Pulane, all sweetness and smiles with summoning tits.

Pulane, sweet delicious pussy.

"I have lots of her pictures," he said.

"Good. How are you feeling now?"

"Bad, Jomo, real bad!" he sobbed.

Pulane, running out on him. *Stealing* from him. No, he refused to believe it.

"Her last name is Kgano. When they get to the village, they should ask for a Kgano ward. That will narrow the search. Jomo, Mark and I sort of fell out. Can you check with him? He can probably help."

"Done that already. Mark left the Chambers' house a month back. Apparently his parents left a chunk of land when they died. He went back home to try his luck at farming."

"Mark giving up city life?"

"There is money in farming."

"Yeah only the smell of money will make Mark give up city life."

"That fat housekeeper seems in the dark too. Pulane only told her she got a fancy job elsewhere but where she didn't tell. This girl has to pay for what she's done," Jomo viciously said.

"What do you mean, pay?" Dean sat up in alarm.

"Since you are blinded by some witch crafting love, I will do you this one favour and settle the score."

"But you can't hurt Pulane, it's not...can't be her fault. She isn't..." his protesting voice trailed off.

Blazing with such rage, Jomo said, "Fucking hell! Whose fault is it then? No, you tell me, whose fucking fault is it?"

"I don't know, but it can't be her fault," Dean said morosely.

"Jesus Christ! Dean, the shit that comes out of your mouth, I'm sick of this, fucking bitch steals millions from you, and you talk such crap! She is a fucking *thief*, Dean!" He was trembling with rage.

Jumping out of bed, Dean furiously screamed, "Stop calling her a fucking thief."

Jomo was so startled that he gaped at his brother.

His towering rage evaporated, and he sat down heavily.

"What has happened to you?" he loudly wondered, completely baffled. He shook his head. His little brother, the only family that meant shit to him.

This shit was all his doing. He shouldn't have gotten that dumb shit job for Dean, it was the worst mistake he'd ever made.

He stared at his brother, unwilling to accept the sorry sight he had become. It looked like Dean had gobbled up all the pride he ever had when he worked a gardener. And as if that wasn't enough, he had gone on to sleep with a house girl and get screwed in the process.

What exactly did this girl have between her legs?

Never before had he believed crap about being blinded by love, he figured it was just a wimpy excuse people clung to when they didn't have a plausible explanation for their mushy conduct.

Could it be possible that his brother had been struck by this blinding witchcraft? This shit was real bad, look at Dean. *'It's not her fault!' Un-fucking-believable!* thought Jomo. *Damn, why can't Dean see this girl for what she is?*

"What you need is plenty of rest. I'll tell Chief you are sick," he gently said as he handed Dean a glass of water and a sedative.

"Are you going to look for her?" he asked.

"Sure," he said, but he didn't explain the rest of his intentions, like how he was going to teach her a lesson she would never forget in all her entire thieving life.

It was terrible, Dean managed to sleep only when it was drug-induced.

Sometimes, when he was home alone and he heard light footsteps approaching he would...Jesus! He was still hurting terribly.

But the fact that Jomo's people were looking helped him along. It was only hope that kept him alive, no kidding about that. When the pain was at its worst, he would picture her back. That helped a lot. In fact, it helped quite tremendously.

God, he really did love that girl.

He felt her way too deep.

The girl was made for him, and she possessed such delicious magic – the magic that had his name stamped on it.

His nourishing soul food.

Even Jomo had come around and had ceased talking crap about Pulane. *About time*, he sighed. He was too weak to take crap from both sides – Pulane's desertion and Jomo's bullshitting.

Pulane.

He truly infinitely loved this girl.

He nodded his head emphatically; it was a forever deal.

No way would he ever manage to get her out of his system. How could he? The girl was part of his system.

She was the virus that no amount of medicine could ever kill.

He loved her so deeply it hurt.

Days passed.

Was it thirty days or thirty-one that made up this month? Well, that passed too.

Then another set of thirty days.

And another.

But Dean didn't budge, he clung to the treasure that no amount of money would ever convince him to give up – hope.

Hope, what will become of us without hope? he wondered.

"I'll be seeing her soon. One way or another, I most definitely will."

Yesterday he had surfaced feeling that today was the day. After lunch Jomo had overheard him telling the maid that when Pulane came to see him she should wake him up. Jomo had looked at him strangely and mumbled out something about going for therapy. He had silenced him with a curt 'shut up'.

Well she didn't pitch.

But he wasn't discouraged. Besides, he blamed Jomo. Jomo jinxed the whole thing up when he said he should consider going for therapy. It showed he didn't share his optimism. Even the bible says you have to first believe before the miracle can surface. It was there in black and white. He had God's word on that. But then if a doubting Thomas like Jomo was with you, well they messed things up.

When she comes back, I'll treat her as the prodigal one. No screaming matches. Absolutely no 'Why did you do it crap', he vowed again and again and again.

Because he figured that would be for his own good. Because when you were this deeply hooked, putting water under the bridge was the way to go – either that or you get drowned.

Who gave a flying fuck about millions?

What he needed was Pulane as in yesterday.

Sure, one or two times he had tried listening to his brother because most of the times Jomo was on the right track. So Dean went out for dinner with him. After they were handed the menus Jomo started lecturing him on how variety was the spice of life. He had nodded agreeably because it was true. Variety really was the spice of life. Then two ladies came over to join them. Well, Jomo seemed to know them – quite good-looking girls. While he had ogled at the one seated next to him, drinking in her hypnotizing beauty, Dean's thoughts of Pulane had suddenly evaporated. But that was only for a full five minutes flat. Then he was back to his staple thoughts.

When it was time to order, he had hesitated. He had suddenly lost his appetite and was looking for something light. That was how it was, actually. When his craving for Pulane was at its worst, he completely lost interest in food. Jomo saw the hesitation and told him to choose a dish called 'good riddance'. At first Dean didn't get it. He had gone back to the menu, scanning for that 'good riddance' dish. It turned out his brother was speaking metaphorically.

He really did love his brother. Jomo had always been there for him. At no point in life had he ever bailed on him. While he sat there facing his brother he felt he had disappointed him enough. So why not, he decided. Went ahead and ordered the good riddance dish. The girl's name was Ami.

But when it was time for the main course, it tasted awful, almost nauseating. *Sorry, bro,* he had bolted back to his staple thoughts.

Pulane.

And even more Pulane.

Once there he felt safe. And yes, soothed, with only one intense wish, to catalyse the reconciliation day.

Fishing out her photo, he listened to the drumming of his heart.

"My staple food," he softly said.

It took Jomo's people nine months and a few days to locate her.

"We've finally located your bitch slut," said Jomo.

"She is not a slut." Great joy erupted all over Dean. He was so happy and relieved that he felt like dancing around the house. He actually had a bright smile on his face, but it froze on his lips when he looked at Jomo's face.

"If you are thinking of getting back with this maid slut, you better think twice because I simply won't tolerate that. I'll personally kill her, Dean, if you don't back off," he said menacingly, pointing a straight finger at his brother.

He took a deep breath, Jomo had such a volatile temper, and it wouldn't do to push him. But Dean had every intention of getting back with Pulane.

"So what is she up to, then?"

"Well this is the hard one. So I'll give it to you straight. She eloped to South Africa with that Mark tramp friend of yours."

Dean struggled to understand.

"They are married, Dean," he said flatly.

Excruciating pain shot all over his body. He gritted his teeth and sank in terror on the couch. Hot burning tears poured from his face into his mouth.

The pain kept on. Stabbing and stabbing.

So staggering was the pain that within seconds he was rolling on the floor in a foetal position. Jomo seemed to be saying something, but his voice sounded so…far away. Through blurred teary vision he saw Jomo pushing a glass of something to his lips. Whatever it was had a bitter taste, and he promptly spat it out.

But Jomo was persistent, forcing it down his throat.

A miracle it was because just when he was resigning himself to the pain in squeezing out his last breath, it drained away slightly. Just slightly. It was still there, but muffled. God he was so scared. Never before had he felt such pain.

Married, did Jomo really say that?

"Did…you say…m…married?"

A firm nod from Jomo.

It turned out the pain hadn't gone after all. It had just broken for more reinforcements.

It was terrible – too, too terrible.

He suddenly felt very suicidal as he stared at his shaking hands. *Nothing, nothing ever goes right for me. So why live, subjecting myself to more?* Jomo seemed to be saying something, what was it? Painfully, he looked up.

"…took us for a ride and she is not getting away with it. If you had told me all along that this girl was involved in that hijack, none of this would have happened."

"So she was never over him."

"Who?"

"Mark, they were…" He shut his eyes, swallowing the knot in his throat. God, it was murder saying it out loud. "They were lovers… once."

"Dammit, Dean! Why didn't you tell me this before? Mark disappears and soon after it's Pulane. Damn! How dumb can you get?"

He painfully looked at Jomo. He didn't have the strength to utter a single word. He was…he shook his head overwhelmed; he was…dead.

"She planned this all along. You falling for her then taking you for a sucker ride."

"I don't believe you!" exclaimed Dean, so shocked at Jomo's theory that he suddenly had energy to scream.

Jomo nodded knowingly. "Of course you don't. She fucked your brains to the pits."

Closing his eyes against the pain, he plugged two fingers in his ears.

"I don't want to hear anymore," he said in a shaky voice.

"Don't be silly," said Jomo, brushing off his hands.

"Jack Daniel's, please," Dean said in a small voice.

He was a completely broken man. His face was that of a man who had suddenly realised what a nightmare life was, and he desperately wanted out.

"Mr and Mrs Mark is how their fellow neighbours address the thieving pair. Own a posh nightclub and a fancy hair salon."

He faintly heard Jomo's voice.

CHAPTER ELEVEN

Feeling quite good, he steadily drove his gold BMW along Livingstone's Way. "And who could have ever figured I would move up like this? Just about to get to the sky." He contentedly smiled.

"Pitiful losers," he said as he passed two men flagging him down for a ride. "If you lack the intellect, there are always other ways." Like his way, not just to sit like a little duck deteriorating in a loser world expecting free ride.

Ha, ha! And look at this one, imagine him reduced to a nothing pedestrian with such hot looks, he shook his head. What a waste! Manoeuvring his gleaming car around a curve, he gloomily told himself that the guy he just passed knew about the goodies his body could buy him. He knew, but 'it's not nice' was enslaving the poor guy.

He sighed, Duncan too liked saying such stuff, 'it's not nice'. Now look at him, with his green overalls and digging forks. *Jeez, does Duncan intend to die a gardener?*

I am no criminal; all I did was cash in on my six-pack. It's a shit world out there. So who was he to hesitate when Pulane asked him whether he had a price tag? Hunger and the sun scorching his back when he was working his ass off at the Chambers' house tuned him on. He didn't even bat an eye.

Pulane, yeah one hell of a girl.

On his way to the club Mark was surprised to find himself thinking of Dean. He couldn't help feeling sorry for him, though. The guy was all right when he first came to the Chambers' house, but then everything changed when he teamed up with Pulane.

In a way he was to blame. It was him who nudged Dean to pursue

Pulane. And Dean probably thought it was a plan all along, but it wasn't.

When he asked Pulane out he was only interested in sleeping with her, and he really thought Dean had the same plan because Pulane had that sex-siren packaged body. One look at her and your head screamed sex. He didn't know Dean would refuse to let go once he sank his teeth into her.

And what was he supposed to do when Pulane started giving him money she swindled from Dean? Hey, he was in desperate need for cash, he couldn't just turn her down. Then she asked him whether he had a price tag.

They struck a deal; he married her in exchange for a good life. But alas she was clever. She produced some papers for him to sign before the ceremony. He was too eager, and he didn't bother with the small print. It turned out she had made him sign an ironclad prenuptial agreement. So it was like that, he walked out on her, he walked with zilch, he stuck around, and he lived a fine cool life.

It was a perfect way of keeping him on her leash. Clever bitch.

"What do they call you, angel," he asked a white girl with exceptional looks.

"Eva."

"Nice name," he remarked. "And what are you drinking tonight?" he asked, signalling the waiter.

"Lemon dry with a tot of Mainstay."

"Get the lady lemon dry with a tot of Mainstay, and my usual," he instructed the waiter, who knew his place perfectly, he wouldn't dare complain to madam.

"Aren't you going to ask what my name is?" he asked.

"Nope."

"How come?"

"I already know," she said boldly. "Did I shock you?"

"No, why?" He grinned at her.

"You are quiet all of a sudden."

"I was just admiring you," Mark admitted.

"I was told you are married."

"Does that bother you?"

"No, not in the least, but I would like a piece of the wife's exclusive," And that marked the genesis of their relationship.

CHAPTER TWELVE

Pulane waved neighbourly at Mrs Smith, but the bloated cow pretended not to see her.

"Stuck up bitch!" she muttered.

She still recalled the first month when she moved to Borrowdale. Her neighbours seemed friendly then. They used to pop in with cookies, welcoming her, so they said. So kindly and sweet they seemed that she warmed up to them. A mistake, big fucking mistake, it turned out they didn't know anything about minding their own business.

She sighed deeply. The last straw was when they came to her house for tea, Mrs Smith and her sidekick Mrs Johnson. While having tea, they started.

"Are you aware, dear, how promiscuous your husband is?"

"What?" Pulane gasped nearly choking on her tea.

"A girl by the name of Connie, dear. The word on the street is that they are pretty cosy with one another."

She completely lost it. She jumped up, spilling tea all over her wifely dress. The tea was hot, and it burnt her skin, which infuriated her even more. She threw the nosy old ladies out.

"Dear, we were only trying to help."

"Such help I don't need," she had shouted, banging the door in their slanderous faces.

She still remembered how she leaned against the door in her demoralised state. It had been pretty hard because she didn't think they were lying. It was just that to hear such kind of talk – in her heart she was Mark's one and only real girl. And hey, that gave her such a warm contented feeling.

But Mrs Smith and Mrs Johnson's talk... she shook her head. It gave her such ulcers, and since this was a free country, she needn't listen to that. Ever since that telling of tales incident, they had never set foot in her house, which was a big okay with her. She knew the situation she was in very well, she didn't need neighbourhood rags putting her on the know – a magnetic stud husband which meant stiff competition with the sluts of this world. She had quickly learnt to treasure the little looks she possessed. Visiting the gym daily and going for facials twice a month were now top of her list of priorities. Manicures, pedicures, the works and only designer wear for her. She may have been a maid, but she had enough brains to know and face the truth, unlike some women, who took marriage as an eternal trap. She knew the truth quite well – especially about a fucking bitch called *Divorce* who would sit at your doorstep waiting to hijack your husband if you had a problem shuffling your wifely cards right.

In life she had learnt one important lesson: never make a mistake of relying on luck rather than learning to create your own. If she just sat tight with her hands folded and waited for luck to knock on her door and change Mark, what then? Supposing one Connie overtook her and grabbed her beloved. The beloved Pulane had every right to keep. No, she had worked hard to get Mark where he now was, and she fully intended to keep him there.

She parked her car by James Court and gracefully entered the elevator to the eighth floor. Her friend Maggie was in, sprawled on the couch.

"So how has it been?" she asked as she sat.

"Not so good," Maggie said.

She frowned and looked at her friend. What was up with her?

"What is it and how is Tim?" she inquired, slipping off her shoes and curling up on the couch. She could see Maggie was a bit down, but mentioning Tim, her boyfriend, had always had an invigorating effect on her. But today none of that came; instead her friend stared at her mournfully.

She took a deep breath. What was this, trouble in wonderland?

"Okay tell me about it," Pulane said, grabbing a prune from the saucer on the coffee table.

"Life is a bitch."

"Yeah," she wearily admitted.

Bursting in tears, Maggie said, "Love, I hate falling in love, opening your heart up to one hell of a heartache." She looked up at Pulane with a tear-streaked face. "Love, you are all the time happy, but then there is," she shook her head, "this *dread* – fear brewing in you, you know it's coming, you know it's on its way. The pain – deep unbelievable pain." Putting her hands on both cheeks, she swallowed. "Waking up in the morning, looking at his face wondering if today is the day when he will lose interest," she said abruptly.

"Men, men." Pulane shook her head stunned. "What is it with them?"

"I found a piece of paper with 'Ursula 0778228153' written on it in his jacket," Maggie said woefully.

"Some people can't stand being happy, they will do anything to get the hurts. Dammit! Mag, what the heck were you doing in his pockets?"

"I wasn't craving for the hurts by snooping. It was a bit chill and I had his jacket on. I put my hand inside the pockets then…" She closed her eyes.

"And what did he have to say about that?"

"I don't want to talk about it anymore," said Maggie suddenly.

"Why not?"

"I just don't want to," Maggie said miserably.

"If you don't let it out, it's going to eat you up," Pulane said knowingly.

"He said it's the name of a boutique in Cape Town. He said it sells one particular aftershave he is interested in trying."

"What?" Pulane laughed so hard her ribs ached.

"I can see this amuses you," said Maggie coldly.

"So what did you do?"

"Nothing. I just kept quiet. There was nothing I could say," she said with misty eyes.

"Did you ask him the name of this aftershave?"

"Said it's a French name he had noted in his diary, which of course happened to be in his office."

"And that was when you kept quiet."

Maggie nodded. "I didn't have the guts to accuse him of lying."

"Why not?" Pulane asked, raising her eyebrows inquiringly.

"I was too scared he'd admit it," Maggie sobbed.

"So what do you think is better, the suspense of not really being sure or the truth itself?" she asked her best chum, handing her a tissue.

Her best pal, Maggie was loaded with money too. Death was a tragedy, but in Maggie's case it was a blessing in disguise. Her aunt nailed herself a rich bugger who kicked the bucket a couple of years after they tied the knot, leaving her distraught aunt childless. Maggie was never close to her beloved aunt, but surprisingly, when the aunt passed on, she left all her money to her.

According to Maggie, before her rich husband met her aunt, she was an outcast, all alone in a cold world, the family wanted nothing to do with her, some even went as far as calling her an embarrassment. But as soon as she got the money, they quickly changed lanes in their attitudes. From a bad joke, she rapidly progressed to beloved auntie, and she soon graduated to their chief sponsor.

Maggie, an only child, deserted by both of her parents who decided to drop dead on her, was raised by her grandmother. And when her Nan finally departed, she was taken in by her rich aunt.

She had sat there and nodded when Maggie told her this story. When it was her turn she told the trusting Maggie that her family owned a chain of supermarkets. She had two big brothers who were involved in the family business. But she decided to move here because they disapproved of her husband.

"I can't say I blame them," Maggie had muttered.

"The suspense is better cos I'll still have an open mind. I can tell myself what he said is true, which really is plausible," Maggie said agitatedly, staring at her well-manicured nails.

"In other words, you prefer to lie to yourself," Pulane churlishly said.

"Lies can keep you going," said Maggie.

"But, Maggie, is that really what you want, living in a trance? What happens when you are jolted back into reality? What about the shock, wouldn't that kill you?"

"I never thought you'd be the one to say that to me," Maggie accusingly stated.

Pulane was now confused, "Why is that?"

"Your life with Mark is a big fat lie."

Pulane vehemently shook her head. "That's where you are wrong," she said, thinking it was about time she put her cards on the table.

"I know for real Mark doesn't love me. These days I don't fool myself with any other story."

"But, Pulie, how can you stay married to someone who doesn't love you?" Maggie sat up in alarm.

"I don't have a choice," she said with a sulk.

"Hey, you have a choice. To walk out and divorce him," said Maggie urgently.

"I can't."

"Why not?"

"I love him and I still want him," she calmly stated.

"But he doesn't love you!"

"So what?" she said, offhandedly shrugging her shoulders.

"No, Pulie, you need to leave him," said Maggie in a serious voice.

Her mind took off as she looked at Maggie.

Her friend was certainly not getting it. She was too one dimensional, she sighed deeply.

'Oh so you don't love me,' rush to your lawyer and demand a quick divorce.

Well, in her life it didn't work that way.

Was it possible to make someone love you?

Well, she already had firsthand experience on that one. If that were possible, Mark would have long ago fallen for her.

And who was responsible for making people love each other?

God.

But was He helping her out on this one?

Nope.

So it wasn't Mark's fault he didn't love her, she silently rationalised.

And Maggie – why should she really listen to her?

Has Maggie ever felt the pain - especially the pain of loving someone? Totally loving that person. And he still couldn't return that love.

Has she ever really felt that emptiness in her heart? The

worthlessness?

When everything in life was so insignificant and you couldn't wait to die, only you didn't have the guts to finish the job yourself.

She loved Mark, but Mark didn't love her. It was a sad fact of life, but after a lot of devastation and a lot of tears, she had finally accepted her fate.

Yes, go ahead and ask, where is my pride?

But I'm my own realistic self, and I know pride doesn't work when it comes to my kind of love. When it comes to Mark, I have gobbled it all up, and it would just have to stay well hidden in my stomach.

What exactly will I profit if I had pride? she asked herself.

Dump Mark and have a broken heart, which would take ages or even the rest of my life to mend. Habitual restlessness.

An empty life with no inclination to go on.

And dignity? What the heck is that really? Would having this dignity accelerate the healing process of my heart?

Would it bring my life back, and exactly how long will that take?

What exactly would it profit to have this dignity when everything in life seems so insignificant to you and all you want is to die?

Yes, he doesn't love me, but he is my husband. Yes, it is pitiful. But at least that is something, not enough, but hey, it's something.

And yes. I'm grateful for the occasional crumbs Mark gives me, and I'll cling to him no matter how sick that sounds, she firmly told herself.

"Pulane, what are you thinking about? Listen to me, I'm dead serious. If you are certain he doesn't love you, then you need to let go."

"I can't," she said stubbornly.

"What exactly are you benefiting in this relationship, Pulane?" asked her baffled friend.

She licked her dry lips and didn't answer.

"Marriage is a two-way street. All you do, Pulane, in this one is give and give, but what about this rat of a husband of yours?"

"Mark makes me happy – the kind I've never been. The kind that is irreplaceable. He has the secret code to my heart – no one else does. Being with him makes me feel good, real good, Mag. He is a bastard, but he happens to be the bastard that I'm in love with. I love him; just lying next to him is enough to make my day. It doesn't matter even if it's Connie he's thinking of."

"You've been holding out on me. So who's Connie?"

"Some cheap bimbo he's currently amusing himself with," she said, taking out the seed in the prune she had just taken from the saucer.

"His cheating doesn't get to you?" said an amazed Maggie.

She shrugged. "I don't stew on it. I've trained my eye to blank such stuff. Because at the end of the day he does come home," she said, popping the fruit in her mouth.

"What if this Connie turns into a permanent thorn?"

"She'll have to be one hell of a girl to get Mark to leave the comfortable life I give him," she said confidently.

"Pulane, you are not the only woman with money."

Exasperatingly she said, "I know."

"You know he doesn't love you, he is only after your money."

"Sure," she said as she stuffed more prunes in her mouth.

"So I still say, dump the loser."

"I told you being married to him is my ultimate goal. He makes me happy, Mag. The kind I've never felt before."

"But the cheating," protested Maggie.

"Which I overlook. All men cheat."

"But he doesn't love you."

"Mark is not the mastermind behind cupid. He can't make himself love me."

"So give him up."

"Then what?"

"Someone right is bound to come by."

"Supposing that someone doesn't come?" Pulane asked.

"He will."

"I'm not going to drop Mark on a gamble. How about I hold on to Mark while we wait for this someone?"

"You'll be distracted, you won't be able to recognise the good thing that he is if Mark is still in your life."

"No, I'm not strong enough to take that chance," Pulane said flatly.

"Pulane, holding on to Mark is just postponing the inevitable. One day as sure as the sun rises every day he's going to leave you for the next best offer that comes along."

She blinked off the tears. "Maybe that best offer won't come along," she said apprehensively.

"You are hurting yourself more by staying with him."

"But in the midst of the hurt, there is that soul-nourishing magic. The hurt is there when he comes home late, or when some nosy bitch churlishly tells me about his new girlfriend, as if I asked to be informed of such stuff. Otherwise, when he's home, smiling at me, giving me those remedial touches, it's all good. I get so happy I could burst. Maybe it's not on the cards for me to live a returned love life. Maybe if I drop Mark anticipating a better deal, I'll wait till I drop."

"I can never stay with anyone who doesn't love me," declared Maggie.

"You are your own person, Maggie. And you've always been surrounded by luck. Not me. I'm way too ill-fated to entertain such hot ideas, I feel that Mark is the best I can ever do."

"Pulane, it's not healthy…"

"Maggie, let's go out for an afternoon movie. You are my friend, and I like you a lot. So stop wasting your breath because no amount of talking can ever make me give Mark up."

"You are heading for the mother of all heartbreaks."

"How about being a pal and letting me experience it firsthand?" she suggested. "Let's talk about this Ursula. Get to the bottom of this. Find out whether Tim loves her or not."

"Love her? He can't love her," Maggie blared.

"Maybe not. She could be just a for-now distraction."

"If Tim has fallen out of love with me, I'll make him fall for me all over again."

"Really!"

"I'll become a real nice person. More understanding, no more nagging," broadcasted a deadly serious Maggie.

"Maggie, you can't make anyone love you. Take it from me. Love comes solely from God."

"Then I'll have to talk to God. He'll just have to understand," she said desperately. Pulane whipped a mobile phone from her bag, "What did you say that number was?"

"I'm not telling you," answered Maggie.

"Come on, Mag, give me the number."

"I can't," she stubbornly refused.

"What are you scared of?"

"The truth," said her friend as she burst violently into tears. "All I have to do is believe. Ursula is the name of a boutique in Cape Town," she said between tears.

"Okay, you know he is lying. So what are you going to do about it?"

"Nothing," she said, wiping the tears. As she saw the naked surprise in her eyes, Maggie said, "Truth hurts."

That shut Pulane up because yes, sometimes truth could really hurt. Hurt too deep.

Suddenly her mind went back to those days when she was a nothing maid. She had wanted Mark the first time she met him.

Like all relationships, it was pure unadulterated joy at the beginning. Just when she was feeling contented and on top of the world, he dropped the bomb. Told her what they had was just a sexual arrangement. She was stunned and the pain was beyond belief. She had to stay in bed for a whole week without moving a muscle. And she tried, really tried to hate him, but she just couldn't. Because when it comes to love, it's the heart that calls the shots. All the shots. There are simply no negotiations. So while she was lying in bed, her body numbed in pain, she thought of the best strategy to win him back. Then she stumbled on a perfect puppy. She still refused to take the blame for using Dean; if anyone was to blame, then it was fate.

At first she fooled herself that Mark would love her, but she soon wise up.

But Maggie did have a point, she silently acknowledged. Sometimes it was the lies that kept you going.

When I lay there, my body numbed in pain back at the Chambers' place, the thing that made me eventually get out of that bed was the fact that I told myself Mark loved me. That was the thing that put the springs back into my feet. Mark had told me without mincing words that he didn't love me, but the thing that saved me was the fact that I told myself otherwise. She shook her head.

But the bottom line was she had been suicidal, extremely

devastated, but as soon as she fiercely told herself Mark loved her, she was suddenly energetic. And dying was the last thing on her mind, yet hours before it had been the one and only thing in her head.

Yes, truth can really hurt. Slice up your heart into smithereens.

The fateful day Mark dumped her was still embedded in her mind. She never imagined anything could hurt that deep. It was unendurable, and she had been certain the pain would wring out her last breath. If she hadn't told herself a couple of lies, she sure as hell would have been buried ten feet under.

She stood up and poured a glass of water, gulping it down. She studied her friend's mournful face.

Yes, truth could really hurt. While she was there writhing in pain, she had changed lanes and quickly told herself Mark couldn't possibly be in love with that girl. He was just a bit confused. It was she that he really loved. She still remembered the remedial effect the thought gave her, like a disturbed child who had just been sung to sleep. She had felt appeased.

She didn't stop there – she pictured him proposing. She had been lying in bed on her back, her hands tightly folded across her chest in a desperate attempt to reduce the gripping pain in her chest. She remembered how mystified she had become because the more she pictured him proposing, the better she miraculously felt. Then she started having beautiful soothing dreams when she was asleep. This time there was progress, they were in church, and Mark was slipping a wedding band on her finger. The dream was so refreshing that the next day she was back to her cheerful self. She felt good and on top of the world. Even Susan was impressed, fondly patting her shoulder.

"You did right by getting that bastard out of your system. I'm proud of you."

And that grade-A bitch Jen couldn't put her down, even the sloppy kisses she fed Mark publicly.

It didn't work.

All she had to do was take a deep breath and bring to mind her medicinal dream. It was magic. It worked better than all the brands of antidepressants put together.

What exactly would have become of her, if she hadn't lied to herself?

She wouldn't have survived the pain, of that she was a hundred percent certain.

Lie to herself – a perfect antidote.

It was because she lied to herself that she survived that time because it had been too, too painful. She couldn't stomach seeing that girl with Mark. She just couldn't. She had to think fast and come up with a plan.

A lying to herself plan to at least get around.

No, she wasn't being stupid; all that she had been doing was trying to survive. She had to think of her job too. Mrs Chambers couldn't just let her stay in bed indefinitely.

Lost in thought she shook her head.

Mark had told her blatantly that it was no big deal. What they had was just sex.

The gripping pain that had choked her then had nearly killed her. She couldn't eat – a big lump just sat there in her throat, swallowing saliva was no more instantaneous, it took a whole minute to swallow.

Then she blocked out Mark's sexual arrangement talk and clamped an amnesia lid over it.

He loves me. Really loves me.

And wow, she could even go to work, humming a tune as she scrubbed the floors.

And she was called a stupid bitch again, this time because she discovered a perfect antidote which she stuck to until she was strong enough, well-equipped enough, to accept that Mark didn't love her, she silently cursed.

"I'm fixing you a strong drink," Pulane said to her friend after giving her a comforting hug.

After two glasses Maggie was back to her cheerful self, even swaying to the music that was playing on the stereo.

"You are such a pal. Next time I'll sit with you when your husband is out."

CHAPTER THIRTEEN

Eva.

It was such soothing song, caressing and expanding his heart. It was amazing really, when he was with this girl, nothing else seemed to matter. He enjoyed spending time with her tremendously. He just couldn't get enough of her. He gave up Connie, with all the transient lot, and concentrated on this rare piece of art.

"Mark, what do you do when you are at home?"

"Most times I'm at the club."

She looked up in suspicion. "You don't sleep with her soon after you slept with me, do you?"

"Are you kidding me? Where would I get the energy?"

"Guess I'm jealous. I know she is your wife and stuff." Looking at him pointedly, she said. "And you still have to sleep with her."

"Hey, there is no reason to be jealous."

With Eva, he had minimised the lies. There were no fictitious juniors crowding him. The lie he held on to was that it was all his money.

The girl was all clued up, no whiny mouth about him leaving the wife. A break. The girl really had herself together. She knew her story, she was real find. Sometimes, when he fell asleep through the night, she would wake him up. Not Connie, never in a million years would she do that. That bitch would hold her breath, hoping wife would kick him out when he waltzed in the house the next day.

But Eva was so refreshingly different.

"It's late, Mark, she is probably worried."

"Only worried about my money," he would grumble.

"She is your wife, Mark, don't do this to her."

What a girl! he fondly thought.

No snivelling scenes of 'I don't see much of you'. Their hobbies coincided. Both were into sensual indoor games.

Flaming, coaxing kisses, spreading those exploratory legs, tongues all out delving into hidden pleasures.

So much to do, so little time.

Still, it was all good really.

The glare from the screen was making her eyes ache. She had been glued to the screen for more than an hour, but she still couldn't figure out the angle of the movie. She pressed 'info'. Shit. She switched channels. She really had to concentrate; otherwise the thorny wondering would resume.

Like how come these days she was always alone in the middle of the night?

Where was he at this ungodly hour? Not the club, she had already checked. Then she would go on to wonder whether his frequent disappearances had anything to do with a woman, and that always tore her heart apart.

She swallowed hard.

Mark, Jesus, why did she have to go on and love him this much?

Bravely, she fought back the tears creeping up into her eyes.

Tears, lately there had been a hell lot of that.

And the pain.

Jesus, the pain, she shook her head over and over again.

No, today she didn't want to take that wondering stinging route. There were too many pricking thorns there. She felt too weak, too spineless to accommodate them – too vulnerable.

And this movie, no, it was what? –Oh, a sitcom!

Damn, if only she could concentrate.

It didn't work. She kept changing channels, but nothing captured her interest.

Was it because she had such a lot on her mind?

She hardly saw Mark these days.

She curled up on the couch and threw the remote on the rug.

This afternoon she checked on Maggie.

"I've left him," announced Maggie before Pulane was even sat.

"Who?"

"Tim of course, who else?"

Pulane was surprised. "So you finally confronted him?"

Maggie nodded disgustedly. "Insulted my intelligence. A boutique. What a rat!" Then Maggie took a deep breath. "Pulane I've been meaning to talk to you. I mean real talk to you."

She frowned. "Don't start on me, Mag!"

"I'm worried about you."

"Don't be. I can take care of myself," she said flippantly.

"You are self-destructing your life with this Mark husband of yours."

"What's with you, Mag? One triumph over dumping Tim and you take yourself for an expert in marriage."

"Don't be silly."

"Silly? Then why are you acting like a martyr? Get off it, Maggie, you are not the first person to dump some cheating boyfriend."

"At least I did something about it," she gracefully said.

"Which was solely your choice, no one pushed you into it. And you did it at your own time."

"Pulane, when are you leaving Mark?" Maggie quietly asked.

"I'm sick of this jazz. Everywhere I turn, 'When are you leaving Mark?' As if walking out is that easy. As if all I have to do is grab my handbag and bolt out. As if I can just switch off my feelings with a single snap of my fingers!"

"Okay, it's not easy, take the first step, do something, throw him out. Do it, you don't need shit like him in your life."

"You all think it's easy," Pulane said with a sulk.

"Pulane, don't you think it's time you saw sense?"

In a hard voice, she said, "Okay, Maggie, let's drop the subject."

"Oh no! We don't, not this time."

"Please," she said softly.

"Mark has no right to walk all over you. But it's only you who hold the key in amending that. We can talk till we are blue in the face, it's you who can really put an end to it."

"Yeah, yeah, by walking out," she said petulantly.

"You are too much of a convenient deal to this guy. You don't even question him on his cheating. He does what he pleases, spending your money. He is having the best time of his life; only there is a major problem here because he is doing it on your time and expense. You are fully servicing him, Pulane, but where is the appreciation? Where is the pay off for such a dedicated wifely service? What's in it for you? A little bit of courtesy? Some kind of gratitude? A thank you gesture from that rat of a bastard? I fucking *hate* this guy."

Pulane flinched at her friend's words. "Okay that's enough!"

"Enough! So now you think you can censor what comes out of my mouth."

"Mag, please."

"What is wrong with this guy? Why can't he at least treat you nicely, why can't he? The other time you were telling me he came home in the morning. What kind of respect is that for someone who took him off the streets, gave him a roof over his head, buys him a car…"

"He was at the club," she quickly said.

"Don't get cute with me, you told me you checked the club."

"But sometimes he's home early," she said, jumping to his defence.

"How often?" probed Maggie.

"What is this, twenty questions?"

"Maybe," Maggie shot back. "You think I'm amused when you call me in the middle of the night crying cos Mark has disappeared into the night again?"

"Okay, I won't call you then," she said sullenly.

"That's not the point, the point is…"

"Maggie, give me a fucking break!"

That was this afternoon, it seemed no one was willing to give her a break when it came to Mark.

She buried her face in her hands.

So what was expected of her?

A fast exit? No, that she wouldn't do. She had invested way too much into this relationship; she was already too attached.

"You seem a bit down. What's up?" he asked, playing with Eva's long blond hair.

"I'm tired of this life," she said edgily.

His stomach tightened. "What life?"

She had never been the one to mince words. "I want you all to myself, Mark. I have had enough of sharing you."

Such a dramatic transformation! Who had been poisoning her mind?

Same old story. "So now you want me to leave my wife," he spat.

She didn't blink. "Exactly."

"Really, how very demanding of you."

She plunged ahead. "I'm not seeing you any more until you leave her."

Not only was he painfully confused, he was also angry.

"But what brought all this about?"

"I want more."

"And you are handing me an ultimatum," he said coldly.

"You can call it that."

"But you knew all along I was married."

"Yes, but I didn't know I would like the taste of you so much," she said.

"You are a selfish bitch! What's wrong in sharing?" he thundered.

"Hey, hey don't talk to me like that!" Her eyes glittered dangerously.

"Fucking hell," he said, storming out. Jeez, what a mouth! When were women going to embrace the good sharing spirit? They were so bloody selfish, wanting the whole meal to themselves.

A bitch! She lured him on, never gave him a hint she didn't like their arrangement. She trapped him into liking her, then out of the very blue, she dropped the greedy bomb on him.

Well to hell with her, so many fishes out there.

Her mind was in turmoil as she stood by the waterfalls in the city park.

Mark didn't love her. She had exhausted all the channels to capture his heart, but still, Mark didn't love her.

Her throat constricted as sadness overwhelmed her.

"Why can't he just love me?" was the thought that obsessed her.

Mark.

Jesus, why did she have to love him this so much?

She was suddenly so emotionally hurting that she sunk to her knees, her heart aching terribly.

Oh God, she so desperately missed her mother.

Miss 'lie down in ma's bed'. Taking deep soulful breaths and staring at the ceiling...

Back then that was how she beat down her depressing moments. Lying down and staring at the ceiling had always been remedial.

Staring at mom's bedroom ceiling.

Then crawling into mom's medicinal bed.

And once there she always felt safe, so heavenly safe and cleansed.

How was she going to beat this one down? How? Breaking down in violent tears.

She felt so miserably alone.

Mark.

Jesus, why couldn't she just let go like everyone said? All this while, all this while she had been living on the crumbs of his traitor heart, right there in the gutter, foraging for the occasional crumbs he threw her way.

Mark.

Christ, he was like the AIDS virus. Stuck in her blood, refusing to let go.

With a tear-streaked face she despondently nodded.

Yes, Mark was indeed her very own AIDS virus.

Nothing seemed to work in curing herself of loving him.

Nothing, she cried powerlessly.

He was the worst mistake one could ever make.

The bastard cheated on her all the time, all the fucking time, so flauntingly, so inhumanly.

She lived under the same roof but hardly ever got to see him.

And the marital sex? That had faded to almost nothing. She was one starved married lady – she painfully shook her head. When did she last have it with Mark anyway? She tearfully wondered as she dazedly got to her wobbly legs, shaking off grains of soil. Two months, weeks? She wasn't sure; it could be longer than that because of the dreams. Sometimes when she was desperate she would dream about it, dream about doing it and...

Still, how did she get herself into this mess? She got married to this alluring stud who was pretty good with his hands, but now she hardly ever got a piece of action because Mark was giving out free fucks. Fucking for zilch. While she had to *steal* to get him, some slut bitches were getting it for free.

Yeah life really was shit, she spat. She stole just so she could finally get a grip on him. The loot she had believed would calm Mark down and turn him into a nice loving husband.

Only the loot didn't do shit. Mark had become more of a rat than he ever was.

Mark.

Oh God, why did she have to love him?

At least he was her husband. A progress, not fulfilling progress but progress nonetheless, she told herself as she hurriedly wiped the tears. And she was well aware of Mark's unfaithfulness. The scary part was what if during the course of his unfaithfulness he met up with a girl he fell for?

Helpless tears sprang out of her eyes.

Maggie came to the house today. Maggie was now in a crusade. Ever since she prised herself loose from the claws of that ratty Tim, she had been walking around like a hero with a know-it-all expression. "If Mark meets up with a girl with more money than you, he will drop you flat."

As if that wasn't enough, Mark had been talking in his sleep last night.

He kept babbling, 'Eva, Eva.'

What does that mean? she anxiously wondered.

Is Mark trying to tell her something – something she couldn't afford to know?

Her heart started to pound.

Eva.

Could it be a new cocktail they were trying out at the club?

Why was Mark all of a sudden babbling 'Eva, Eva' in his sleep? She wailed.

Was he dreaming and this Eva happened to be in the dream? It was probably just an acquaintance, part of her rationalised.

But he kept on muttering her name, only her name.

Why?

By right, wasn't it her name Mark should be chanting?

Damn, a shit world this was. Why couldn't he utter a name like Joe or Dean?

A man's name.

Safer ground.

Why this Eva?

Why?

She started crying even harder.

Supposing Mark had fallen for someone else, possibly this Eva. The anguish that surfaced…

"But that would be unfair," she gasped.

Pulane get real, when has life ever been fair?

Fear gripped her already aching heart.

"Why couldn't he say my name out loud? Why, this Eva? Why?"

The fear of the inevitable deepened.

Somehow, he just couldn't go cold turkey on her. He was already in way too deep.

He tried his utmost to steer clear, but a magnetic force summoned him to the Southampton house, Eva's flat.

"One hell of a situation I've gotten myself into," he brooded.

How could he possibly drop Pulane?

But damn, he was so into Eva.

He irritably kicked a lamppost outside Eva's flat.

What am I to do?

Eva droves a Ford Fiesta – a tramp car.

So who would provide for him if he listened to this alien feeling?

Hooked he probably was, but a moron he was not, he admitted.

"I'm going to have to lie to her. In the meantime, me and my heart need to talk economics, think smart cos leaving Pulane is not negotiable," he said out loud. *Losing my mind over some stupid love, oh no!* He shook his head vigorously. The stakes were too damn high.

Jumping in the lift he pressed Eva's floor. *Eva, the girl is…good, very good in bed, Eva, Jesus Christ!*

Just the thought of seeing her again raced his heart. Damn, what was happening to him? Sexually, the girl was a real deal. She knew her moves, knew how to make use of those long legs. There was sweet delicious magic between her legs. Honestly, she was woman enough for him; it was just that there was the money issue. He warily rang the bell, was she going to swallow his story? This was no Pulane who never – the door flew open.

"Come in," she said coldly, looking at him up and down. "But don't make yourself too comfortable unless you have something meaningful to say."

"Okay, fine, I'm leaving her," he said, raising his hands in defeat.

"Really?"

"Eva, please don't make this harder than it already is," he softly pleaded.

"You didn't seem so eager last time we talked."

"Last time was last time. I had to sit and digest the whole thing," he patiently said.

Raising her voice in anger, she said, "You called me a selfish bitch."

"Hey, I'm sorry," he said, holding her hand.

She shook off his hand. "I trust you've talked to your wife then?"

"Oh yes, I have."

"What did she say?" She had her hands on her hips – this girl was it, man, so fucking sexy.

"Hey, what's with the interrogation? Isn't it enough that you are getting me?" Fuck you, Eva! he wanted to scream. Give me a fucking break. I ain't here for a fucking conversation. I want an in, in that magic pussy. I haven't had you for two whole weeks now. I'm pussy starved!

Fixing him with her blue seductive eyes, she said obstinately, "I want details."

"Why? You want to know if she cried and begged me to stay? Don't be a bitch! Anyway, cos she didn't sign any fucking paper, she has me by the balls."

Suspiciously she asked, "What do you mean?"

"My lawyer says I can play her along and pretend there won't be any divorce. Then start selling some of my properties and hide some of the assets. That way she wouldn't take much, but this one is on you, babe. It's up to you, if you can't wait a couple of months till everything is all sorted, then okay with me, but know that she will *walk* with plenty. She already she has me on adultery." He looked pointedly at her.

"But…"

Working himself up in rage, he shouted, "No buts, Eva. That money is mine. I can't just let her walk away with it; she doesn't even contribute a cent. She tricked me into marrying her by saying she was pregnant, and after I put a wedding band on her finger she conveniently had a miscarriage!"

"She lied about being pregnant?"

"And you want me to pay her for *that*?"

"So when are you starting to sell?"

"Soon, I'll start with the club. My lawyer is drawing up the papers."

"How are you gonna do it without her finding out?"

Things have changed round here, he thought bitterly. Such a long interrogation and no sex. Cutting down on the sex and she wanted exclusive. Ha! Wearily he said, "My lawyer will look for the buyer, but I won't sell all the shares in the club. That way I remain in control of majority shares, and she won't have room to be suspicious until it's too late."

Eva crashed onto the couch. "So we must wait," she said, pouting.

Mark sat next to her and kissed her on her neck. "It's up to you, babe, but I think we should wait. Look, it's not like I have kids with her, so why should I give her more than half of my money? Hey, let me take you to my lawyer so he can explain the whole deal to you."

"That won't be necessary, Mark, I believe you."

"As soon as he okays this, I'll move in with you," he promised.

"But how long will this take?"

"I don't know, hon. But if you are a bit impatient, that's also okay. We'll just take our chance. I'll file for divorce, but the fact that I'm living in adultery will make the court favour her. And she could walk away with plenty."

"No, we can't let her do that to you. It's your money, and she has no right to it, especially since she trapped you into marriage with a pregnancy that never was," said Eva determinedly.

"I'm sorry, honey, I really wish there was another way," he said taking her in his arms.

CHAPTER FOURTEEN

It was two and half hours past midnight when he left Eva's flat. He quickly drove home, not that he was expecting trouble from that puppy he married. But sometimes he was riddled with guilt because this puppy wife also happened to be the luck of his life. If it wasn't for love beating her hard-core heart – he shuddered – he would still be pushing that degrading wheelbarrow.

A man ought to appreciate his luck, not continually attack it.

There was absolutely no chance of him ever leaving Pulane. How could he possibly walk from such comfy insurance, an insurance that had been handed to him by fate, free of charge? He smiled brightly. And the best kick being he didn't have to spring cash for the premiums. Nope, the godsend love had seen to that too.

He drove on and heaved a deep sigh of contentment.

What a beauty this love thing turned out to be. His wife's brains were nicely scrambled to a yes puppy.

Pulane, nurturing a dumb hope that one day he would change.

Poor, dumb, hoping Pulane.

When he came home this late, she gave him the look, then the sulks. But that was as far as it got. "No screaming matches, just a harmless sulk," he laughed.

And there was naive little Eva dancing in her dreamland. What was it with Eva – deficient brain cells? Did she really, really think he would give up a good, money-loaded Pulane for her? Yes, he did love her, but there was one major hitch, Eva, Miss High Expectations, didn't have a good commercial package. One thing you needed in life was good commerce to get you along. The girl drove a pitiful Fiesta for Christ's sake. She lived in a little one-bedroom flat with minimal furnishings. No, he shook his head, he hadn't lost enough of his marbles to leave his wife for a shit stinking beggarly life.

Besides, Pulane was very allowing. He could count on her to take *all* his crap, so love or no love no one could walk out on such a sweet deal. Him, ha! No, not him.

Life was fine as it was; there was no need to crash anything. He had the very best of both worlds; he happily hummed a soft tune while he quickly changed gears.

A man could have it both ways, as long as he knew how to make use of that spade in that deck of cards. Eva was cool and all-woman for him. Sex with her was good, mind blowing in fact. Those long exploratory legs, and that sweet wet pussy, virginal muscles gripping him so – fucking hell, should he make a U-turn? No, mustn't let Eva know she had him by his dick and…heart. Once a woman knew that little secret, you were finished. He loved her pretty bad, but was love going to take care of his bills? Yes, it was one hell of a great feeling, but what use would it be when he was starving to death?

He sighed as he glanced at the clock, it was very late, and he cursed Borrowdale for being so far out of town. Snobbish bastard choosing to live as far away from the common people as possible – he frowned, a car was flashing its lights, signalling him to stop.

He didn't recognize the metallic green sedan. "Ah well, probably an acquaintance from the club." He stopped on the side of the road.

Pressing down the window he waited. He glanced at the clock again. Fucking hell, it was really late – maybe he shouldn't have stopped.

A short heavy guy got out and walked towards him with a big grin.

"What's up, Mark?"

"Cool and–"

It happened too fast. In a flash his door was open. He tried to fight, but it was no good. He was quickly dragged out of his car and a soaked cloth thrust to his face. The chloroformed cloth remained pinned on his nose till he was forced to inhale. And soon he was floating in darkness…

When he came to it was still dark. He was lying on the ground, thorns pricking his back.

Shit! What the fuck was this? He was in the middle of nowhere, his legs and hands tied tightly with a thick rope.

What the fuck was this shit? Hadn't they taken his car? What more did the bastards want from him, a ransom?

Shit! He looked up.

His heart completely missed a beat, banging against his ribs with sweat bucketing out of him.

He took another terrified look.

Dean!

"Hello, Mark." In his hand was a baseball bat, and his face was twisted in diabolical rage.

Mark suddenly had difficulty breathing. He opened his mouth wide to gulp in the oxygen, but the damn air refused to get to his lungs. His eyes nearly popped out of their sockets as he saw Dean nodding to the guy who chloroformed him. That guy too was holding a bat.

"Dean," he tried to plead his case but no sound emerged.

He was already screaming before the bat landed on him. More blows rocked him, tearing his flesh with blood pouring out. He howled, this time full blast as more blows landed on him. He kept on screaming in gruelling pain, blood spilling out.

Finally he welcomed the darkness that beckoned him.

First thing he said when he surfaced was, "Dean, I'm really sorry. But it's…Pulane…who…"

With his eyes blazing, Dean growled, "Shut up!"

"B…but…"

The chloroform thug instantly got to his feet and sealed Mark's mouth with adhesive tape.

His whole body was… he started bawling like a baby. Blood still pouring out, both his legs and hands were still bound.

Fearfully, he stared at the blazing bonfire in front of him. Dean was out of control; no way was Mark going to get out of this one alive.

"Get me beer," an all-out for revenge Dean ordered.

Beer came, and after taking mouthfuls he smirked and kicked Mark in the groin, "You do know, Mark, that it's a tradition to tell a folk story round a bonfire."

In a cold deadly voice he said, "I'll tell you a short story, Mark."

Not wanting to risk another kick, Mark quickly nodded.

"Once there was this nice guy, a real nice guy. He fell in love, but it turned out the girl he fell for was just a scheming grade-A bitch. The bitch teamed up with this guy's supposedly best buddy. They stole his money and took off. But this guy, who really was a nice guy but could turn real nasty if provoked, tracked the thieving couple down. He caught up with them, *finally*!

"So, Mark, how about using those thieving brains of yours. What do you think this nice guy did to this couple when he caught up with them?"

In violent rage, he said, "Talk, you piece of shit!"

He tried to scream, but the adhesive tape muffled the sound.

Dean suddenly stood up.

"Of course, he taught them a deadly lesson."

He grinned deviously. "Well, that's the end of the folk story, Mark."

Then he stared at Mark's feet menacingly.

"Those are nice sneakers Mark. You've developed such classy taste with my money, huh?" He aggressively shook the sneakers off Mark's right leg and stripped off the sock too.

A wind of apprehension blew all over Mark as the chloroform thug abruptly stood up.

"Your feet used to be so coarse. What softened them, Mark? Is it the missus's deceitful tongue? Does she lick your toes one by one and suck them like a lollipop?"

The jealousy in Dean's eyes made Mark shudder uncontrollably.

"Pulane needs someone to take care of her. How about shifting her to you," he mimicked.

"And poor naive me played right into your calculating hands. A fucking plan all along," he shouted.

He wanted to cry because it sure looked like a plan all along, yet – damn he violently shook his head. He desperately needed to get through to Dean. *Okay I'm going to die; the least I should do is leave a clean slate behind.*

But the damn gag. He tried to talk, tell the truth as it was. Back at the Chambers', they were good buddies. Dean never did him any harm. But God how he tried. He remembered that first time Pulane came to him asking for a second chance. She bluntly told him Dean could go to hell for all she cared. He had angrily called her a cold little bitch, throwing her out of his room. He tried, Jesus he really tried, but her fucking claws were tightly screwed on Dean's balls.

He tried to talk – muffled sound.

"Let's hear what he has to say for himself," said the other thug.

"No, whatever it is, it's a lie," spat Dean.

Mark swallowed. Once again he had tried a shot at doing the right thing, but still it didn't work. Dean was still the same, very obstinate, and still obsessed over Pulane – nah that couldn't be, Pulane had played him far too much for a sucker, and no one could be that pussy-whipped. No one.

Closing his eyes Mark dreadfully waited for the end.

They roughly untied his feet and grabbed his right foot, planting it in the middle of the blazing fire.

He gasped and gasped, but the intense pain kept on, biting into him, reaching to his heart. He tried to pull his foot back from the devouring fire, but the bastards had that covered. They grasped it firmly. Never in his entire life had he had such bone-crushing pain. Struggling for breath he watched in terrible agony as his foot burnt, willing to be anaesthetized to the terrible pain. But the unbelievable pain carried on, and got even more excruciating.

Through teary eyes he watched in horror as his nails melted to black gravy. He watched in shock as fat from his foot burnt with black smoke boiling vigorously in the fire.

I...can't...take...it...anymore.

Finally darkness came for him, hugging and embracing him. Taking him under its wing, shielding him from the hellish pain.

She had stumbled out of the hospital after the doctors had fully assured her Mark was going to be all right.

God, how she hated hospitals. The sick medicinal smell, the sudden realisation that there really was no escape. One day as sure as the sun rises daily, fate would see to it that she too ended up in there, writhing over some inexplicable ailment that had no right feasting on her.

"No escape at all," she muttered. Mark who had been in perfectly good health all along, but now his health was impaired by diabolical thugs. And you would think her wobbly legs would sympathise with her? It wasn't enough that Mark was in some intensive care ward after some low-life took it into him to beat him to a pulp and satanically roast his foot. Oh no that wasn't enough at all. Her damn legs had to turn on her, mounting her problems with a sprained ankle.

Not giving a rat ass about the superficial image of what people might think, she abandoned the high-heeled shoes and hobbled on.

Her mind was set on one thing.

A drink, yes that. Hadn't she learnt from past predicaments what perfect mood toner vodka could be?

"Are you okay, ma'am?" a girl who waited on tables inquired, looking at her bare feet.

Not getting how a peasant waitress could help, she had razor-tongued her back to her lowly place.

She slumped on the seat and ordered vodka straight, on the rocks.

All those machines hooked to Mark, with Mark not looking like Mark.

She sucked in her breath.

Her heart kept on, dancing to its devastating beat, crumbling down her shielding defences. The searing pain that tore her insides reduced her to a whimpering wreck.

More burning tears spilled out.

But who could do such a horrible thing?

She plunged her shaking hand into her handbag, found a tissue, and hurriedly moped up the tears.

The drink came. Gratefully she gulped it down and promptly ordered another one.

Yes, Mark had his faults, that she wouldn't dispute but foot roasting, she dejectedly shook her head, whoever did this murderous act deserved a lead voice in the devil's committee choir.

Another drink was put before her.

She took a mouthful.

The doctor said it was a miracle none of Mark's bones were broken. If whoever did this had killed Mark – her heart lurched.

Someone gentle tapped her on the shoulder. She ignored whoever it was and stared at her drink tragically.

"Poor Mark."

Another gentle tap.

What was this, a woman drinking alone and automatically she was on the prowl?

"Leave me the hell alone," she said in a surge of anger without looking up.

"Pulane."

She whirled around in shock. "Dean!" she exclaimed in horror.

"Yeah."

Jumping out of chair, she repeated, "Dean!" Her mouth was completely dry.

"Yes, Mrs Mark, it's me."

Damn, where the hell was her acting capability? She grabbed her drink and gulped it down. She had to get it together. This was Dean after all, the same Dean she could twist around her little finger. She still remembered how a simple word phrase 'I love you' could work wonders on him.

"You seem terrified to see me, Mrs Mark. Now why is that?"

Her eyes automatically filled with tears.

"Please, don't call me that. I hate that name."

"Really." He was not buying into her act.

"Pulane will do," she firmly said.

"And why is Madam Pulane scared to see me?"

What was with Dean and this grating sarcasm? He never used to be like that. Or maybe he had wise up. The thought filled her with cold dread.

"Scared! How could I possibly be scared of you? I was just taken aback, that's all."

"Really."

"You seem to have fallen in love with sarcasm, Dean."

"That could be true. Beats falling for a woman."

She tried another angle. "I hope you aren't referring to me," she said, bursting into a flood of tears.

"I am," he said flatly.

Fuck, today really is one of those days. First Mark gets barbecued and then this creep spring from nowhere. A creep she didn't know how to handle seemed to be a clever creep this time. He wasn't even moved by her tears. Unbelievable!

They were still both on their feet.

"Dean, I'm so glad you are here," she said between tears, hugging him.

Another big surprise, no gallant hug returned from her once upon a time pawn. Shit!

She sat down heavily, managing to keep the tears flowing.

"I've been in so much hell, Dean. I'm so happy that you finally found me," she gasped between sobs.

Dean just stared at her, unruffled. He sat down and remained mute. So what else could she do? She kept on with the crying.

More tears rolled down her cheeks. Crying wasn't so hard really. All she did was picture Mark's swollen body hooked to those horrible machines – all purple, his flesh torn. Damn. And life, full of shit it was. Where the hell had this bad joke sprung from? She had so much on her hands right now; Mark was in hospital, and he would need her undivided attention. Sure, Dean had been good enough to sponsor their marriage, but he really was the last thing she needed right now. But then Dean wasn't so hard to please; just a couple of 'I love yous' and he would come in plenteous joy.

Still…

Damn!

Deep down she felt she owed Dean nothing. If it hadn't been for her, Dean wouldn't have pulled that hijack; it was that simple. She was the one who planted the idea, sweated a great deal caressing his fragile ego, and nursed him back to believe in himself. One hell of a tough job, and she deserved *all* the credit, especially when she resurrected his balls, which he apparently lost when he became a gardener. And what about all those nights she spent spread-eagled, servicing his out of control hormones? Bastard didn't even repay her with one decent orgasm.

Wiping off the tears, she took several deep breaths.

"This place is depressing. How about we go somewhere else?"

"Shoes?"

"Um, a sprained ankle."

He shrugged. "Let's go to my hotel, then."

"Sure," she said.

She relaxed slightly. It was the same old Dean, her sucker of all time, waltzing to her only tune, always in complete agreement to whatever she said. She confidently linked her arm through his and together they went out.

"Are you driving?" she asked once they were outside.

He nodded steering her to where his car was parked. They silently drove to his hotel.

When he switched on the light in his room she was alarmed at the expression on his face. He stared at her in murderous wrath with his eyes blazing – shit, they were daggers. She was suddenly numbed with fear, to the point of nearly peeing on herself. Had she underestimated him! Damn what was she to do now? Dean used to be such an agreeable puppy.

What the damn fuck happened?

"Before you say anything, I want you to know that it was me who beat up your beloved husband."

"What?" she gasped.

"I roasted his foot. Now start *talking*," he thundered.

Insane rage seized her.

"How could you do such a horr…" she stopped just in time.

"Go on, finish your sentence," he dared her.

Damn, she nearly blew it. *I have to think straight. I have to really, really think straight.* But knowing it was this heartless bastard who nearly killed Mark – it was hard.

Very, very hard.

"I am waiting, Pulane!"

He sat on the couch and stretched his long legs. So intense was his rage that he started shaking, but he didn't move an inch. He waited for the lies. He was curious about how she was going to bluff her way out. He didn't have a long wait as words tumbled out from her pathological lying mouth.

"I can see you are really angry with me. You have every right to be. But, Dean, I didn't have a choice. Mark found out about the hijack. He blackmailed me to elope with him for insurance."

A stony silence with a murderous look from Dean.

"It's been real hell, Dean. All this time missing you like hell. I wanted you so much it hurts. But Mark knows I love you. That was his trump card. It was either I went with him or he called the cops. What could I do? He knew I would never risk him calling the cops on us. He knew damn well I could never subject you to hell in prison."

Something snapped in him. In a fog of anger, he grabbed a chair and blindly hit her lying slut body. When the chair broke, he didn't hesitate, he went on, hard at work, this time disciplining her with his fists. He was out of control, and he kept hitting. He beat her senseless, blooding the lying bitch. The thieving bitch screamed her slut lungs out, but he quickly solved that minor problem by playing some funky music louder. He went back to her, intent on beating all the lying crap out of her. He could hear Jomo pounding on the door, but that didn't stop him either. He landed another one on her face with the full intention of rearranging it. She tried to protect her lying face by covering it with her slut hands, but it didn't work. More blood poured out of her slut body, making his hands slippery. Without batting an eye, he switched to another tactic. He drove his Timberland boots into her calculating body.

He stamped and kicked. He kept on kicking, not bothered by the blood pouring out.

Then his interfering brother kicked the door in.

"Get out," Dean said menacingly at him.

But Jomo grabbed him.

"It's enough," he said in a firm voice.

"This is between me and her," Dean said through clenched teeth.

"I know, but like I said, it's enough," Jomo said as he drag his brother away.

Shaking free Dean walked out. He kept on walking, not really knowing where he was headed. Eventually he stumbled upon a bench and sat himself down. He gulped in the fresh air. He sat there drinking in the air, his mind completely blank, staring at the ground. With his blooded hands resting on his lap he nursed his anger. The throbbing pain he felt in his hands gave him great satisfaction, the pain meant the cheap scheming slut got plenty.

Good, he nodded.

Soon he found himself drifting into a light sleep.

Trudging back to his room two hours later, Dean found the lying slut sprawled on his bed, her face bloody and swollen with multiple scraps.

"I'm not going anywhere," announced the champion slut. She was lying in bed with only one blanket; a bundle of sheets drenched in blood lay in a heap at the foot of the bed. She had such a nerve, he told himself in aggravation.

He looked at her, the murderous rage back. Then he looked at his bed, the bed that had been a source of comfort to him was now contaminated by the lying slut.

"Get the hell out of here," he said, his voice thick with rage.

"You can kill me if you want, but I ain't going nowhere," she stammered in fright.

"Out!" he screamed, trembling in rage.

He slapped her pathetic swollen face. She gasped, but she didn't move an inch.

He slapped her again.

"You know he has always been too into money. Well, he frightened me when he confronted me. He was probably just suspicious, but I blew it when I confessed to the whole thing. It was the damn fright that clouded my senses and I'm so sorry," she said between hysteric sobs.

Another slap.

She painfully sat up, buried her hand under a pillow, and produced two documents.

"Here take a look at these," she said.

"Get the fuck out of my room!" he thundered. Just to make sure she knew he meant business, he punched her lying face. Blood poured out, but still she didn't move.

"Ouch," was the only response he got.

"I…called…my…lawyer…when…you…were…out.…he delivered these. P…please look at them."

Why not, it was only a cat that curiosity killed. He grabbed the documents from her shaking hand, casting a suspicious look at her. Christ, what a bitch! Running off with his friend! I have to control myself and see what this is all about. He opened the first document.

"I'm the recipient in your will!" he gasped.

"It's your money, Dean," she said, clutching a Kleenex to her face.

He looked at the date on her will – it was the same month she ran out on him.

"So what's this supposed to make me feel, good?" he sneered.

Aha! So it was still the same sucker story. It wasn't about the money, it never was. The bastard still loved her; he was still tangled up in her.

"Mark signed a prenuptial before he married you!" he exclaimed at the second document he was suspiciously scanning.

"Yes, I conned him into signing that. He thinks he's smart, but he can't even read his name, and when we divorce he won't be getting a cent of your hard-earned money," she said smoothly. *Mark divorcing me!* The gasp was out before she could stop it.

"What's wrong?" he frowned.

"It's nothing, Dean. Just a little pain where you disciplined me."

"I don't trust you, Pulane," he said as he sank into a chair.

"Understandable, but, Dean, I didn't have a choice," she wailed.

"These documents are probably not real."

"That's where you are wrong, Dean. These are legit. Ask Jomo to check them out for you."

This time she was telling the truth, the papers were real. That was the only truth; the rest was of course something else. If she ever let on about her deep love for Mark, this maniac would kill her, of that she was dead certain. So the truth had to be changed a little for a good cause. So he was still obsessed with her. It was a bit of a drag, but at least that would guarantee her life. So the best angle was to pretend Mark didn't mean shit to her, and that it was he who really counted. Pretending would be damn difficult, she acknowledged. It seemed her acting talent had waned; otherwise she wouldn't have gotten beaten up. That was the shit thing about having money; you lose your street-smart sixth sense and get too damn complacent.

"How could he be so stupid in signing a prenup?" he still couldn't seem to get over it.

"Mark is stupid," she said heatedly. And the will, well, she wrote that because if you still wanted to live, then you didn't underestimate anyone from Snoop. She had known a possibility of Dean tracking them down existed, no matter how small, and if it so happened, she had figured that would be her life insurance.

In a silk soothing voice she said, "I didn't waste any money, Dean. It's all invested; there is nightclub and a salon. I think we are even worth more."

"We? That is my money, Pulane," he said viciously.

"I'm sorry, you are right, it's all yours."

"Why didn't you trust me enough to confide in me?"

"And risk Mark calling the cops on us?"

"A lot of ways exist of killing a cat with equally the same result."

"I'm sorry," it seemed the right thing to say.

"If I hadn't come…"

"Oh, I've been working on that, I was just about to contact you. It's been months of hell, but God has finally answered my prayers. I've been hesitant though because your anger would have blinded you to rationally deal with Mark."

"So how is your married life?"

This was dangerous territory; this was where she had to be alert.

"It's not marriage, Dean. I'm just the dog on his leash. He doesn't care about me, has a chain of girlfriends."

"And what about you, do you love him?" he cut in.

"How can I be in love with such a cold-blooded bastard?" She managed to sound hurt.

"So what are you going to do now?"

"The beating would probably scare him off, and then I divorce him of course."

"Really." Not even a ten-year-old could miss the joy in his eyes. What a champion sucker!

She took a deep breath. It was now time to cement her supposed love for him and seal her life insurance.

"Dean, I love you so much. I know I will be asking a lot if I ask you to take me back. But I really love you, and I pray that one day you will find it in your heart to forgive me."

Not a word came from Dean.

"We'll talk to the lawyers and hand right of ownership to you."

"Yeah, I want that club in my name," he said recklessly.

"Everything is yours, Dean, even the salon. And the houses."

"No, I don't want the salon."

"Well you can always sell it," she said.

"I don't care much about the salon, you can have it."

"Thank you, Dean," she said grateful.

Then he dropped the bomb.

"I like this country and I've decided to live here."

"Ohh," she said cautiously.

"Sure," he said, all smiles. Ah, men, so easy, so stupid. All it took was a little play, a little mystery, a little stinginess with what was between your legs and oh yeah, he would fall for you like a ton of bricks. Once a man fell for you, really *fell* for you, it was a done deal. A man would believe anything that came out of his woman's mouth because in his double-standard mind, it was only him with talent and the right to lie.

"I guess I should go."

Disappointment written all over him he said, "Go! Where to?"

Jeez, did the dangerous thug expect her to sleep over? "Home," she said.

"I'll drive you there," he offered, conveniently forgetting the brutal beating he had just given her.

"I would appreciate that, Dean."

"Come, let's go."

She tried to get up. "Ouch."

"Shit, I beat you too hard. Lie in bed; I'll call you a doctor."

"Thanks."

He looked at her. "Does it hurt?"

To keep herself from losing it, she took a deep breath. "Not as much as I hurt you, I don't blame you for beating me, though. I should have trusted you enough to deal with Mark. It's just that I felt I'd put you in enough trouble already. I felt I should protect you, I felt it was the least I should do."

Before she fell asleep she thought of Mark. What if this foot roasting was too much for him? What if the beating scared him off? "I…wouldn't be able to…" The sedative in the painkiller the doctor had given her taken over, and soon she was in deep dreamless sleep.

"So, dearest brother, tell me, are the documents legit or what?"

"They are genuine, but I still don't trust her," Jomo said.

He broke into a big winning smile.

"She is one hell of a great girl," Dean said dreamily.

Jomo gaped at him, dumfounded.

"She feels real bad for what she did. She's even handing me the rights of ownership to everything. She tricked that rat Mark into signing an ironclad prenup. What a great girl she is."

Jomo gaped at him in stupefying shock. "What are you trying to tell me?"

"I am taking her back, Jomo," he said quietly.

"Don't even think about it," Jomo warned.

"Sorry, bro, but I am taking her back. Why don't you wait till I tell you the whole story before you paint a distorted picture of her," he pleaded.

"So what did she have to say for herself?"

"It was that bastard Mark all along. Somehow he found out about the hijack. He confronted Pulane, who lost her nerve and confessed to the whole shit. So he blackmailed her. Either she run off with him or he goes to the cops."

Jomo looked up at him. "What's the smile for, Dean? You think it's some kind of picnic being played for a sucker once more?" Jomo asked bitterly.

"Jomo, stop being so paranoid. I'm cool, Pulane is not the scheming bitch we mistook her for."

"Really, what is she then?" Jomo asked icily.

"A nice girl who fell victim to that blackmailer. I fucking hate Mark."

"She is a thieving bitch, and I don't buy into her little victim act. If Mark had the brains to be a blackmailer, then he would have the brains to know the impact of signing a prenup. I'll say the victim is Mark on this one," shouted Jomo.

"I don't like that kind of talk," Dean said, sulking.

"Come on, Dean, can't you just think rationally for a minute? If Mark is the blackmailer, then he is calling the shots, all the shots, Dean. Why would he marry Pulane when he already had everything he ever wanted?"

"Marrying Pulane was insurance in case I came looking for them. The bastard knows I love Pulane," Dean muttered.

"Yes, Dean, Mark knows of your pathetic love for this bitch. And he knows you will never rest if she runs out on you. He knows you will move heaven and earth to track her down. So why would he be stupid enough to tempt fate by grabbing her instead of just approaching the two of you and getting his blackmail payoff to live happily ever after? Why saddle his free self with her? *Why?*"

"Because he is a greedy pig and he wanted it all."

"She is lying to you," Jomo said flatly.

"You never ever liked Pulane. You'll say just about anything to turn me against her," he said glumly.

"Dean, how long do you intend to play a sucker's game? Haven't you had enough?"

"No, I haven't," he snapped.

Shaking his head and reeling in shock, Jomo asked, "What the fuck is happening to you, Dean?".

"I'm sorry," he said once again. He slumped on the chair, suddenly drained of energy. He was so full of energy when he waltzed in here, but Jomo and his sucker-talk had drained it all. *Am I really a sucker?* he wondered, scratching his head.

"This girl has been the bane of your life. You need to forget her, Dean," Jomo said urgently.

"I love her," he said.

"You have to forget her, Dean. It will be the best thing you will ever do. Okay, I understand it will be hard, but come on, man, you can do it. Take it as if she's dead and buried, ten feet under."

Viciously he said, "No!"

"Dean," pleaded Jomo.

"Can't you understand this? I can never live without her," he wailed.

"No, I cannot understand that," said Jomo coldly.

"I love her," Dean whined.

Jomo shook his head. He made a mistake bringing Dean along. He should have just come alone and taken the money, after teaching her a lesson of course. Once again, he blamed himself. He shouldn't have underestimated the blindness of this witch-crafting love.

Rage began to burn inside him. He hurled the glass he had been drinking from at the door.

Bringing Dean along had been one hell of a mistake. It seemed Dean wasn't burnt enough. Damn, he could still remember those days when that maid bitch ran out on him. He closed his eyes. Dean was a mess – completely crushed. It was a tragic sight; just looking at him would make you want to weep. It was something he wouldn't even wish on his worst enemy, and Dean was heading for that again.

Restlessly pacing across the room he asked himself for the umpteenth time, why had he insisted on Dean working as a gardener?

What if Dean didn't survive more heartbreak? What then? What the fuck would he do?

"Jomo, please don't be mad at me, I love this woman," he pleaded in a tiny emotional voice, feeling very uneasy. Yes, he did love Pulane, but he also loved his brother. The brother who had always been there for him, the brother who at countless stages even became his mother. The uneasiness deepened.

"Jomo, please."

"Take the money and leave her," Jomo said.

Leave her, no that he couldn't do. He wouldn't be able live, not with her out of his life. He stared at his shaking hands, not saying a word.

After a while, he wearily stated, "I can't live without her."

"How about those months she disappeared? Yes, you suffered, Dean, but you survived, that is the most important thing."

"But I was in pain all the time," he protested.

"But you managed to live," Jomo insisted.

"It was the hope of seeing her again that kept me going."

Damn! Jomo wanted to scream. *What is it with this stupid cunt of a maid? Why can't Dean see her for the devious scheming bitch that she is?*

"Leave her while you still have your balls," said Jomo in a serious voice.

"I can't," he cried.

"This girl is no good, Dean."

"That's cos you don't really know her," he said.

Jomo stared at him silently, then he said, "I could order a hit on her, but…no. The best thing is to leave you to see for yourself what exactly this girl is made of. Experience it firsthand," was Jomo's last word before he left.

CHAPTER FIFTEEN

The terrible agony.

He been hospitalised for three whole weeks. Three fucking weeks, almost a month, fucking hell!

He stared at his bandaged foot – finally it clicked why God has opted to use fire in hell.

He shuddered uncontrollably as he recalled the entire episode of his foot roasting. He still had chilling nightmares about that.

So Dean wasn't into bluffs, provoking him further by staying with Pulane would definitely be the end of him. Damn, he and Dean used to be so cool, but because Pulane preferred him to Dean – he shook his head uneasily. Such injustice. It was Pulane who came to him, practically begged him to marry her, baiting him with all that money she stole from Dean. But who got punished? Him, while the real culprit got off with only a couple of punches.

He shifted his eyes to his foot again. He wondered whether the nails that were all burnt would grow back. The doctors said yes, but why should he take their word? The swelling of his entire body was gone. He was still blue in certain parts and the torn flesh, oh, that had been stitched too. There were stitches in his head where the bastards had split it open, they weren't going to take long to come out though, they told him. Jesus, he was marked for life; there would be scars on his head the doctors had said. No more brush cuts, all time he would have a shaved head! And there were headaches, nasty ones. He figured he was flawed for life. Hey, what was his crime? Alluring charm and a flexible tongue that bewitched women into thinking he was the 'one'. Fucking shit stinks of prejudice, was it him who stole the money?

Nope. But it was him whose head had been split with bats while Pulane was still up and about, oh no, Missus Pulane was hardly touched because there was witch-crafting candy between her legs that Dean couldn't get enough of. That was another mystery to him because as far as he knew… Ah well there was no accounting for the taste of pussy.

Still, Dean? What was going on in his head? Pulane had really played him about, messed him real bad, used him to finance her married life with another man. But oh no, Dean was still not getting it. Dean was still forgiving Pulane and fucking Pulane. "Is Dean fucking mental?" he had asked Pulane. "Don't you feel bad about what you did to Dean?"

She had looked at him all wide-eyed. "He slept with me, Mark, I deserve some kind of compensation." It showed you couldn't trust women!

The scratches on his face were not much, the pain was still there, but compared to when it was administered, you could say the pain was now trifling. He still wanted to live, so he turned his full attention on Eva, no gangster skeletons waiting to barbecue him with delightful Eva. Of course she probed and asked who could do such a horrible thing. An emotional 'I don't know' set her in line because much as he loved her he still had to tread carefully. When she saw how upset he got, she had told him the best thing was to put it all behind them. Let bygones remain what they were. It was a terrible ordeal, and mentioning it was upsetting enough, she had said. That suited him fine he reflected.

Then he told her how his near-death experience had wise him up. Which really was the truth, Eva was the kind of woman you could count on when it was dark and cold, and she didn't talk crap either. Life was too short to trifle upon. She mattered too much to him. He was finally leaving his wife; he didn't care about the money. For all he cared she could take it all, as long as he got the chance to be with she who mattered was what he told her. Also he missed the sex, he wanted it all the time, loved being inside her, and oh yes, the after cuddles – delicious kisses drinking in sweats off each other, plus those reassuring whispers in the dark, no chance of *that* if he kept flip-flopping around. Then there was Dean, yeah Dean, who was bound to kill him if he remained with Pulane.

He hurriedly packed the clothes he needed to exit fast; he didn't want to risk another foot barbecue.

"Mark what are you doing?" she yelled.

Looking up at her, he answered, "Ah, Pulane. I didn't hear you come in."

"I came from the hospital, Mark," she said, dropping her car keys on the dressing table and looking at him mystified. "Why didn't you tell me you'd be out today? Who brought you here? They said you refused an ambulance."

"A friend of mine gave me a ride," he said.

Slumping on the bed, she took off her heels "What friend?" she asked suspiciously.

"Pulane, let's go in the lounge. Me and you, we need to talk."

Looking at the half-packed suitcase, she stammered, "This t...talk – is it going to be heavy?"

"Let's go," he urged, leading her to the lounge with the aid of his crutch.

"Mark, you mustn't let Dean intimidate you. I love you and together we can fight him."

"So how is Dean?" he asked once they were seated.

Bitterly she said, "Still the same bastard of a rat."

"I thought you said he forgave you," he said frowning.

"That's what he says."

"He must really be in love with you," he remarked.

"What did you want to talk to me about?" she asked.

"I want a divorce," he said straight out.

"What?" she said, blinking rapidly.

"I am serious, Pulane," he said, this time there was an edge in his voice.

In a strangled voice she asked, "Why?" It had to be a dream. Should she pinch herself and find out? She didn't dare.

"I'm in love with someone else."

"But...but..."– It was her very worst nightmare! The blood drained from her face.

"Because of Eva I've suddenly realised how precious life is, and that there is more to life than money," Mark pleasantly announced.

She was now speechless.

Huh? Mark was speaking an entirely different language, a language she didn't – couldn't – understand.

How had this come about?

"I know this is hard on you. But try to understand," he softly told her.

She finally summoned the guts to pinch herself.

She wasn't dreaming!

More to life than money, when did Mark learn that language?

Eva, the creature's name is Eva, she dazedly kept thinking. Eva you bitch of a cunt. The rage that seized her was so intense that she started quivering uncontrollably.

Eva, Jesus, what is she? Who is she?

She shook her head over and over again in disbelief.

Divorce.

Eva, husband-thieving bitch!

Mark calmly stood up and poured her a glass of water to drink. "Are you all right?" he asked after she had taken a few mouthfuls.

She nodded weakly. "Mark, please, I can't live without you," she heard herself wailing.

He adamantly shook his head. "No, Pulane, we are over."

The palpitations that were usually triggered by caffeine intake started attacking her.

"Sorry, Pulie, but this is something I should have done long back."

So staggering was the shock that she had to briefly shut her eyes.

Eva.

She didn't say a word, what could she possibly say? Mark's mind seemed set on walking.

Standing up, he casually announced, "So I'm like moving out now."

Her breath came in laboured gasps. The heartless bastard wasn't even giving her time to digest this nightmarish info.

"Can't…you…at least think…about it first?"

"I've already thought about it."

"Who…is…s…she?"

"You don't know her. She is white and her name is Eva."

"Really." Why did Mark feel the need to tell her this woman's skin colour, she wondered seething, the pain temporarily forgotten.

She tensed. "Is it cos she is white?" she asked because no matter what they said it always came back to your skin colour.

Mark looked at her blankly, shook his head, and climbed the stairs.

She sat there, more shocked than hurt at Mark's sudden announcement.

A white girl he said.

So what was this? A couple of smiles from her and Mark was acting all crazy, an infatuated puppy throwing his life away. It started off with him singing her name in the middle of the night and now this. She started breathing hard in rage that suddenly flooded through her.

So what happened when this girl decided she would rather baby-sit her own than a nothing nigger the likes of Mark? What then? Did Mark expect her to stick around, waiting to hold his hand? Damn! She jerked to her feet, surprised at such intense rage. She wobbled to the bar and poured a stiff drink.

Her eyes started flashing with the force of her rage.

Eva.

A white girl.

No, no, she fiercely shook her head. Mark had always been an unfaithful bastard of a rat. She mustn't let colour issues blur her rationality. White skin or purple skin, Mark was walking and she'd be husbandless. Raw undiluted pain is what I'm going to endure even if it were a sister who snatched my husband. No colour gradations when it came to a broken heart was what she was desperately trying to get through to her dazed mind.

She walked to the couch and sat. Mark had been upstairs for quite a while now. She dialled their bedroom extension.

"What's up with you?"

"Keep your cool, I'm about to finish."

Mark was such a self-absorbed bastard! She mustn't think about Mark, she mustn't, she rebuked herself. It was too painful, she frantically decided.

She shrugged helplessly.

Well, she was Pulane, a nothing girl with her multitude of blunders. The sucker of all time was what she was called on the streets. Some had even infuriatingly told her it was people like her who were making it hard for other women, giving men more ammunition to trample on women, making things worse than they already were. But you would never find her in screaming matches with those people because yes, anyone who could tolerate Mark's bullshitting deserved those disgusted, pitying looks. And she was not going to feed anyone anything sloppy like, "I don't mind his serial cheating," because she did mind, only she was a too coward to take that big step. And yes, she would admit it; she was no hero.

Now what? Mark was walking, but what was she going to do, sit here with her sorry hands pathetically folded, clinging to a 'for better or for worse'?

What the fuck was she going to do?

She heard footsteps descending the stairs. Her heart lurched, Mark was coming. She looked up to see Mark enter with two bulging suitcases.

He left.
Just like that.
He casually walked out of her life.
She numbly watched as he left with the bulging suitcases.
He didn't even hug her goodbye.
He didn't even look back.
I'm not going to cry, she whimpered to herself over and over again.
I refuse to shed a single tear because how long has it been now fully at his service?
How long had it been?
She had started working at the Chambers' house four years and two or three months back. And Mark how long before... yeah two months and six days precisely. Then of course he asked her out. And it was all– good, in fact more than perfect then, this time tears spilled out.
So how long had it been then? Three years and some months if she took out those months she spent recruiting Dean.
Three years fully servicing him.
Three years of utter waste.
And no goodbye hugs.

He just walked out with not as much as a look back.

But I said I wasn't going to cry…

Somehow the vodka helped, a bit, just for her to get on her staggering feet.

She got in the car and drove haphazardly, she couldn't see straight because of her tearful eyes. But she got there in one piece – well physically. She double-parked in front of a small building between 14th Avenue and George Silundika Street. She was still shaking.

It was hard. So unbelievably hard.

"Oh God, why do I love Mark so much?" she whimpered.

She lurched into the office of the private investigator her friend Maggie had recommended. Efficient and discreet she had been told. Exactly what she need. He was an ex-cop who went by the name of Edgar Martin.

"Excuse me, madam."

Her problems were endless as it was, and she had no time for a stupid receptionist. She threw her a scathing look and staggered to the door the PI's name was marked on.

A beefy man sat behind a huge desk.

"I'm sorry, sir, but she just…"

He waved the receptionist off.

"It's okay, close the door behind you."

"Afternoon, miss."

Mark had left her.

He really had left her.

Left her for an Eva.

She sucked in her breath.

The shaking resumed.

"You look pretty shaken. What should I get you, juice, or something stronger?" he asked softly.

More alcohol would get to her head. She had to be on her guard, especially now that bastard of a rat Dean was in the background.

"Water will do."

He nodded before going to a small fridge in the corner and taking out a bottle of water.

"So how may I help?"

She didn't waste time. She requested surveillance on her major enemy.

"Her name is Eva. I want you to find out everything about her. All the skeletons in her white closet."

The PI men nodded understandingly.

"What's her surname, ma'am?"

"Don't know."

"Her address?" he asked, pen poised on the notepad.

She shook her head in agitation.

"This – Eva – she is having an affair with my h…husband."

"I'll start tailing the husband then. Give me his cell phone number."

After noting the number down he said, "Give me a week, I'll call you as soon as I have something."

"I want a divorce."

The impact of Mark's words had slapped hard where it hurt. She tried to drag her lead legs, but she couldn't. She suddenly was so physically sick.

"I love her," he had said. Not 'I love you Pulane' but 'I love her'. She bit her lip so hard she tasted blood.

Eva the super bitch. She had sabotaged the only dream Pulane had ever had.

And God?

I prayed till I was blue in the face, but what happened? You decided Mark was better suited to this Eva. And the worst thing was… She gasped loudly.

This Eva never prayed, not even once for Mark's heart. She wouldn't have minded if she was handed someone else.

But no, it had to be Mark, the Mark you know I love. The Mark I knelt down and prayed for. But that didn't count, right? You decided Eva, who didn't even ask for him, was better suited to him.

God handed Mark to her just like that – on a silver platter.

A heart-wrenching sob rose in her pained chest.

Eva – Pulane was still amazed at her unbelievable luck.

Never prayed and pleaded for Mark's heart.

Yet, she emerged a triumphant winner.

Probably dished out an ultimatum.

A divorce or…

And lucky Eva was with Mark right now. Having champagne – celebrating.

And all the while I sunk to my knees, praying I thought You would come through for me. I really, really thought You would do that one thing for me, she sobbed.

But no, it was Eva You came through for.

She started crying even harder.

"Is something wrong, dear," she faintly heard,

But that didn't stop her. She cried even harder because it wasn't just something, it was everything that was wrong.

After a while she dragged herself to where her car was parked.

That thug had scared off the one thing that mattered to her. How she wished Dean would just get her out of his clingy system and leave her alone. She was willing to give him half of everything, hell, even three quarters of it, but the bastard seemed to have a different agenda. He didn't seem to give a damn about the money. He never even bothered to see lawyers about changing the club title deed to his name.

He was only interested in her divorcing Mark and marrying him. Like she could ever want to *marry* such pathetic shit.

She was still working on a plan to rid herself of Dean once and for all. But for now, she would play along. She knew damn well it was her supposedly love for him that was currently cooling him off.

"Hey, hey, your eyes are all puffy. Have you been crying?" he asked, all concerned.

With a small smile, she admitted, "Yes."

"Why?" he asked in alarm.

"I feel bad about all the pain I caused you – I keep thinking I should have trusted you. Anyway, you'll be happy to know we are finally free," she said.

Unbuttoning the first three buttons on her blouse, he remarked, "You don't seem to mean what you say."

"Jesus Christ, Dean!" she exploded.

"I like your boobs," he stated, his hand plunging into her cleavage.

"Mark got himself this white girl, and he is happy. He moved in with her."

"Mark can never be in love with anyone," he said flatly.

"Who said anything about him being in love?"

"A white girl, you said. She's probably loaded," he said.

Loaded! That meant she had seen the last of Mark unless the girl decided on a change of a scene.

She took a deep, boosting breath. "It's not important what this girl is. The bottom line is Mark is out of our lives."

"Even if he hadn't met up with this girl, he was still going to get out of our lives," he said viciously.

"So when are you moving in?"

"Today," he promptly answered.

Her eyes widened. How could she have suggested that he move in with her? How was she going to pretend with him hovering over her twenty-four hours a day?

Damn, damn, damn!

Before the week was up, he had the full report.

"She is a straightforward girl who seems to be in love with your husband. She used to date a lot before your husband appeared on the scene, now it's only him." He dropped pictures on the desk.

She took a look.

"Beautiful slut," she bitterly admitted.

She picked another one. It burnt her, and she instantly dropped it. It was of the happy couple kissing, not just kissing, soulful kind of a kiss, and the way Mark was looking at her... Mark had never looked at her like that.

It hurt too much.

Her heart was in shreds. As if Mark's desertion wasn't enough, she had Dean living with her fucking her every day. She burst into a flood of bitter tears wondering why this was happening to her.

The PI handed her a Kleenex, soothed her and gently squeezed her hands.

"Nobody can be this perfect. What exactly is it about this girl that makes her so irresistible to my husband?" she said, wiping the tears with the back of her hand, ignoring the Kleenex on her lap.

"Probably it's her being white, some people get off on that," said the PI.

"How much is she worth?" Pulane asked warily, very much aware of the jolt in her chest.

"Nothing. It's not the money. She's a clerk in a law firm and studies part time in a college. I wouldn't worry about her, soon the novelty of her white skin will wear off, and you, my dear, will be back with your husband."

Finally she could exhale. No money. Good, very good.

"I need something that I can use against her. Something that can shock my husband into running back into my arms," she explained.

The PI stared at her for some time then said, "I have no sympathy for home wreckers. So it's like this, I can help, but it will cost plenty."

"How would you help?"

"We can construct the shadiness. Anything," he said, shrugging his broad shoulders.

"Really?"

"She is studying A level maths in some college called Foundation. Her dream is being a chartered accountant. But she is having such difficulty in maths. Always flunking the subject, still, she is determined to make it."

"But what has that got to do with me getting my husband back?"

"Everything," he smiled mysteriously.

CHAPTER SIXTEEN

Looking up at her, a tall blond guy said, "Sorry about that."

Judging from his physique, which was enormously arresting, he was in his mid-twenties. He had the kind of looks one was forced to notice and marvel at. His eyes were hypnotically blue – piercing all the way to the heart. When he collided with her, scattering her books, she was initially annoyed, but when she looked up, ah well….

"No problem," she answered with a bright smile. With your kind of looks you don't need to say sorry to anybody. She happily bent to pick up the textbooks scattered on the floor.

"May I?" said the young man, picking up the books and handing them to her after patting off whatever dust they picked up on the floor.

"I'm very sorry. This is my first week here and…"

"I know the feeling," she said, nodding her head sympathetically.

"I hope I didn't mess your books up."

"That's okay," she assured him. "Hey, you are in my class?" she asked.

"I'm not sure, but I'm here for upper-six A level maths."

"Yes, you are in my class. I've seen you," she said.

"So we are in the same maths class," he said conversationally.

"Yes, and I'm Eva," she said, shaking his hand.

"I'm Ray," he said, smiling at her.

"Well, nice to meet you, Ray."

"Likewise," he said.

"I sit at the back in class to avoid Mr Dow's incessant questions, that's probably why you didn't see me," she explained.

"Oh."

"So what do you think of maths?" she asked.

"I like maths. It's actually my best subject," he said.

"That's nice, but studying maths is such a drag to me. I find it irritably hard, and yep, I do flunk the subject quite often," she said, opening up to him.

"Shame," he sympathised.

"So tell me your secret."

Blinking, he looked up at her. "What secret?"

"Of being a success in maths."

"Oh. Spend more time on the subject. Do as many questions as possible, when you get to something you can't solve, don't just skip it, and hand it to your tutor. Put up as much fight as you can, even if it takes days to get the answer. The thing is if it's you sweating, you won't easily forget. Sorry, I'm talking too much," he suddenly said.

"No, please go on. You are being so helpful. But sometimes I try really hard."

"At least make sure you know where you went wrong before you hand it to your tutor. It's very important to know where you went wrong, not just the fact that you were wrong."

"I see. So where are you from?"

"Kenya. My folks came here last month." He paused, focusing hypnotic eyes on her. "Work."

"Well, welcome to Cape Town, Ray. This town isn't that bad, pretty soon you'll find your way around."

"Thanks," he said brightly.

"We have a lot of movie houses and nightclubs that are really cool and the beach."

"That's nice." He looked at her shyly. "Do you know where I can get a Bostock and Chandler textbook?"

"Which one?"

"Core maths."

"Sure, Kingston bookshop. It's opposite Barclays Bank main branch, 10th Avenue."

"Thanks," he said, gratefully scribbling the address in a small diary.

"Anyway, see you tomorrow," she said as she got into her car. Wow. Sometimes just looking at a good body was an instant high in itself, feasting your eyes on a rare piece of art. Just that, looking with no X-rated agenda.

"I've finished marking your test on integration, and I'm very disappointed with you," Mr. Dow indignantly announced.

"The highest is Ray with ninety percent, which was a surprise since he only joined us last week and didn't even learn the entire topic."

"He obviously learnt it where he came from," said another student.

"Shut up, now let's do the corrections. Eva I suggest you end your conference and *concentrate*," Mr Dow said, looking at her. He went to the board and copied the first question.

"Integrating exponential functions is not so complex. Just a reverse of differentiation…"

"Well done," she said after the class.

"Thanks," Ray said shyly.

"Guess what I got, twelve percent," she said sourly.

"You mustn't lose hope. Next time you'll do much better."

"I really revised for this test, but I guess I don't have the brains for this," she said grimly.

"Don't ever make a mistake of giving up," he warned.

"I have very limited brains," she moaned.

"I don't think you do," he gently said.

"I don't know what to do," she said bitterly.

"Anything, but not the giving up," he said encouragingly.

"I need a pass in maths to get a bursary, but it's so hard!"

"Listen, I can help if you want," he offered.

"Really?" she said, brightening up.

"Sure, but you have to promise to do all the work I ask you to do."

"Yes, sir," she said beaming.

The following day two men were walking side by side on the wooded slats in City Park.

The younger one grabbed a handful of pebbles from in between the slats and playful threw them at a couple of trees.

"So how is it going?"

"Slow, but I'm getting there."

"Whatever you do, don't come on to her. Remember, you are a nice guy and the last thing on your mind is girls."

"What if she doesn't play along?"

"She will," was the confident reply.

"Whatever you say."

"Girls have enormous ego. That's the angle we are going to work on. To them a platonic deal has to be dished by them. If it's from a guy, it gets to be a challenge. 'Platonic, so he thinks he is too good for the likes of me. We'll see about that'," the beefy man mimicked.

"And make sure she knows you are straight but not seeing anyone. Available but not interested."

"Okay."

"Try speeding things up, the client is getting anxious."

"She's beautiful," the young man said dreamily.

"Never mind her beauty. Act the part of a nice guy, ignore the beauty."

"It's hard to ignore such beauty."

"Hey, hey, don't start with that sloppy shit on me. Besides, you'll have plenty of time to do something about her good looks. Only the time is not now."

"Okay," he said, throwing more pebbles.

Frowning at the young man, he said. "Stop that, will you?"

"Why?"

"Because this is important and you are not concentrating."

"Sorry," said the young man, dropping the pebbles on the slats. He shook his hands and nodded to his beefy companion.

"Give it your best shot in teaching her and make sure she really learns this maths. And stand firm in your platonic ground. The first move has to come from her. The fact that you are not taken in by her looks will get to her, enough to go after you – it's nothing to do with love, just a stupid ego point to prove."

"And when she makes her ego point to prove move?"

"The crossing of that bridge will only be done when we finally get to it."

"She is hopeless in maths."

"And you are a miracle worker," stated the beefy man.

The young guy shrugged. "I'll try."

"No, don't try, do your utmost. The key to this case is maths. You need to use maths to win her over. She failed maths in high school two years ago, enrolled in this Foundation college, rewrote last December only to get an unsatisfactory grade once again."

"She got an F twice!"

"You only fail if you don't try hard enough. There is no such thing as a *failure* unless you embrace and accommodate it. Now this Eva – she is a fighter, she is still trying when most people would have thrown in the towel."

"But-"

"She can pass this maths cos she *wants* it."

"An F twice!"

"You need to want something in order to succeed at it. That, my friend, is the trick of life."

"Can you just cut the sermon and listen to me. This is a two-year course of study and she is in her fourth year, still getting twelve percent!" Shaking his head, the young man continued. "We need to change tracks, she will never pass maths!"

The beefy man patiently said. "You need to help her in the one thing she wants the most. This girl is pretty; she can get any man she wants. You need maths to have a hold on her."

"Pretty, and she had to go for a married man."

"She seems to have a weakness for unavailable men, according to my source she chased after this Mark, frequented his club and offered herself to him. So you will *not* be available to her and you get to work, unlock her potential and get her a pass in maths."

The young man nodded resignedly, "Okay, but this is a tough one."

They found an empty classroom and sat at the back.

"Today we'll look at Newton's law of cooling."

He quickly scrawled on the notepad.

$D = ae^{-kt}$

"That's Newton's law of cooling."

"I don't understand. What cooling you are on about?"

He took a deep breath.

"When a person dies, the temperature of the body cools. And the temperature of the body at any time after death is governed by this equation," he said, pointing to the equation.

"Is this A level maths?"

"Of course, we are using an A level textbook," he said, showing her the cover. "It's still integrating exponential functions but a bit tricky," he said. "Mr. Dow is starting this topic next week, and I want you to be more familiar with it. No need to memorise this equation, it's included in the booklet of formulae in exams. All you need to know is how to apply it."

She nervously looked at him.

"Come on, it's not so hard. Separation of variables to two simultaneous equations, and finally integration of course."

"Which I dismally flunked."

"Don't worry, if we encounter problems, we'll go back to simple integration, only let's give it a try."

She gratefully nodded.

"Let's go back to the equation. The D is the temperature difference between the cooling object and its surroundings. Let's be more practical," he suggested and opened another page.

"Good, here is the question. The cops arrived at the scene of murder at 10 am. On arrival the temperature of the body was 30°C while the temperature of the room was 17°C. This was taken to be the moment when t = 0. At 11 am when t = 1 the body temperature was measured at 25°C and room temperature still as 17°C. Estimate the time of death."

"That is too hard!" she vehemently protested.

"I don't want you to ever say that word unless you want me to quit helping you," he said coldly.

"Sorry."

"Let's go back to the equation. Remember, D is the difference between the cooling object and the room." He started scrawling.

"So D= 30-17 when t=0, and D= 25-17 when t=1. Now let's substitute in the equation, so when t = 0 then D = 13. Which is 13 = ae^{-k0} this is our first equation, when t = 0." He looked at her. "What is e^0?"

"One," she answered.

"Good, so our first equation when t = 0 is…"

He was a ruthless tutor, and he worked on her mercilessly. But she was willing, and she worked just as much.

The next time she got sixty percent in her monthly test. Even the teacher was surprised. Once again Ray was top, and this time he got everything correct.

"Thanks," she said gratefully.

"This is just the beginning. Soon you'll be much better."

"You think so?"

"I know so," he said. "I can't believe I'm about to reach my dream."

"So how come you are always so serious?" she asked.

"That's how I intend to be until my dream is fulfilled," he said, winking at her. "I don't want to get sidetracked."

"What's your dream?" she curiously asked.

"Too personal, can't tell."

"Mine is being a chartered accountant."

"Not too bad. So you should choose statistics as your option paper."

"But Mr Dow advised us to take Paper 2 as the option paper. He said it contains not so deep statistics and mechanics."

"He was saying you have limited brains, and you should take a paper that doesn't cover the deep topics of both subjects."

"So Paper 2 is a safer insurance then."

Shaking his head, he said, "No, it's not because it covers two subjects. The time you spend learning about projectiles in mechanics you could be plunging ahead with your statistics, doing variances, and when you finally do your chartered accounting, you won't encounter any hiccups."

"Yes, that make sense now. Then I'm taking the statistics paper. And you?"

"I'll take mechanics," he said, smiling at her.

"Damn, who is going to help me with statistics?"

"Statistics is not so hard, Eva," he said, frowning.

"Maybe, to you," she muttered.

"It's just a series of formulas – pie charts, probabilities. It's pure maths where you need to apply your utmost cos once you flunk Paper

1 your fate is sealed. They won't even bother with your option paper. And look at how nice I am helping you with that."

"For which I'm very grateful."

Soon they were the best of friends and started confiding in one another other.

"I'm in love with a married man."

"A married man, Eva!"

"I can see you disapprove," she said glumly.

"Of course I do. What about his poor wife? Don't you care about how much she is hurting?"

"She is a witch. She only married Mark for his money."

"How do you know that?"

"Mark told me."

"And whatever this Mark says is the truth, how sweet."

"He would never lie to me," she said agitatedly.

"But, Eva, if he could leave his wife, what makes you think he wouldn't leave you?"

"Ray, please, don't talk like that," she said in a small voice.

"Sorry, I just don't want to see you hurt," said a concerned Ray.

"How could I get hurt? He is divorcing her to marry me."

"Well, just be careful," he said.

"I will. Now enough about me. Are you seeing anyone?"

"I'm not."

"You're kidding, right?"

"Nope," he said seriously.

"How come?" she asked.

He just shrugged.

"When was your last relationship?"

"Six months back. I've been in a single boat for a while now," he admitted.

"Did you love her?"

"Of course. What do you take me for? You think I can just go with a girl I don't feel for?" he said, slightly irritated.

"Some guys do," she pointed out.

"And I'm not some guys," he retorted.

No girlfriend on the scene. Nice charming guy like this. If it wasn't for Mark, she would sure as hell grab this one.

"Tomorrow is my birthday," he calmly announced.

"And you are only telling me today?"

He shrugged. "It's no big deal."

"And who are you spending your birthday with?"

"My folks. Haven't made many friends yet."

"But I'm your friend!" she stated, sounding hurt.

He smiled at her. "Yeah, my only friend."

"Shame, not even a single girlfriend to spend your birthday with," she teased.

"What's with you and this girl thing?" he asked.

"I'm taking you out tomorrow night for a nice birthday dinner, and I ain't taking no for an answer," she said in a firm voice.

"What? I don't want to hang around married men, Eva. Especially one who deserted his poor wife."

"But he is doing the right thing, letting her go by divorcing her."

"It's not the right thing, Eva," he said quietly.

"It is," she insisted.

"I wouldn't want my parents to divorce."

"Me neither, but when the love is gone…

"Whatever, but it's my birthday and I call the shots."

She hesitated. "How about I take you out, just me and you?"

"Tempting, but what about him. You can't leave him by himself. He would probably run back to his wife."

"Don't be silly. Mark is a nice guy, he'll be cool when I tell him you'd feel uncomfortable in his presence."

"He'll think I have something to hide."

"But you don't. I'll just tell him you are uncomfortable among strangers."

"Okay," he said reluctantly.

It must have been the birthday dinner alone that started it all, or possibly the maths lessons – it was never quite clear what actually started it. Or maybe it was the piercing eyes – well, it could have been anything. The guy had such good, exceptional looks; ones you were forced to…well…do something about. He was charming as well. So gallant, so real, so cute. And did she mention his height? One of those heights that seem so right in a man, perfectly built. So what was she supposed to do?

Only human, that's what she was.

After the birthday dinner she felt it wasn't enough, so she asked him out for a weekly dinner, again without Mark. In between were the maths lessons. She talked to Mark about it. How the guy was new in town, and she was just showing him around.

But she didn't mention the emotions that stirred up inside her when she looked at those piercing eyes. And Mark, Mr Nice, had nodded understandingly. Well, since Mark was such a nice understanding guy, they put going to cinema in their already crammed schedule. She ached to hold his hand while they were walking. She tried that a couple of times, but he pulled back. Damn!

She started taking a critical look at her own physical self in the mirror. She didn't look bad. So her expectations of him getting attracted to her were well, not baseless.

A week later she changed her hairstyle. Mark loyally showered her with compliments. She eagerly went for her lesson that evening, not single compliment from Ray. She could have kicked herself, but it was out before she could stop it, the desperation.

"Don't you like my hairstyle?"

He just shrugged, "It's okay."

Damn!

'Okay', word seemed so bald, so lacking. She hadn't gone to all this trouble for a mere 'okay'. 'Okay'! Fucking hell.

She heard him complimenting one girl on the perfume she was wearing. The following day she threw her Tommy girl scent in the dustbin.

"What are you doing?" exclaimed Mark.

"I don't like it."

"But it's a good scent," he said.

She looked at him and for the first time realised Mark was...well, not much of a bargain really.

She rushed to the shops and bought the Angel perfume the girl from yesterday was complimented for wearing.

Any compliment from Ray? Nada. Her pride was wounded. She

was totally convinced her mirror was playing tricks on her. If she looked this yummy, then how come…? It was all so bewildering, and miserably depressing.

She invited him for a walk in the park one evening. It was weird that all the invitations came from her – what did that mean? Was it because – she clamped out the frightening thought.

They stopped by the waterfalls and locked eyes.

No one spoke a word. The night was beautiful. Drizzling and nicely misted, plus the sight of such beautiful flowers fuelled her feelings. She stared at those blue eyes and was lost in them. She waited and waited for him to…at least touch her, help her out in extinguishing the blazing flame erupting in her.

He didn't.

She reached out for his hand.

He pulled it back.

It was suddenly too much for her. She burst into tears, tears of desperation.

"Why can't you hold me, Ray?" she cried.

She didn't wait, she couldn't afford to. Her hands were already on him, pinning him to her so hard that she could hardly breath.

"Why are you crying?" he asked in bewilderment, wiping her tears with his fingertips.

She slowly licked his fingers. Then she progressed and kissed him. At first he didn't return the kisses, but then…well, he was only human.

They kissed and kissed.

Then he abruptly untangled himself from her.

Damn!

"What's wrong?"

"I can't do this."

"Why the hell not?" She was almost shouting.

"You have a steady boyfriend, and me, my dear, don't want to get hurt."

She swallowed hard.

"Eva, I do love you, but I can't go out with you."

"Why not?" she asked glumly.

"Mark."

"But it's you I love," she stammered.

"No," he said flatly.
"I love you," she firmly repeated.
"You love me! What about Mark, do you love him too?"
"He has given up so much for me. I can't just drop him like that."
"I see," he said icily.
Damn, she felt like screaming. "Ray, please."
"I'm taking you home, Eva, and I want you to forget all about this little episode."
"But I can't forget," she wailed.
"Hey, no worries, Mark will help you forget."

"It's taking so long?" she complained.
"These things take time," he patiently explained.
"Are you sure it will work?"
"Absolutely."

Outside she irritably kicked a stone on a sidewalk. Dean and his 'I love yous' every fucking morning were sure as hell doing her head in. As if she could ever be interested in loving a rigid gangster rat like him. The PI better hurry up with his plan.

And Mark.

She so terribly missed him.

So terribly needed of him.

Oh, Mark, where are you?

Do I ever cross your mind? Because you cross mine all the time. You have to get me to cross your mind.

You have to, Mark.

Get me to cross your mind, not just once.

All the time.

Get to miss me real bad.

Get to deeply yearn for me. "Oh God, am I losing my mind?" she asked herself, bursting into helpless tears.

"She kissed me last night," he announced.
"Yeah?" the PI said, grinning knowingly.
"Said she loves me."
Leaning forward he asked, "And?"
"But she still can't drop him."

The beefy man thoughtfully tapped his pen on the notepad.

"You haven't slept with her?"

He shook his head.

"Don't."

"Why not?" Ray asked, frowning.

"Don't," he emphatically said.

"What now?" the young man wearily asked.

"Mind games. Do a disappearing act for a week or so. When you appear back on the scene, tell her you've done some thinking. You can't teach her maths anymore. You'll ask someone else to help her."

"Explanation?"

"'Unlike you, Eva, that kiss meant a whole lot to me. It stirred up deep emotions in me. Emotions I never knew I had. I'm sorry, but I can't pretend nothing happened between us.' That's what you say, and cement that with one or two tears."

"I'm not stupid," young man retorted.

"I know."

"I still don't understand why I can't sleep with her," he complained.

"You will, but not now."

"Why not?"

"What if it's nothing deep? What if it's only you stinging her a piece of you that makes her lose her mind? And once you give in – no, we can't take that chance."

How come I'm the only one initiating the dates and phoning? she wondered. Still that wasn't conclusive enough to think he had zero interest. The guy just needed some encouragement, she told herself. That she never had a problem doing. Some guys don't take kindly to women who take over the dating lead, a woman is supposed to wait till she is asked out, otherwise she is grouped with the slut A bitches.

No, not Ray, he was nowhere near that. Ray was a nice understanding guy. He wouldn't expect her to suffocate in her wanting-him feelings because of some stupid rigid belief. No, Ray would expect her to cough up her feelings – come clean, cleanse her spirit. Straight talk right, who did it ever hurt really?

She swung her hips to the full-length mirror. "I really look good.

I'm assembled gorgeously, delicious to any pair of eyes."

She stood by the mirror and practice her arresting smile – the one she intended to use on him.

Widen my eyes – big eyes, good seduction tool, better go buy a Wonder bra. Yeah, she would widen her longing eyes to get the message across, she decided. She needed to sleep with this guy, clear her head, figure this thing out, it could be love, but first things first – sex.

She blamed her loose mouth for Ray's inflexible stand. She shouldn't have mentioned live-in lovers. Bad move. But Mark was just a boyfriend; there were no vows that were being broken. She was still fair game.

What if Ray isn't taken in by my come ons? she wondered. Well, a flat no would be better than this suspense. She thought of him – all day, and at night she was burning up, yearning for him.

She dropped into bed and sprawled there. Still the emotional distance between them was too far. What she needed was – what? Yeah, an emotional reaction speed catalyst.

Sure, it would hurt if he didn't reciprocate, but at least it would be better than this burning up suspense. She was wasting the creative side of her brains in imagining all sorts of fun with him. She was exhausting her creative side before realising her dream of hitting it big in the literary jackpot. Her secret dream – not a lot of people knew about her dream of writing a hit movie script. Long ago she used to be so free in blurting out her dreams. Not anymore. That was before she got wind of the laughs.

"Eva still talking big with her everlasting failures."

"Hah hah hah."

She fought back the tears. She had learnt the hard way. If you had dreams, seal your mouth shut. Make them your deepest personal secret. Leave them untold except to God. No, not because you didn't believe you had it in you. Not that, she fiercely shook her head. Because if you weren't careful, the incessant laughter ringing in your ears could scramble your brains to breed that crippling belief. You really were a champion failure. Amen.

Seal your mouth shut, she told herself. That was the way to play it in a world where the reigning goal was lazing around feasting on benefits. Where you set out to have a ward of babies with a trail of different fathers for a council flat reward.

She had confided to Ray about the hah hah's.

"Who exactly is laughing at you?" he had quietly asked.

"Everyone I know."

Ray had looked at her completely baffled. "A person who has absolutely *nothing* going on for her laughs at you, and it gets to you!"

"The great following of my laughing sitcom is…"

Ray had cut her short. "Don't let the laughing get you down. There is nothing worse than a person who is content in being a total failure. That's even worse than death, Eva!" He shuddered. "Because no matter what bullshit people say, if you work hard, you can achieve anything you want, anything. Content with the little nothing life, working a dumb-shit job and drinking your ass off, married to a bartender in the village, those are the people who are quick to laugh at us when we are down on our luck, but see, you have to keep on because you cannot afford to wind up like them. You simply cannot, Eva!"

She sighed.

Ray was an exceptional guy. She suspected that was when she started to really like him. And now, she nodded her head, she wanted him.

Sure, maths talk was fine, but a little something on the side would hurt no one, she told herself.

Except, she shook off the guilt trip that tried to ride on her.

Her heart didn't give her a break.

It kept on and on.

You want him, want him so bad, her heart pondered, giving her somersaults.

The yearning got so deep that she decided to take matters in her own hands.

"I just have to have him," she said determinedly.

According to him, he slept in the servant's quarter of his parents' mansion. He needed his privacy he had explained.

"Perfect," she said triumphantly.

"Where are you off to?" asked Mark.

She scowled at him. What was with him?

"Out," she said curtly.

"I can see that, the question is where?"

She looked at him darkly. "Hey, hey, I already have a mother."

Then she stormed out. Mark was no fun anymore maybe she should…

It was after eight when they sneaked into his home. It was perfect timing because according to him that was round about the time he would be having dinner in the big house. A concerned friend who was in the key business accompanied her. A nice and understanding friend who understood what it was like to want someone. The friend had a skeleton key, and within seconds they were inside. Her friend locked her in – mission accomplished.

Now to the real business. She stripped naked, took out bottled perfumed oil and started massaging her whole body. She wasn't in the least embarrassed. If you didn't take that first step, who did you expect to take it for you? Ray was blatantly ignoring her at college. It was as if she had a contagious disease. "Well enough of that," she said firmly as she slipped into sexy lingerie.

"You are being such a slut," a rigid part of her cautioned.

She dismissed the stupid voice. When the pining was this deep, you couldn't care less about name-calling. She told herself she was doing the right thing. She was taking care of her rampant heart. It hadn't given her a break since the day they kissed. Exactly what was she supposed to do? Her life was falling apart. She couldn't concentrate on her studies, and at work it was worse. She had tried to forget. She had stayed at home and watched Mark's not so enticing face. It didn't work.

"What?" he said when he got back.

She ignored the what! She plunged her tongue inside his mouth. He started to protest, but he didn't stand a chance. Within seconds he was returning her kisses. The air around them was electrifying.

"Make love to me, Ray," she said huskily.

The kissing abruptly stopped.

Damn!

"No," he said. His hands shook as he lit a cigarette.

"Please?"

"No," he said flatly.

"Why not?"

"I don't play spares."

"But you are not," she said desperately.

He looked at her. "Really, then what will sleeping with you make me?"

"What do you want from me?" she cried in frustration.

"I want you all to myself," he said quietly.

"But..."

"I can't take Mark's crumbs, Eva."

In mounting desperation, she pleaded, "Can I at least stay here with you just for a couple of hours?"

"No," he said, shaking his head. "I have loads of studying to do. How did you get in here, the door was locked?"

"I asked a locksmith mate to open the door for me."

He shook his head at her. "You are bad."

"Ray, please?"

"Sorry, I do want to make love to you. I want to do that so bad, but hey, I'm not into a cheap thrill!"

"Ray I really need you."

"What do you want from me, Eva? A snatched hour with me, then you rush to your live-in boyfriend," he shouted.

"But I made him leave his wife," she whimpered.

Dismissively he muttered as he lit another cigarette. "Sure, babes, I understand."

"What about the lessons?"

"I'll ask someone else to help you."

"Why?"

"I need to get you out of my blood, Eva."

She burst into tears. "Ray, I really like you."

"Can you just go, please? Your married boyfriend is waiting for you."

Damn!

"Last night she broke into my room. Practically on her knees begging me for sex."

"That means she is getting desperate." The beefy man grinned. Looking up at the younger man, he said, "Any talk of leaving him?"

"Nope," he said, shaking his head.

He thoughtfully stared at the ceiling.

"Time to start putting doubt in Mark's mind. Write her a letter; she is into you deep enough that she wouldn't throw away the letter. She'd probably just hide it. When she is out of the house with her lover boy, we plant the letter where this Mark is bound to find it."

"You mean kind of a love letter?"

"An incriminating one. Something like how good you felt when she told you she loved you the other day, and mention the soulful kisses. Put the proper date on it. We wouldn't want her to wriggle her way out by claiming you were an old boyfriend."

"He doesn't strike me as anyone who can read."

"Why? Because he is black?"

"Touché, touché."

"Well maybe we have reason to get touché, touché," the beefy man said heatedly. "That slavery stunt your parents pulled on our people."

"My parents!" exclaimed the young man.

"Yes, your parents," the beefy man said edgily.

"Cool it, Ed. Anyway, I don't think that will be necessary, she is already into me."

"Sure, but just for insurance in case she doesn't kick him out."

"Do you think this Mark will leave her if he sees the letter?"

"Maybe, but things will get strained, trust gone. Mark won't buy her story when she says she's going for her lessons. There'll be a screaming match, finally he'll grate her nerves, and that will convince her that lover boy Mark isn't such a hot deal after all."

"So what do I do now?"

"Call her tonight. Tell her you can't live in limbo. Ask if she's decided to leave lover boy cos if she hasn't you are moving on with your life, and in your life they is no such thing as going back."

"Okay." He nodded.

Never before had she seen him like that. He was curled up in a ball on the couch. A couple of empty vodka bottles were on the floor. He wasn't crying, but when she saw the red-rimmed eyes and the puffiness, she could see there had been quite a lot of tears.

"Mark!" she exclaimed, troubled.

"Call room service, I need another bottle."

"No, you've had enough."

"Please, Pulie, I need it to numb this pain," he said as he clutched at his chest.

He was completely crushed. She swallowed the lump in her throat, so Mark was really into this Eva girl.

But why? she pondered.

She fought back the jealous tears and quickly controlled her emotions.

"Mark, get a grip on yourself," she sternly told him.

He squinted his eyes at the vodka bottles.

"Isn't vodka supposed to have a calming effect?" he asked.

She ignored him and dutifully ordered a cup of latte coffee for him.

"Coffee! What's with you, girl? I ain't drinking that, what I need is something stronger. Whiskey would do," he said, slurring his words. She kept quiet and stared at Mark, not only was she hurt, but she was also baffled to see such grief.

What exactly is it about this girl that hooked Mark so bad?

She stood up and started pacing around.

The girl didn't have a cent, she was a clerk at some second rate law firm.

"I think I'm going to die of a heart attack," he said, bursting into tears.

Mark was reduced to racking sobs.

Okay, so he really loved her.

She put both of her hands on her cheeks and hot scorching tears came out.

All that time I spent in praying and working on my patience.

She squeezed her eyes shut.

A discreet knock sounded on the door. Room service, she hurriedly wiped her face and answered the knock. She sternly told Mark to drink the coffee.

"No, I need whiskey."

"How am I supposed to help if you don't do as I ask?"

"But…"

She cut him short.

"Hey, whatever this girl is, she can't be worth this much."

"How do you know it's a girl?"

Oops, gotta be careful. "What else could work you up like this except the white trash you dumped me for?"

He drank the coffee.

"Eva left me," he said.

She couldn't help herself. "Why, Mark? You seemed quite convinced she was the right girl for you."

"Apparently it wasn't mutual," he hiccuped.

"She left you, that's so insane. What did you do, cheat on her?"

It was as if she had struck him on the face.

"She is the one who did the cheating, then she dumped me," he said, his eyes tightly closed.

"But I don't understand this girl of yours. Any girl would be crazy to leave you."

"She dumped me for this white guy called Ray, said I was a mistake," he said with tears streaming from his cheeks.

"Shit! So you were just an experiment. She wanted to see what it was like to fuck a black man, huh?"

He numbly nodded. "Yeah, an experiment that ended up being a mistake after all."

"She found out black dick doesn't do it for her. Mark, this girl of yours seems so bitchy. Why did you leave me for her? The only reason I let you go was because I thought she was a nice decent girl."

"I love her," he said.

"What? You still love her after the devious stunt she pulled on you!" she shouted.

"I meant I loved her," he hastily amended.

"When are you going to learn, Mark? Never trust a white person," she said emphatically. "They profoundly believe they are better than us. They will always look down on us, no matter what. It's in their blood!" she shrugged. "Who knows, probably her mates told her off when they found out she was sucking a black dick. Maybe it's her mum and dad."

"Her parents didn't have a problem with me."

"Ha! That's what they always say in front of us, but what about when they are alone with their darling daughter? Honestly, Mark, dating a white person is like you are on trial. Imagine such feelings all your life. Hey, she might be okay with you, but those guarded looks from her mates. Jesus!" Accusingly she said, "And you left me for her. Am I jinxed or what?"

"Pulane, your gangster lover came back. What did you expect me to do? You think being beaten with baseball bats and having your foot roasted is some kind of picnic? Be reasonable, Pulane, if the situation was reversed, would you have hung around?"

So it was never really about this girl, it was that dangerous animal that catalysed Mark's sudden exit out of her life. *I fucking hate Dean,* she silently cursed.

"Sorry," he said.

Yeah right, sorry indeed.

Cheat and cheat, and all that he had to do in return was mumble 'sorry'. He fully expected her to swallow this sorry. Fucking bastard.

"Pulane I said I'm sorry," he whined.

She took a deep breath.

"If I come up with a plan that will guarantee Dean leaving you alone, will you come back to me?" she asked.

"Dean is too much into you, Pulane. He will never stomach you with someone else."

"I asked you a question, Mark, answer me."

He looked at her. "Pulane, why are you so obsessed over me?"

"It's not an obsession, Mark. It's called true, unconditional love, only you can't see it because you always manage to get yourself distracted."

"Dean will never let you go," he said.

"We'll see about that."

She rented an apartment in Kavalla Court at the corner of Ninth Avenue and Livingstone's street. The apartment was fully furnished with a full-time maid. She stationed Mark there.

Pulane, he sighed deeply.

Once again she had come through for him. It was such a pity he didn't feel anything deep for her. But this time he was really appreciative, to the point of being nice. He was wise enough to know he couldn't play it any other way; especially now that devious foot roaster was hovering in the background.

He had accepted his fate that Pulane was the only woman for him, but his heart insisted on an entirely different story. So what? He was through listening to his dimwit heart anyway.

Look at what transpired when he listened to it.

A mistake, my foot. Bitch just wanted to taste a black dick.

It was quite hard getting back on his feet. One time after heavy drinking he dialled her mobile number and declared his unending love, but the bitch cut him off.

"Ray is new in town, and he doesn't know a soul. I'm showing him around." This was what she had said.

Only he misread her. There was no town this Ray was being shown. What that Ray bloody rat was being shown was her deceitful body. Right there on exhibition to do as he pleased. Mark cringed – surprisingly it still hurt. She would come home in the middle of the night clutching an armful of textbooks. "After the lesson, Ray helped me with my pure maths." Yeah right, pure maths indeed.

No wonder she stopped wanting to make love, she was one satisfied bitch. While he tossed and turned, that bitch would be there chanting her slut lines.

"I'm tired."

"I have a headache."

A lesson learnt indeed; once a woman started chanting headaches, she was getting it elsewhere. He could kill himself for being so trusting. He should have read between her deceitful lines and caught her at her own slut game.

The funny thing was, as hard as he tried he still couldn't work up enough hatred for that little bitch.

But he was working on it.

I guess I'm really lucky to have someone like Pulane in my life. But how come I don't feel lucky? How come I'm still so depressed?

Ah, his heart again, still into that honky slut.

"I hate her," he said with all his might. He expected an angry ear-splitting voice to follow, but what emerged was low and hesitant.

"What's going on?" he wondered, suddenly frightened.

"I hate her," he said over and over again. That would be his therapy, he decided. Every day he would sing that a hundred of times until his stupid heart got the message. It was embarrassing the way his heart carried on. Jumping about to its dense beat every time that cheap slut came into his mind. It was about time he showed it who the boss was. He was sick of this shit; his heart ruling his life without consulting with him, making a circus clown out of him like that time it drove him to make that impulsive call.

Because at the end of the day who got jeered at?

Who got to be called pussy whipped?

Who took the rap for its dumb antics?

No, this time fucking traitorous hearty was going to listen to him, really listen to him.

CHAPTER SEVENTEEN

"I finally came up with a perfect plan to chuck that bastard out of our lives," she told him triumphantly.

"Huh?" he asked, not really believing her.

"It's like this. Confront him and tell him about his sidekick Ivan. Threaten him, tell him that if you go to the cops, they'll rubber hose this Ivan to confession."

"Pulane, are you crazy. If I came up with a story like that, Dean would kill me!"

"You think he can go that far?"

"He is a Snoop, it sure as hell wouldn't be past him," he said matter-of-factly.

She slumped on the chair and brooded.

"How about if you tell him I confessed to everything on tape? And that you've instructed your lawyer to hand the tape to cops if you happen to get killed."

"What if he wants to see the tape?"

"Dean is stupid, my word is enough to fully convince him there really is such a tape," she said confidently.

"So you'll confirm the tape exists. He'll ask how come he is only hearing about it now."

She shrugged her shoulders. "I'll say I was too scared to tell him."

"Do you think he'll buy it?"

"Dean buys anything I sell him."

"It might work," he admitted, grinning in admiration.

"I just want him to leave me alone," she said glumly.

"Do you think that's really possible?" asked Mark in disbelief.

"What, him leaving me alone?" she asked.

"Yeah."

"Of course, tell him you still want me, and that there will be no divorce. If he cooperates, we give him half of everything, and he *fucking* disappears out of our lives."

"But Dean is way too much into you. He'll never let you go," he protested.

"He is going to have to," she said flatly.

"But, Pulane, Dean, loves you. He treats you like a queen. What's so bad about that?"

Glaring at him, she said, "The fact that I don't feel him but have to sleep with him is bad enough," she snapped.

"Why not just let it stay this way, stay with him and visit me here?"

"Meanwhile, I will be fucking him, right? What the fuck do you take me for, Mark?"

"The plan is not so bad, though," he said, deep in thought.

"Hey, about that girl who experimented with you. Do you ever think of her?"

He was so startled by the drumming of his heart that he hastily got to his feet. Fucking hell, when would he get that bitch out of his head? His heart still jumped about at the mention of that bitch. Honestly, he just didn't get it. This girl really messed him about. She found him too black for her liking and dumped him. This is bullshit, he fumed as he poured himself a shot of brandy.

"I asked you a question, Mark!" she shrieked.

After gulping the brandy down he looked her straight in the eye. "I never think of her," he said.

When she left Mark's flat, she felt so good, so jubilant. Aha, things were now back on track. It was finally happening for her. If I was an actress, I would have long won an Oscar, she chuckled. Dean was so certain this stupid love he felt for her was a mutual thing.

"Ha! Stupid gangster rat," she muttered.

But underestimating him was out. That beating had wise her up. Time for more tears, break down and call Mark a devious bastard. She would scream, slam herself against the floor, and make it look like going back to Mark was the last thing she wanted. Then she would subtly advise him to go back home so she would be able to see him every time she went there on the pretext of visiting her relatives. She wasn't stupid. She knew that as long as she declared her undying love for him and let him occasionally get on top of her, grunting like the pig that he was, he would stay in line. Minus that, she started shaking. They would be fireworks and this time their spark would bury her ten feet under. She had no intention of worms feasting on her prematurely, no, not if she could help it. There was just so much to live for.

And that PI, he was simply the best, she grinned.

"We need to fuel her believe that she is in love with our boy. She might not really be in love with Ray, but we need her to keep *thinking* it's him she is in love with. Meaning shrugging off your husband if he tries to get back with her."

"So?"

"We leave Ray to fuck her for one more month."

Anxiously, she said, "What if she realises she doesn't love Ray? Won't she go back to Mark?"

"It depends how soon she realises the fact, by then your husband would have given up on her. That's why the first few weeks Ray has to give her his undivided attention. We double his expense account to take her out and stuff, then just when she least expects it, 'boom!' he dumps her."

Fair deal, she took the advice. So she hadn't left darling Eva in the lurch, she wasn't so heartless after all. One more month was enough to help her along, and if by the time the month was up and she hadn't managed to nail Ray, it wouldn't be her fault. Pulane did her utmost.

Sure Mister Mark still didn't love her; that was one thing she had learnt she could do zilch about. It took quite a lot of tears, but she had finally accepted him not loving her, but not the giving up part, that she could never do. They could talk till they were blue in the face trying to muddy her mind, but leaving Mark was out. At least she has something he needed, money, and that kept him around. So her strategy was fattening the money. She intended to be richer than this; let his greedy mouth water even more. She would wisely invest her money in real estate; grow richer with Mark's greedy eyes as big as that of an owl waiting to pounce on her riches, only he wouldn't because if he walked, he walked with zilch, thanks to that prenuptial deal he signed. Imagine if she hadn't insisted on him signing it, she shuddered at what the consequences would have been.

They all say money cannot buy happiness, but that was just disgruntled talk. Sure it can't buy *all* happiness, but some happiness is buyable. Look at her now. If it weren't for money, Mark wouldn't even give her a backward glance. Of course, he didn't love her, but it was she he was married to. Some people who had it all would never understand how one could settle for this. But that was just it, they had it all, and it was okay for them to talk, but what about her? Mark was the closest to happiness she had ever had because if that wasn't the case, where was her better option? Where was he? Not Dean, who always left her with such a dry irritable feeling. No, life without the occasional crumbs Mark fed her would be worse than hell, she decided. Sure, Mark was a shit bastard, but hey, this was the bastard who made her want to fly. So she decided to use her only weapon, making more money, meaning Mark stuck around. Sure, she dismissively lifted her shoulders, it sounded like a load of bullshit to other people. To them she was pathetic. People were all talk, so full of shit – she shook her head.

Everyone has been down this road. Loving someone who messed them about and friends telling them to leave him, but no one listens – not right away. They take their time, hoping he will change. And eventually yes, they leave. Eventually, she repeated to herself. Everyone had been down this fucking road.

So hey give me a fucking break. When I feel it's time to walk, I will. Only I don't feel that time is now. Fucking selective amnesia! she silently fumed. Pulane had long realised the unfairness of life, and knowing the futility of crying and beating herself up, she had decided to make things happen for herself. Sometimes being good didn't pay. Yes, she sabotaged Mark's relationship with that girl, and no, she didn't feel bad about it. Hadn't she tried God? Prayed and prayed, but what happened? It got even worse. Mark dropped her for a white girl. He left without a goodbye hug, without even looking back.

So, what was she supposed to do then? Cry? Ha! No, not this time.

He decided meeting him at the club would be the best insurance.

"What's up, Dean?" he said with a broad smile.

"Hey, Raditonki, what brings you here?" he coldly asked.

Fishing out long forgotten names from the woodwork – a ploy of intimidation probably. He shouldn't have bared his soul to him, such a big mouth he had then. He said, "We need to talk."

Viciously Dean said, "There is nothing I can ever talk to you about."

But he did talk. It was such satisfaction to see blood draining from Dean's thuggish face. All of a sudden he was interested in what he had to say.

"It's quite simple. Mr Chambers needs to be told he was taken for a ride. He thought he was doing his supposedly good friend Jomo a favour by taking in his loser of a brother." Shaking his head bleakly, he said, "Hmm, sometimes being good doesn't pay."

"Hey, don't talk shit! My brother had nothing to do with that!"

Smiling triumphantly, Mark continued, "Sure, but do you think Mr Chambers will buy your brother's sob story? Poor Mr Chambers does the good deed of hiring you, recommended by your bro, and six months later all hell breaks loose. The thing is, Chambers will not be amused. Anyway, who the fuck cares about Chambers? It's the insurance I will be talking to. I hear they have good private investigators," he said meaningfully.

In a cold calculating voice, Dean asked, "Hey, how is your foot?"

"Listen, you don't scare me anymore. I have dynamite info I will be happy to trade to the cops. You think your fucking brother can buy all the cops in the country. You fucking roasted my foot, you devious bastard!" he furiously shouted at him.

"What do you want?" Dean wearily asked.

"I don't give a fuck about that Pulane of yours. She is not for me," he said frivolously. "Too desperate and only you would want such stifling shit. I will be happy to divorce your mistress as soon as you hand me the five hundred thousand, hard cash in *dollars*."

"You're blackmailing me!" said a stunned Dean.

"Blackmail!" Mark exclaimed. "I say it's compensation for that foot roasting you did on me."

"Get out of my club, Mark!"

"Hey, I would be happy to go elsewhere with this."

"I'll call you," Dean said, dragging Mark to the door.

Shrugging indifferently, Mark said, "I know you can put a contract on my head, but hey, that's life. My lawyer has this nice confessional tape and letter and if I happen to die, that's it," he grinned at him. "Don't say I didn't warn you," he said on his way out.

He whistled a tune, quite exhilarated by all that money coming his way. No way was he going to ask Dean to leave town because that would mean him remaining clamped to Pulane. If there was any leaving of town to be done, then it would have to be him, he decided.

"Sorry, Pulie, but it's quite a drag tied to your leash, cramps the little style that I have." If Pulane had more sense, she would thank God he was finally out of her life because if the truth be told, he had never been anything to her except pure miserable pain.

"One hell of a favour I'm doing you, Pulie. An about time exit out of your life. Save you from more of my crap. You will even have a good chance to explore your relationship with Dean. He could be exactly what you need. The guy loves you more than life itself," he said to himself as he stretched on the couch.

Five hundred thousands worth of victory. He pleasantly congratulated himself for twisting Pulane's plan to his own advantage.

"A five hundred thou advantage."

He looked at the cheap polyester couch. It was trash that needed to be covered in a rug in order not to prick him. He had shouted, "I'm supposed to be the love of your life, and I get to stay in this dump."

She had hushed him down. Telling him that if Dean found out he was staying in a posh place, he would start wondering who his sponsor was. This was just a temporary measure while she was still trying to figure out what to do, she had said.

Well, she did figure it out. Nicely figured it out for him to a have a five-hundred-thousand pay off.

He remotely played the radio. Good quality sound filled the room. His sponsor knew he got off on the sounds, and this time she didn't trip. She got him a high-quality Sony home theatre. Such a good sponsor this girl was.

Pulane is sure going to react badly to my leaving, he reflected.

The problem with babes was that they were too into emotional challenges before *checking with their hearts first.* They were fooled into thinking emotional challenges were some kind of fashion trend like those tight jeans they prance around in. A good, nice guy who played it straight was hardly considered because to them he was a placid fool.

Well, hadn't he too tried a shot at Mister Nice when he first hit the bright lights of the city? A one-woman man he had been then. No standing up pranks. And nah, that was not just to reserve someone who would nurse the frequent tightening in his pants. It was no bluff; he really did dig that girl. He felt her real deep.

But what did honey girl do? She told him to quit calling her so much. She said his whimpering calls were… he silently shook his head.

The calls he made out of the deep lovingness of his soul. They were calls he treasured more than anything else because, believe it or not, her voice, just her saying hello, had been enough to make his day. He briefly closed his eyes as he recalled how crushed he had been then.

So he did exactly as honey babe said. He cut out his whimpering 'I love you' calls. She had on numerous occasions mentioned his placid side. Hey, who liked being called a bore, especially in the now era? So he spiced up his life with those variety games. Surprisingly, she had had the audacity to call that cheating on her. *Cheating! Like I have the bitch's name tattooed on my dick. Don't talk shit,* he had blustered.

Now this was the strangest part. The girl started being nice and sugary, trailing after him, coughing up money. The girl bought him a nice mobile phone and loaded it with credit.

"Please, Mark, call me."

The girl actually said please to him. That was a first.

Still he didn't buy into her new buttered-up manners. When he called, which wasn't often, it would be just to make an appointment with her flexible giraffe legs.

"I want to fuck you tonight," he would say straight out.

She would start on him with her whiny mouth, "You never call me."

"What is it I'm doing now?"

"You don't love me anymore…" He would cut her off. Call more clued-up girls. Girls who understand how short life was. There were a lot of them around, only you had to know where to look.

The next day, who knocked on his door? It was giraffe's cousin, practically on her knees. "Why are you doing this to her? She is in a bad way."

"I don't take kindly to emotional blackmail."

"Mark, please be nice."

His bad boy attitude had finally earned him some kind of respect. The girl and her bunch of relatives learned to say please to him.

"More often than not, being good does not pay," he firmly told himself.

Was it any wonder then that he ditched the Mister Nice and buried it ten feet under?

And now Pulane, he sighed.

Never would she be thankful for this great favour he was doing her. To be quite honest, Pulane was too good a convenient deal to simply walk out on, but ever since that Eva bitch, there was no pleasure in it anymore. The bitch was still haunting him. He thought of her all the fucking time, he cringed.

Why? He still didn't know the answer to that one. He had played it straight with her, but no, she…damn! He was still hurting.

Don't think about it.

He took a deep breath.

Goodbye, Pulane. It was a big break for her, but was Pulane going to appreciate such a good compassionate move and shake his hand? Maybe send him a postcard?

Would she say, 'I spend most of my time on my knees thanking God you are finally out of my life'?

No fucking way! What Pulane was going to do was shout all kinds of profane complaints and call him names.

Women, he sighed. Before checking the strength of their hearts, they impulsively jumped into emotional challenges. But wait till a real challenge came along. They instantly crumbled to whining cows, assembling their girlie group to gang up on you. "You are a shit bastard, Mark!" Tear-facedly playing the victims, conveniently forgetting the fact that they were the ones who volunteered to jump into this stewing pot. Hell, it wasn't like Pulane didn't really know him before she let herself fall for him. For two whole months she saw with her own eyes the man he really was. She should have run for her life then. But she didn't, with her eyes wide open she had said yes to him. Her biggest mistake, the very first warning you get in a relationship you should takeoff before your heart starts running interference in you. Before it turns the screws on you, you run. That's where the sucker trap hibernates. Where you get to be a blundering fool. Where you see a grade-A bitch as Mother Theresa.

A heart, because a heart always has its own treacherous agenda.

Some bitch spreading her legs to some bastard Ray, and the moronic heart is saying, "We still need her, she is the source of our being happy." Dumb fucking hope!

Fuck that shit! he blazed.

Like that time it forced him to make that humiliating call, only for the bitch to cut him off. Why not? She had finished her experiment.

Pure miserable pain was what he really had been to Pulane, he mused.

And Pulane never once threatened to walk he marvelled.

Never even coughed out ultimatums to at least scare him into getting his act together.

If she had, would he have bought into her threats?

Maybe. Still, she could have tried.

If Eva had asked for another chance would he have said yes? "Welcome aboard, Eva, all is forgiven."

He winced. "I don't want to think about her," he viciously said to the empty room.

And all time pain to Pulane.

Continually letting her down dismally. He slept with the hired help – anything. He would have slept with the neighbours, only the ones they had had grown too fat and were too ancient.

So while he was busy serving his out of control libido outside the marital boundary, Pulane had stood back, playing the perfect wife. "I know it wasn't your fault, Mark," then she expertly covered up for him.

Yeah, for real with Pulane he could get away with *anything*.

Eva, fuck you! I refuse to think of you.

Maybe bolting out of this country would finally make him forget....

"What?" exclaimed a shocked Pulane as her head started spinning. She sat down heavily.

"Are you sure that's all he asked for?" she stammered.

"Of course I'm sure," he said, frowning at her.

"Why didn't you tell me he recorded you when you foolishly confessed?" he asked fuming.

"I was too scared to tell you."

"What the fuck, Pulane?" he screamed. "You should have told me."

"So that you could beat me up like you did that time."

That cooled him down.

In a resigned voice, he said, "I think we should pay."

"No," she screamed hysterically.

"Calm down, babe."

"I fucking hate him, why can't he just leave us alone?" she said, bursting into tears. Inwardly she was all confused. *What is going on?* Could Mark be heartless enough to hijack her plan? What was the five hundred thousand for? If Mark got that money, he would be independent, and she would never see him again.

She started shaking like a leaf.

"Pulane, you are shaking. Shit, this must be quite a shock to you. We'll have to pay, Pulane. We don't have a choice," he rationally explained.

She shut her eyes as she felt a big jolt in her chest. It was imperative that Mark didn't get the money. She tried to gain her composure by boosting herself up with more gulps from the glass of Johnny Walker Dean handed her.

She stared intently at Dean and said urgently, "If we give Mark the money, it will not be the last time. You know damn well he'll milk us dry."

"You are right, but I don't see us getting out of this one."

"Stall for more time," she desperately suggested.

"More time for what?"

"Maybe something will come up."

"I think…"

"What's wrong with you, Dean? How can you so easily give in to blackmail? Do that, Dean, and Mark will remain the god of your life. Today, it's five hundred thou, how about next week, how much is he going to ask for then?"

"I'll try stalling for more time and think of a way out."

She exhaled heavily.

The following day she was at Mark's flat. She didn't waste time; she greeted him by throwing a vase at his head. It missed him by inches. She grabbed the decanter that was on the coffee table. This time she didn't miss; it was a pity nothing was in it. It shattered on his head. It was the sight of blood that brought her back to sanity. She silently cleaned up the wound and applied an antiseptic ointment on his lying head.

"What did I do?" he wailed, chewing two aspirins.

"That was my plan, Mark," she shouted, about to lose it again.

"But I did exactly as you told me."

"Really!" she said, fuming.

"Yes, Pulane, but you know what he's like. A thorough thug to the core. He threatened to torture me if I don't just take the money. It was him who even came up with that figure. He is too obsessed over you, Pulane, and he told me he would never give you up. Sorry if I messed things up."

"You should have insisted on my terms," she scolded.

"But he laughed at me and asked whether I wanted another foot roasting. He told me straight out that he knew all kinds of pain he could administer on me till I spill the name of the lawyer who has the tape." He paused. "And imagine if I had called it a bluff, and he went ahead with his threat. I could have spilled all our secrets, and we'd both be in deep shit," he said.

"Stop exaggerating to excuse your own behaviour," she said coldly.

"Exaggerate! He beat you, Pulane, imagine him beating up a woman. Something even I wouldn't do, then he roasted my foot. And you still say I exaggerate!"

"So what happens after you get the money?" she asked, dreading his answer.

"Well, I start afresh," he said guardedly.

"Afresh, what's wrong with your life now?"

As if she didn't know.

"Dean for starters."

"And this starting afresh of yours doesn't include me."

"I'm scared of Dean, Pulane. He is way too dangerous an animal, and I did try my best to make him leave you alone, but you know Dean, he didn't budge. He called you his one true love and said he would give up his life first before he could give you up."

"One true love my foot. Dean and this shit love of his gives me such fury. Damn, I never should have slept with him!"

"It's not the sex, Pulane, it goes further than that."

"Oh really, how would you know that?"

"We used to be pals, remember. He loved you long before you slept with him."

"Well, I still think sleeping with him worsened the situation."

"I couldn't understand how he could fall for you before the sex. We used to argue about that a lot. Sex is meant to be the deciding factor of whether to love or not to love; I used to tell him that."

Looking up at him, she said, "That explains your seedy affair with that bitch, she must be one hell of a dancer in bed. Do you think I should ask her for lessons, Mark?"

"I don't want to talk about Eva, Pulane," he said viciously.

"You should have been adamant on what we agreed on," she said stubbornly.

"He threatened to roast my foot again."

None of this shit made sense. Mark was saying this, while that bastard was saying that.

"Who has reason enough to lie?" she pondered.

Dean and this sick obsession he had on her. But Dean was a Snoop thug. It was so unlike him to succumb to blackmail. Unless Mark presented a foolproof deal, and Dean was trapped with no way out. And that meant what? Mark had the upper hand so what was this talk about blackmailing money? Could Mark... no Mark was a rat but not to such a devious level.

When she got home that evening she found Dean pacing around.

"I just had a call from Jomo. Apparently my dad has had a heart attack. He's in coma."

"Shame, I'm so sorry." Who gave a flying fuck about his dad? She had enough on her hands right now, like this blackmailing puzzle.

"It's been ages since I last saw my dad, but like Jomo said, he is still our dad, despite his shortcomings."

"Of course, sweetie. But how did Jomo know? I thought you and him have exiled yourself from the rest of the family."

"He has ways of finding out things. Just as he found you and that blackmailing rat Mark."

"And I'm glad he did, sweetie," she said smoothly.

"I'm flying back home to see how he's doing."

"That's a good idea," she said in a silky voice. A big relief, finally she would be able to do her own thing without the thuggish bastard breathing down her neck.

"We are going together."

Damn, what did she do to deserve this shit?

Tried to reason. "But, Dean…"

"We are going together, Pulane, end of discussion," he said flatly. He was a controlling bastard of a rat. No wonder she still couldn't find it in her to at least like him a little.

So what was the sucker rat up to now?

Exhibit her to his mafia grandmother.

Damn!

They flew to Francistown that very night. His gangster brother came to pick them up from the airport. Not a single 'hi' came from him. That was fine with her. As if that wasn't enough, Dean paraded her to his bunch of peasant relatives as his fiancée!

Fiancée! Ha!

It was hard to pretend. She had to summon all her acting capabilities. The bastard forced her to stay there for a whole long week!

Then thank God the mafia dad was removed from the intensive care. And there was Dean walking around like he had just won an award with a stupid smile plastered on his face. He called the whole shit a blessing in disguise – he was finally reconciled with his family.

Ha, who gave a fuck?

Damn, she missed Mark terribly. And boy, was she glad when they finally left for Cape Town.

As soon as they arrived, she left on the pretext of checking the salon. Her mobile phone rang just when she was about to reach Mark's flat. She frowned, it was the PI.

"Afternoon ma'am. When can you come over? Something has come up."

"What is it?"

"It will be better if you come here."

"I'll be there in ten minutes," she said as she made a hasty U-turn.

Her knees were shaking as she faced the PI.

Why was her gut feeling warning her that something was terribly wrong?

"Is Ray blackmailing us?"

"No, not Ray, he would never pull anything like that."

"Then what could possibly be wrong?"

"You do remember that the agreement was for Ray to ditch that girl after a month."

"Yes," she said impatiently.

"Well, Ray did just that. To hammer the point home he changed college. But last week he bumped into Eva. Only it wasn't the Eva we expected, she was all smiles, claiming to have gotten back with Mark. And their relationship is as strong as ever. Ray didn't buy that and figured it was her way of licking her wounds, but he nevertheless passed their little chat on to me."

"She was definitely lying," Pulane said dismissively.

"But in my profession there is never smoke with no fire lurking somewhere. So I broke into Eva's flat and planted a voice-activated tape recorder. Now let's find out the real story," he said as he inserted the tape into a portable player.

He pushed the play button and sat back.

"I still feel bad about what I put you through," the voice from the tape said.

"Eva, I really love you, and I'm glad we are back together."

"What the fuck?" Pulane jumped to her feet in shock.

The PI pushed the stop button.

"Should I bring you a glass of water?"

She dazedly shook her head. The PI pushed the play button again.

"Mark, you gonna have to give up that flat and move in here. Save unnecessary overheads."

"Whatever you say, sweetheart."

"Thought you'd go back to your wife when we broke up."

"I couldn't."

"Actually that was what brought me to my senses. I realized then that you loved me just as much."

"This time I ain't bluffing. I want a divorce pronto. Marry you and, Eva, I want a couple of mini us."

A small scream escaped Pulane's lips.

"A family!" a voice from the tape exclaimed.

"Eva, please don't deny me that."

"Of course not, darling." Pulane felt so light-headed, the kind you feel whilst in a lift. Unsteadily she gripped the oak desk.

"Stop the tape," she said in a quivering voice.

The PI man raised his eyebrows inquiringly.

Like a little kid she said, "If I hear more of it, I'm g…going to die."

The PI understandingly nodded as he pushed the stop button.

She burst into heart-wrenching sobs. "I think this girl is a witch."

The PI man gentle sat her down.

"What a…am I t…to do?" she said between sobs.

"Personally I feel you should let it go. They are too much into each other, and whatever we do would just fuel their love for each other."

It was as if a knife had been plunged into her gut because even through her teary eyes she could see she had finally reached a dead-end. It had been a long painful road, and she had emerged a dismal loser.

"So, there is nothing you can do?"

"True love is serious shit. Yes, we could do something to break them up, but the break-up wouldn't last. They'll always get back together, it's pretty strong. More magnetic than even the magnet itself."

Hadn't they all told her to let go?

"Pulane it's a lost cause, he doesn't love you."

But what did she do? What the fuck did she do? She cried even more violently.

"What the hell do you know?" was what she had said.

It turned out they knew much more than her. It turned out they were right all along. She would have saved herself from more humiliation, more pain and the 'I told you so' crap she knew would soon be tumbling her way. She wiped the tears and staggered to her feet. She had been stupid for too long; it was about time she wise up.

"Thank you for everything. It's hard, very hard to accept defeat, but if there is anything I've learnt in this, it is that it pays to listen. So this is it. We leave them alone."

The PI nodded.

"I'm glad you followed up on Ray's info, or I'd still be in the dark."

She shook hands with the PI and left. It was still hard to come to terms with Mark loving someone else because, God, she really loved him. But at least the veil that had been stuck over her eyes had finally been lifted.

Mark and Eva. The PI was right; whatever those two had, it was serious shit. Still, it hurt.

CHAPTER EIGHTEEN

"Mark called me up, he gave me till tomorrow night to come up with the money."

"I told you not to give him a cent!" she furiously exclaimed.

"We have to pay him, there is no other way," Dean calmly explained.

She was about to grill him when the maid announced dinner was ready.

"I'm starved, let's go and eat," he said.

As soon as the maid was out of earshot, Pulane continued, "We are not having dinner till this is settled once and for all."

"But it's already settled, we are paying."

She leapt to her feet in alarm. "Paying?"

"Why not? It's not like he is asking for a lot."

"And you think that would be the last we hear from him." Asshole, no wonder she still couldn't return his feelings.

"Since you take yourself for a fancy millionaire with an urge to give away money, don't you think charity would be a better cause?" she snapped.

"Why are you being so nasty?" he asked, perplexed.

He still didn't get it.

"And why are you being so stupid?" she retorted. A dim-witted question, when had he ever been anything else except that? The sucker of all time.

"I'm merely being realistic," he explained.

Realistic, quite an interesting word he had come up with. She was actually taken aback that the wimpy rat had it in brain vocabulary.

Realistic, how about exercising that over this sick obsession you have on me?

She sighed. So Mark wanted the money to live cosily ever after with that home wrecker. Unlike the pathetic creature facing her, she was no fool. What Mark had with that girl was too deep; the kind of shit that never dies. But she would be damned if they thought they could get her to finance their little honeymoon. Mark had used her for far too long, it was about time she put her foot firmly on the ground.

Mark was an emotionally devious bastard. If he hadn't strung her along with his lies, she would probably have long ago given up.

Still, she couldn't believe she had been so stupid.

After she listened to the tape at the PI's office, she went to Mark's flat. The bastard looked so relaxed, so unconcerned, as if nothing was wrong. He had plunged his deceitful tongue in her mouth; his version of 'I missed you, honey'. He told her he had been going crazy missing her. She asked him whether he had heard from Eva.

"Pulie, that girl played me for a fool, and I can never forgive her for the bitch stunt she pulled on me. I fucking hate her, and I curse the day I met her. You are the one thing that matters to me, and I'm glad that cheap slut is out of my life. And to answer you, no, I haven't, and I'm very okay with that."

She had gaped at him stupidly. She was speechless, she never knew he had it in him to lie so blatantly.

Love, what a load of shit. And marriage was not even enough. It wasn't that big assurance because the bastard could still walk out on you. It didn't matter whether it was the first or fiftieth anniversary, he could still walk, she shuddered.

Christ, she really felt like crying because she still hurt. *I was willing to live a second-rate life with him, and it didn't get me anywhere except a post-dated broken heart.*

She took a deep breath and managed to gain her composure.

"Leave it to me, I'll go talk to Mark."

"Do you think he'll listen to you?"

"I can try," she said.

She couldn't eat. She left Dean wolfing down his food like the dog that he was.

Her heart. God it was aching so terribly. She got in her car and drove around with no particular destination in mind.

Tears pricked her eyes.

Mark – she tried so hard not to think of him. She helplessly beat the steering wheel with her clenched fists. If only she could get the bastard out of her blood. But how, move to China?

Nights were the worst.

She couldn't sleep, not when she knew so much about entwined games. She knew about how mighty the paradise of night could be, full of kisses and cuddles. That lucky slut Eva was wrapped into happy Mark, while she had the rotten luck of being saddled with a clingy gangster rat who still couldn't give her one decent orgasm. Life really was a shit.

Last night it had been the worst. She had eventually managed to catch some sleep. She woke up screaming. It was a murderous nightmare.

Mark in church.

Mark in a tux.

Mark saying out his vows.

Mark slipping a ring onto… the piercing scream and Dean shaking her had woken her up.

She had refused to sleep afterwards. She hadn't dared sleep since then. For some inexplicable reason she was totally convinced if she slept, the dream would come true. That night she had staggered downstairs and gone for her nightly ritual – vodka drowning. It was true about vodka. Right there in the middle of that bitter taste lies the anaesthetic magic.

As she took glass after glass, the pain would get muffled, and yes, it still mattered that Mark had preferred someone else to her, but the vodka was a medicine in itself; it made her feel it was a big deal, but not that much of a big deal. In the morning they found her sprawled on the couch in an alcoholic stupor reeking of vodka but not blacked out, vodka was more familiar with her now. It was embarrassing for the help to find her like that, but she had decided what the fuck, she could live with that.

And that rat Dean wasn't making things easier for her with the suffocation and his daily inquiry of what was the matter with her. Last night she nearly blurted it all, it was only when she remembered the beating he once gave her that she reconsidered. But one of these days, she would let him down gently, not the truth about her real feelings for Mark and how she capitalized on his moronic love. She couldn't risk her death with such confessional stories.

Damn, Dean just didn't do it for her. If only he had the right orgasmic moves in bed, but it was routine passion-less sex. Yuck, who needed that shit? Of course she had tried taking the lead to spark up their sex life, but he had abruptly disentangled himself and berated, "If I had wanted to sleep with a whore, I would have checked the streets." Imagine such shit!

She really should unload him.

Wow, the park. She stopped the car and decided to take a walk around. She thrust her hands deep in her coat pockets and walked heavily.

Such titanic pain, she winced as she took a swig from a vodka bottle she had brought along for company. Screwing the lid back on, she put it back in her coat pocket.

A post-dated broken heart thanks to her stubbornness. If only she had known. If only Mark had come clean with her long ago, "Listen, Pulane, my heart is smart, it will never fall for a pathetic little shit like you. Try little junior, he is not that particular, give him some loot and in he will plunge."

God it hurt, she muddled on, screwing her eyes tight against the pain.

If only he had sternly told her the bitchy truth from the start. But he went along with her, horribly played her.

"Hi, Pulane."

She silently cursed. Just her luck. She had come here for peace of mind and look who she stumbled into? Hadn't she suffered enough?

"Eva, this is Pulane, my ex-wife."

Her eyes widened, ex-wife, was the divorce through already? She looked at them; hands over each other as if they didn't get enough of one another, or was it their way of gloating? She wouldn't put that past them.

She still loved him. *Oh God I think I'm going to die.*

"Hi, Pulane," Eva said, offering her hand. The bitch was all calm.

Pulane ignored the offered hand.

How come she still loved him? Oh God she so wanted to – weep.

"Oops, a grudge," Eva said with a chuckle.

A chuckle, she painfully swallowed the lump in her throat.

"So how is Dean?"

She closed her eyes. What was with Mark and this Dean shit? Was it a pathetic attempt to cushion his guilt? Her eyes automatically filled with tears because she suspected there was no one else in the whole wide world who had been taken for such a sucker ride.

"Pulane?"

If she said anything, her voice would emerge shaking. No way would she give them that satisfaction.

"Honey, let's go."

They left her like that, exactly like the fool that she was, standing in the middle of the park in her miserable sorry state. She looked around, there were couples everywhere – she was the only lonely figure.

Another stab of pain. The pain that was long overdue, she would have had it long ago, and today it would have long healed. But it wasn't happening because she thought she was the clever one.

She slumped on a nearby bench.

She felt so miserable – so overly depressed.

Everyone she knew told her to let go of Mark. But she didn't listen.

She shook her head miserably.

They had mumbled a sick song of them standing on a sidewalk and the whole lot just talking to hear their own voices, since talk was so fucking cheap, it wasn't even VAT chargeable. Stubbornly she had told herself she knew better.

It turned out she didn't know shit.

She really had the right to this pain.

She had dug her own grave.

She had made her own bed.

Tears spilled out because she wished she could turn back the clock. But the clock refused to turn; it kept chiming, on and on. God, everything was so against her these days.

All this time she had wasted, refusing to let go.

Her head started to pound as she recalled those days battling as a maid. How she used to bath with a dish detergent. She frowned, did she really do that? No, she shook her head; her mind must be playing tricks on her.

Okay, Pulane, take the denial route; nobody is as competent at it as you.

She fidgeted uneasily because she was suddenly so embarrassed. Embarrassed enough to wish the earth would gobble her up. She took out the bottle again to numb the embarrassment and the pain.

The pain, she started crying again. There was just too much of it.

And that time when he dumped her, calling what they had a mere sexual arrangement. And yet she had clung on. She had become his whore, sacrificing her body in order to recruit Dean into being a sucker. It turned out the biggest sucker was her.

What exactly didn't I do to trick Mark into loving me? she wondered. The truth was, she did every single humiliating trick she could come up with, but what did she get in return?

Apart from the lies and the crumbs of his heart.

Pain.

And even more pain.

With Eva having the time of her life laughing at her.

The pain deepened as she recalled the amused expression in her blue eyes. Painfully she breathed heavily and glumly admitted that Eva was right to laugh at her. If ever there was anyone out there who deserved to be jeered at, it was Pulane. She was the definite laughing stock. No wonder Mark was never into comedy movies, he never even watched a sitcom. She still recalled one time when she had asked him why. She bit her lower lip as she remembered how Mark had stared at her like it was the most stupid thing to ask. Well, now she knew why.

"Why should I when I live with one big comedian?"

"I'm the funniest joke ever invented," she said, violently sobbing so hard she thought her heart would break.

Although the cold intensified, culminating in frostbite she didn't leave, she just sat there on the bench. Where else could she go? Home and face that clingy rat?

Unreturned love. Was it some kind of punishment because nobody deserves this shit?

The bastard had blown her heart into smithereens. But she still loved Mark. Damn. She clutched at her chest.

I have to find a way to get him out of my mind. I just have to, she cried between mouthfuls of vodka.

She stared at the sky; it looked like it would be raining soon.

Did love have to be so overwhelmingly powerful and blinding all at the same time? And this blindness shit was the worst. Making marshmallows out of her brain. She wouldn't be in this predicament if it weren't for this witch-crafting blindness. She would have long ago seen him for the lying rat that he was if this blindness crap hadn't interfered with her sight and rationality. She would have long ago busted him for the low-life, cheating, pathological lying rat that he was.

Why did You give love such utmost power over us? Culling all the shots and forcing us to do stuff we wouldn't do otherwise.

God, it was so cold, she shivered.

Why couldn't You at least make it just powerful but not blinding? she wondered, very much puzzled because it just didn't make sense.

None of this would be happening.

Grand deceit.

The dumb hope.

The unending pain.

Why did You have to give it such an upper hand?

Such power.

Is it really necessary? she wondered.

Rain poured furiously out of the sky, but she didn't move an inch. She stayed right there on the bench because it was the not knowing why that made the pain even more unbearable.

The not knowing why she could had been that stupid.

The not knowing why she got to be such a fucking moron.

The signs had been there all along, brutally glaring at her. Plus good Samaritans had warned her off.

They had told her Mark was an emotionally devious bastard. They had told her she was better off alone.

Why was I so blinded I couldn't listen, is what I need to know.

She figured if she knew the reason, then it wouldn't be so unbearable.

It got even chillier with the rain pouring down on her. But she sat there, determined to have an explanation. The explanation she felt she rightly deserved.

"You owe me that much," she said with her teeth chattering.

She sat there and waited.

How did she get to be such a fucking moron?

She waited for someone out there with more wisdom than her to talk to her – enlighten her. The pain was still there as raw as ever, but still it didn't make sense. Especially now when she knew the kind of rat Mark really was, but she still loved him! Jesus Christ!

Why?

He was the lowest rat that there could ever be.

She had the right to his heart, that was what she had forever blabbered to her friends. Devastated, she shook her head.

Now what was that about?

Right to his heart? Where did she get that rubbish?

What right? she pondered.

Deliberately playing dumb hoping that would…what? Earn her his heart!

Only she never got the heart.

Painful indigestible crumbs were all that she earned; she squeezed her eyes shut as another pain shot through her.

It was two in the morning when he was jolted by the doorbell. He hadn't slept. He was worried to death not knowing where Pulane was. He had tried her mobile phone countless time; the damn thing just rang.

He padded to the main door. Pulane had no reason to ring the bell – she had the damn keys.

He yanked the door open.

"Jesus Christ! What happened to you?"

"Hello, sir, I found her walking aimlessly in the rain in the city park."

"Walking in the rain?"

"Yes, sir."

"Thank you, officer. Pulane, your clothes are soaking wet!"

"She seemed to be in shock. She kept babbling about someone called Mark."

"Ex-husband, he caused her a lot of grief."

"Shame, she must have loved him a lot," sympathized the officer.

"What?" exclaimed Dean.

The officer handed him the car keys.

"Well, I guess she's in safer hands," said the cop at the door.

"But what about you, how are you getting to the station?"

"I'm all right. Patrol car followed us."

"Shit, let me change her clothes. Bye, officer, once again, thanks."

Gently he led her to the bedroom.

"Oh, Pulie, baby. What has happened to you?" he said as he took off her drenched clothes.

"He never really loved me. Didn't even like me a tiny bit."

"Huh?"

"Never loved me."

"Pulane, stop babbling like a fool," he said, wiping her with a thick towel. "I can't risk putting you on a shower when you're so wobbly."

"So horrible. Called the best thing we ever had a sexual arrangement. It was more than that. It really was."

"Okay, this is bad. I'm calling the doctor," he said as he gently put her in bed after helping her into her pyjamas.

"And Susan told me. Told me long ago. My heart bleeds for you, that's what she said."

Damn, he hurriedly crossed the room to the phone. He dialled quickly.

"Doctor, it's about Pulane. She is incoherent, her pupils are dilated and she is shaking real bad. I'm worried she might have caught pneumonia. Can you please come and check her. Thanks doc."

He replaced the receiver.

"Why couldn't he just love me? Why couldn't he? I had the right to his heart."

This was real bad. She must be hallucinating about her teenage life, thought Dean.

"Oh, baby. You are so cold," he said as he fondly touched her cheeks.

"Why couldn't he?"

He took the remote for the air conditioner. He activated it and pressed 'Heat'.

He then jumped into bed to keep her warm.

He took her in his arms.

"I knew you'd come back to me, I knew it," babbled Pulane.

"Of course, sweetheart," he soothed.

"Oh, Mark, I'm glad you came back to me."

Coldness swept through him – his hands went limp.

"Oh, Mark, it has always been you. I love you so much."

He jumped out of bed, his mouth hanging open, shaking and shaking.

"I hate that devious bastard Dean, he's the one who scared you off."

Dean stood there, frozen in his tracks, his heart thumping so hard.

"Pretended long enough with Dean. I can't do it anymore, Mark. I just can't." Pulane sobbed.

He dragged himself to the phone again. He had changed his mind about the doctor coming here. Voice mail. *Shit!*

"I love you, Mark. I really do."

The blood drained from his face.

Then the doorbell rang.

"I wish this bastard Dean hadn't come back."

A loud painful gasp escaped his dry mouth.

The doorbell rang again.

She woke up with the mother of all headaches. It felt so stuffy, and she felt so sick.

"What's wrong with me?"

"Doctor gave you a shot of something. He said something about you being in the cold for too long. Damn doctor didn't listen to me. I told him to leave you alone. I told him confession is good for the soul. He insisted and just when you were about to reveal all, you fell into a deep sleep," he shouted.

"Dean, stop screaming at me. I have a bad headache…"

He slammed his fists hard on the headboard table.

"I don't give a fuck about your headache!"

She blinked, "Dean, you are scaring me."

"Now, start talking, real talk about this love you've for Mark and how you curse the day I tracked you down."

"W…what are your t…talking about?"

He jumped on her and grabbed her arm. He twisted and twisted till he heard the crack sound.

"Deeeaaan!"

Eyes glittering daggers, he growled, "I'm going to count to three, Pulane. Only to three, and if by the time I reach three you are still not talking, so help me God."

"One!"

Ouch, the gangster bastard had broken her arm.

"Two!"

She fearfully looked at his eyes – he meant business.

"Okay," she whimpered in pain.

"I've never really l…loved you, Dean. It –w…was Mark all along. I was never over him."

Her arm, damn. She looked at Dean, who was standing over her in a towering rage. She didn't know why, maybe it was too much pain in her arm, but she suddenly didn't care anymore.

"I am waiting, Pulane," he roared.

"So I told myself that if I land enough money, Mark would love me. I was young and stupid – no, let me not make excuses. So I decided to use you. Well, you know what I did. Finally, I had the money and we eloped. Then you found us. You nearly killed Mark, and that beating you gave me. I figured I underestimated you, so I went back to my pretending."

"You never loved me," he said in a strangled voice, his eyes in glassy shock.

But she was on the roll and it was true about how talking about it helped. So talk she did.

"Yes, Dean, even today I don't. One of the last tricks I played on you was telling Mark to blackmail you. I told him to claim a tape existed, and I'd vouch for that. My plan was to give you half of everything and you leave us alone, but Mark double-crossed me."

"My brother was right all along."

"There is no such tape, Dean, let alone a confessional letter. It was all a lie to scare you off."

"So I was nothing to you, nothing at all," he said in a dangerously quiet voice.

"I don't love you, Dean," she said weakly as the throbbing pain in her arm worsened.

"I was nothing but a damn pawn," he said, taking a faltering step towards her.

"Ouch, Dean, call the doctor."

"A fucking pawn," he repeated in a deadly voice.

"All those 'I love yous' were just to marinate me to be your fucking pawn."

"Would you stop going on about it. I'm in pain here."

Another faltering step forward, his shaking hands stretched out.

"Just a pawn to fix up your life with Mark."

"Dean, please, my arm is hurting."

"You lied to me, Pulane," he said quietly as he reached the bed.

"Sorry," she said weakly. Shit her arm.

He seized her around the neck.

He clasped his hands and crushed her long neck.

"De…" She tried to fight him, really tried.

Her breath stopped and darkness descended.

He kept crushing.

It was only when she went limp that he let go.

Eyes flashing, still burning in murderous rage, he stood over the lifeless body.

All those 'I love yous', they…they didn't mean shit to her.

She was just buttering me up so I could fix up her love life.

And if she hadn't paraded in the rain unconsciously blabbering it out, he would still have believed in her love.

He frowned. The murderous rage had evaporated, giving way to a troubled feeling. A very troubled feeling.

If he hadn't bullied her into confessing, he would still be in the dark. He would still be calling her lovehoney. He would still be calling her the love of his life.

The troubled feeling deepened.

They told me right. They said she was the bitch of all trades, they said - if fate hadn't intervened, he choked on his breath as pain flooded through his entire body. He dropped to his knees on the carpeted floor.

He would still be calling her his one true love.

Shaking his head over and over again, he said, "Oh Lord, where were You? You were supposed to warn me off - tell me to…"

As more pain tore into his heart, he buried his face on the floor. Bitter tears poured out, scorching his cheeks.

She played me.

She really, really played me.

He gasped loudly as his big brother's words finally hit him.

"How long do you intend to play a sucker's game?"

THE END

www.ingramcontent.com/pod-product-compliance
Ingram Content Group UK Ltd.
Pitfield, Milton Keynes, MK11 3LW, UK
UKHW041257180426
11947UKWH00008B/539